Raven's Fall

World on Fire, Book II

by

Lincoln Cole

This is a work of fiction. Names, characters, organizations, places, events, and incidents are either products of the author's imagination or used fictitiously. Any resemblance to actual persons, living or dead, or actual events is purely coincidental.

No part of this work may be reproduced, or stored in a retrieval system, or transmitted in any form or by any means, electronic, mechanical, photocopying, recording, or otherwise, without written permission of the publisher.

Published by Lincoln Cole, Columbus, 2017
admin@LincolnCole.net
www.LincolnCole.net

Cover Design by M.N. Arzu
www.mnarzuauthor.com

Table of Contents

This one is for my mother.

"It is better to conquer yourself than to win a thousand battles. Then the victory is yours. It cannot be taken from you, not by angels or by demons, heaven or hell."

Buddha

Prologue

As soon as Abigail stepped outside the house, she knew something was wrong. She no longer stood alone, although she couldn't see anyone else around her in the immediate proximity. How could she know? Nevertheless, she felt certain.

Alert and alarmed, she slipped her gun loose and crept toward her car, scanning the area around the house. Dark and cloudy, she couldn't see anything.

When she drew closer, Abigail noticed that the vehicle rested lower than it should have. Someone had slashed the tires.

Not waiting for the trap to spring on her, she sprinted to the right, running toward a fence leading into an old horse paddock. A shout came from behind, followed by a gunshot. Abigail ducked and dashed to the fence, climbed over it, and dove into the tall grass below.

Years of horses walking over the muddy terrain had made the ground uneven. Luckily, the grass stood several feet tall and disguised her entire body, especially with such little light.

Abigail landed hard and rolled, ducking into the grass as more shots fired behind her. She kept moving, crawling low through the grass and, occasionally, glancing back the way she had come.

Near her car, three people ran toward her. Although Abigail couldn't recognize their faces, she knew them from the way they moved: Colton Depardieu, Jack Wright, and Anong Sao.

It looked like they had come to finish what they had started back in Lausanne. Colton raised his pistol and fired into the grass. The shot fell behind her, but not as far away as she would like.

Abigail flinched, ducked again, and continued crawling. On this breezy night, the grass wafted in the wind and masked her progress. She moved fast, staying low, and went another fifteen or so meters. When she checked again, her pursuers had made it through the gate and into the field. They combed the area slowly, spread out to fan the entire field, and worked their way toward her.

Abigail held onto her revolver. At the least, she could drop one of them from her hiding spot. Anong stood closest, oblivious to her. They hadn't prepared for her to retaliate, and she could put a bullet in Anong and still (probably) crawl away without the other two being able to find her immediately.

However, she didn't. These were Hunters, her brothers and sisters, and killing them felt ... wrong.

Though she might well regret it, Abigail slipped her revolver away instead and belly-crawled through the weeds and toward the fence. There, she found an opening that she could crawl under and slid outside the field. Abigail couldn't see any other houses or vehicles in the area, but an old barn sat only fifty meters from her.

It looked like it had burnt up in a fire years ago, probably due to lightning or hooligans, and only half of it remained standing. Still, it gave better cover than nothing.

Abigail moved cautiously, crouching low, and made her way to the barn. Once there, she ducked inside, out of sight of the fields, and let out a quiet sigh.

Chapter 1

(A few weeks earlier)

"What are you thinking about?" Frieda drew Haatim out of his thoughts and back to the world at hand. He stood staring out of the window at the mountains and countryside as they flowed past. Headed through Switzerland, the beautiful landscape slid past their train. In only a few more hours, they would reach the Council buildings where they would stay for the next few months during Abigail's trial.

Snow had fallen in the region, leaving a light dusting over everything. At just the beginning of winter, conditions would get considerably colder before spring thawed everything out again.

His mind drifted far away in his thoughts and memories. It would be the first time since the aftermath of Raven's Peak that he had spent more than a few hours in the same room with his father. He couldn't decide if he looked forward to the prospect or not.

On the one hand, Aram had raised him. Taught him right from wrong. Helped him grow up and shown him how to be a man.

Haatim kept thinking of the little things, like how to tie his shoes and shave. He loved his father dearly and missed listening to him tell him stories about the wide world and all of the places he'd been.

Yet, on the other hand, Haatim could hardly believe how much of his true self that Aram had kept hidden from him. The sheer volume of lies he'd told his son since birth felt staggering. His father had withheld everything that mattered and kept him in the dark. All of those fairy tales that his father had told him about the world had just been stories.

A fairly large part of Haatim felt furious at such complete deceit. His father was his blood, and if he should have been able to trust anyone in the world, that person should be Aram Malhotra. And yet, he'd come to find out that his father made for exactly the sort of man he couldn't trust.

How the hell would he ever explain that to Frieda?

"Just thinking about life," Haatim said, realizing how vague his words sounded. "Nothing in particular."

Frieda sat on the railcar seat opposite him, studying him in a way that always made him uncomfortable. The woman never seemed to smile, but he also found her quite beautiful despite being many years his senior. She had an austere and pristine grace that captivated.

Right now, she wore a gray business suit with a white blouse and high heels. A mole sat on her left cheek, and she had her blonde hair tied up in a bun. It amazed him that she could always dress so immaculately, even in the craziest of circumstances. He'd never once, in all the months he'd traveled with her, seen so much as a hair out of place.

"Are you worried about confronting your father?"

Haatim cursed her intuition. She always seemed to know exactly what thoughts held him in thrall.

"It is a concern," he said. "Aram ... my father kept so much from me—from us. I don't think he told anyone in my entire family about this secret life he leads. I doubt he told my sister anything before she passed away, either, and I know my mother is in the dark. I just never knew he could lie to us about so many important things."

"It doesn't mean he doesn't love you."

"No," he said. "But it does make it harder to trust him. I never even guessed he would keep something from me, let alone something like *this*. I think that says something about me as much as him."

If he'd expected Frieda to disagree, he'd find disappointment. "It's a wonder the things we can convince ourselves of when we have a stake in maintaining our false reality."

Haatim looked back out of the window, tapping his fingers lightly on his knee. "I'm also worried about Abigail," he said, after a few moments. "I haven't seen her in months and want to make sure she's all right. Are you worried about seeing her?"

Frieda hesitated. "I suppose I am a little bit, and about what comes next. The evidence your father's built up will make proving Abigail's innocence quite challenging."

"You can do it, though, right?"

"Of course," she said. "Abigail has many faults, but at heart, she's one of the greatest people I've ever met. I'll never regret the decisions I made to trust Arthur all those years ago."

Haatim wanted to ask her what she meant. All the time, she made vague statements about Abigail's past, but whenever he questioned her more deeply about it, she closed up and refused to speak to him at all.

He decided not to try and get more information right now. If he'd learned one thing over the past few months of traveling with Frieda, it was that he shouldn't press his luck. Frieda would tell him when she wanted to.

"She did save my life," he said, instead. "When I tell them what happened at Raven's Peak, they'll have no choice but to release her."

"Maybe," Frieda said.

"You said I would be allowed to testify."

"You will, and your father is on the Council, so your words will carry weight, but I fear that some of the evidence against her will prove hard to overlook. I feel certain that I can prove she's a hero for what happened in Raven's Peak, but that doesn't mean she's not also guilty of many other crimes. She has broken our laws and disobeyed orders. My job is to show that she's still redeemable."

"Dumb laws," Haatim said before he could stop himself.

Frieda shrugged. "Many of them are, and I would love to remove or change half of them. But, just because they shouldn't exist, doesn't mean we can ignore them. You can't change a system if you refuse to play by its rules."

Haatim returned his gaze back through the window just as the train went over a bridge. An enormous canyon stretched into the distance, several hundred meters below them. He couldn't even see the bridge next to them, just the emptiness.

Part of him sat in awe of it, and the other part felt terrified. Heights weren't his thing, and he couldn't keep his fingers from tapping.

He'd never been much for riding trains, but this seemed like something else entirely. The tracks ran up and through the mountains, passing innumerable pristine vistas, unlike anything he'd ever imagined seeing. To call it awe-inspiring gave a disservice to the true power of what he experienced.

Beauty, he'd come to realize, could also terrify all too often.

"Would you like a drink?" Frieda asked.

"Sure," he said.

She stood and walked to the bar near the middle of their railcar. They rode in high comfort in one of the luxury cars. Each ticket cost more than the monthly allowance he'd had while he lived in Arizona. On these travels with Frieda, he enjoyed comforts he felt unaccustomed to.

However, he could get used to them with little effort.

Frieda returned a moment later with two mixed drinks.

"Kirsch," she said, handing him one.

He took a sip and winced. It tasted sweet but incredibly harsh on his throat. When he glanced up, Frieda had an amused expression on her face as she watched him.

"Takes some getting used to." She stirred her drink with a finger, and then took a sip. "We're almost to Lausanne."

"I can't wait." Haatim took another cautious sip. "We've been cooped up in these seats for too long. I still need to do my stretches."

Frieda nodded. "Every day," she said. "But I won't be able to do them with you anymore."

"You mean because of the trial?"

"Yes. I won't be able to teach you anymore."

"I understand," Haatim said.

For the last several months, Frieda had trained him in how to defend himself. Basics of hand-to-hand combat and the use of fairly common weapons like pistols and shotguns. He wouldn't have considered himself ready for a real fight by any stretch, but he felt better prepared to defend himself than he had a few months ago.

"I've asked someone else to continue your training, and he will be able to help you tremendously with your fighting and survival abilities; far more than I ever could."

"Who?"

"Dominick Cupertino. A dear friend and incredibly loyal."

"Okay," Haatim said. "Does he know about …?"

Even without finishing the thought, Frieda knew what he meant. She shook her head. "I would advise discretion. I trust Dominick completely, but some things are best kept secret."

They spoke of the events in the factory at Raven's Peak. Haatim had faced down a demon in a violent confrontation. It had tried to harm him, but he had chanted a stream of litanies and prayers that he'd learned through his years of studying religions. Somehow, he'd managed to walk unharmed through a tornado of dangerous objects that the demon threw at him.

He'd told Frieda about it and felt surprised at how readily she'd believed him. The woman had heard stories about people with abilities similar to what he had demonstrated, but knew few concrete details about just what happened. It lay outside her expertise.

Frieda recommended that he keep the details to himself until they could better determine what had gone down. Fine with him. The only people that knew were himself, Frieda, and Abigail.

To be perfectly honest, he didn't feel totally sure if he believed anything strange had happened. When he looked back through his memories, he thought it more likely that the demon had simply gotten overconfident and Haatim exceedingly lucky.

"I'll avoid discussing too much with him," Haatim said. "He'll teach me to fight?"

"He'll beat the hell out of you," Frieda said. Haatim thought she was joking, but she didn't smile. She rarely smiled. "Hopefully, you'll learn something about fighting along the way."

Her statement didn't reassure him.

They rode in silence for another ten minutes before reaching the city. Small and quaint, it had a lot of short buildings spread out into the distance. The station sat on the outskirts of the city, little more than a platform and series of ticket booths.

The train pulled to a stop next to the platform, and people filed out. Not a lot. The train appeared about half-full, right now, of bundled up adults and children. Haatim watched them disembark, and it took him a moment to realize Frieda sat watching him.

"We'd better go," she said, finally. "The train won't wait around forever."

"Where's it go now?"

"Basel," she said. "But it's a long trip through the mountains."

He nodded and stood, grabbing his duffel bag. Toiletries and a change of clothes the only items he'd packed. "Are you ready?"

"Welcome, welcome!" a man said, as they exited the railcar onto the platform. He looked medium height and well-built, muscular and athletic, with brown hair and eyes and a winning smile. Most of the other passengers had gone already, heading off to their rides or a nearby rental office to get a car.

"Hello, Dominick," Frieda said, greeting him with a modest hug. "It's nice to see you."

"It's been a while." He walked over to Haatim and stuck out his hand. "You must be Haatim."

"That I am." Haatim shook it. Dominick had one hell of a grip. Haatim took care not to wince.

"I've heard a lot about you. Nice that I finally get to put a face to the name. Do you guys have any bags you want me to grab?"

"No," Frieda said. She held up her bag, and then gestured at Haatim's duffel. "We travel light. Martha will come with the rest of our stuff in a few days."

Martha worked as Frieda's assistant, and a highly competent one at that. Haatim never noticed her, but she always seemed to be there whenever Frieda needed something. She had stayed behind in Germany for a few extra days, wrapping up business, before following them.

"All right," Dominick said. "Right this way."

He led them off the platform and into the parking lot. He kept talking, but Haatim barely noticed what he said. He felt fatigued from traveling so much over the last few days and didn't have the energy to converse about the weather.

They stuffed their bags in the trunk, and then climbed into the cabin. Frieda took the front—fine with Haatim because it meant she would do the talking. A moment later, they headed into town.

Most of the buildings looked old like they had a lot of history. Snow covered the streets, and the going proved slow, as the tires skidded across slippery patches. Luckily, with most people preferring to stay in, not much traffic used the roads. The city didn't seem to be in any hurry to clear the snow.

"We'll fly in," Dominick said. "The roads to the hotel have closed until we can hire someone to clear them. It's expected to keep snowing for another few days, and then we'll have good weather for several weeks."

"Have you spoken to Abigail?" Frieda asked.

"I have," Dominick said. "She's struggling. Being locked up for this long hasn't been good for her."

"Aram keeps postponing," Frieda said. "He wants to put as much time between the trial and what happened at Raven's Peak as possible."

"Why?" Dominick asked.

"So no one thinks about it when the trial starts. Raven's Peak wasn't a good day for the Council, but people can justify their actions more easily over time. He's also trying to make it harder for Abigail so that she doesn't testify so well."

"It's working," Dominick said.

"Not for much longer. I'm here now, and the Council won't allow him to postpone again."

"That's good," Dominick said. "We're also pulling in a lot of mercenaries."

"I know," Frieda said. "I don't like it, but Aram is in control of security right now."

"Are you vetting them?"

"As much as possible," she said. "Most of them have shady pasts, though, so I'm not sure who to trust."

"Have things gotten so bad?"

"We aren't recruiting, and our numbers have dwindled. We have three Hunters on site, counting you, and the rest out on assignment. We don't have the soldiers to manage our security."

"Things have changed a lot since I first showed up," Dominick said.

"They'll get better," Frieda said. "We've had a rough couple of years, and the Council is trying to solve too many problems economically and diplomatically, but we are considering starting a new recruitment push. After Raven's Peak, I think I have them convinced that we've neglected our army long enough."

Dominick didn't reply, and they drove in silence for a while. Frieda didn't often talk about the affairs of the Council, and certainly never with such negativity, which meant that she did trust Dominick.

And himself, Haatim realized. It surprised him how quickly Frieda had come to trust him, considering how new to all of this he was. Maybe because he offered an outside perspective and didn't have any stake in what they discussed.

Either way, it felt good.

"We're here." Dominick pulled the car into the airport. The tires crunched across the snow, and he drove up to a private helipad and parked.

Haatim and Frieda shuffled out of the car after him, following across the snow toward a gray and plain helicopter without any visible insignia or markings. It looked large, about three meters tall, with a pilot's door on each side and a passenger door entering from the right.

"Meet Spinner."

"Spinner?"

"Yeah," Dominick said. "This is my baby. Climb in. Haatim, you can ride up front and be my copilot."

"I don't know how to fly."

"Neither do I," Dominick said. "But it hasn't stopped me so far."

Haatim hoped he was kidding. He climbed up front and buckled himself in. Dominick passed him a helmet with a built-in microphone and headphones.

"Can you hear me?" Haatim asked, aligning the microphone to his mouth.

"Yeah," Dominick said, flipping controls on the dashboard. "But, if you want me to hear you while we're airborne, you might want to flip on the microphone."

Haatim felt around the helmet, finally finding a switch under the left ear. He flipped it, and everything became much clearer. "That better?"

"Much," Dominick said, and his voice came through loud and clear.

The engine kicked on, and the blades rotated, but the headset blocked most of the noise. After a few minutes of prep, they got airborne. Gradually, the city shrunk beneath them until the buildings looked like tiny specs. It seemed like a snow globe to Haatim, beautiful and packed under mounds of snow.

"Haven't flown much, have you?" Dominick asked.

"I have in planes," Haatim said. "This is something new, though."

"Beats the hell out of planes if you ask me."

"I flew once before," Haatim said. "When we left Raven's Peak. They flew us out, but I don't remember much. I fell asleep."

"I was in Germany when that happened," Dominick said, shaking his head. "Hate that I missed the party."

"Definitely crazy," Haatim said. "How far are we flying?"

"About a ten-minute flight to the hotel," Dominick said. "Your rooms are all ready to go."

Haatim watched the mountains slip past beneath, as they flew away from the city. The mountains looked jagged and uninviting; he'd never seen nature so pristine and foreboding.

He didn't see another structure until they reached their destination. A huge hotel sat tucked away in a small valley, surrounded by trees and forest and barely noticeable. A single road ran to it, dead-ending into the hotel and almost completely buried under mounds of snow.

It reminded him a little of the hotel in The Shining, but he pushed the thought away.

"That's where we're staying?"

"Yep," Dominick said. "Home sweet home."

He lowered Spinner toward the lawn out front. The ground rose to meet them until he finally touched it down. The landing pads sank about two feet into the snow. The blades above slowed when he powered down the engine until finally coming to a stop. Everything fell silent. The absence of the engine rang in Haatim's ears.

"I hope the roads clear in the next couple of days," Dominick said, taking off his helmet. Haatim followed suit, setting it on the dash. "But, until then, we're stuck here."

"I can think of worse places to get stuck," Haatim said, climbing out.

The snow came up to the middle of his shin, making it difficult to walk.

They made it to the lobby, and warm air came out to greet them. Frieda closed the door behind them. "Where's Abigail?"

"Down the hall," Dominick said, pointing. "On the left side. You'll see Jim and Mike parked out front."

"Aram is using them as guards?"

"For now," Dominick said.

"I'll put a stop to that today. If he's bringing in mercenaries, then he sure as hell isn't using Hunters to babysit."

She headed off at speed, striding down the hall in the direction that Dominick had indicated. Haatim thought to follow her but decided not to; he would let her have some time alone with Abigail before interrupting them.

Instead, he shook out of his heavy coat and warmed his hands. Though so miserable outside, he hadn't realized just how cold he'd become.

"At least the furnace works," he said.

"You're telling me," Dominick said. "They're spoiling us out here."

"I'm not a fan of cold weather." Haatim rubbed his hands some more.

"Me neither," Dominick said. "Give me a beach and martini any day. The cold does have its uses, though."

"Yeah?"

"It'll make your training a lot easier."

Haatim didn't like the sound of that. "What do you mean?"

"You'll find out. Get some rest. We'll start in the morning. Want me to show you to your quarters?"

Haatim shook his head. "No," he said. "First, I need to talk to my father. Do you know where I can find him?"

"Upstairs in Conference Room B," Dominick said. "It's his office for now."

"All right," Haatim said.

"You're on the top floor." Dominick handed him a keycard.

"Isn't the place mostly empty?" Haatim scrunched up his face. "Why not the first floor?"

"Because you're going to get real good at taking the stairs," Dominick said, smiling. He headed off before Haatim could respond, disappearing down a side hallway.

Haatim glanced at the keycard and sighed before sliding it into his pocket.

Time to go see his father.

✳✳✳

Haatim hesitated outside the door to the conference room, gathering his courage for the confrontation surely about to ensue. He wanted to see Aram, but also felt worried about just what sort of a yelling match such a meeting might entail.

He could turn around and head to his room instead, but that wouldn't help anything. Sooner or later, he would still have to see his father and, if anything, he'd rather just get it over with. Like pulling off a Band-Aid.

He knocked on the door.

"Come in." The heavy wood muffled his father's voice.

Haatim opened the door. His father sat at the head of an expansive conference table. The room had a vaulted ceiling and looked expensive and tasteful. The only person inside, Aram worked with multiple sheets of paper spread out before him.

"Yes? What is it?" Aram asked, not looking up.

"It's me," Haatim said. "Hello, Father."

Aram glanced at the door. When he saw Haatim, his face lit up. He jumped out of his seat and hurried across the room to his son. Aram wrapped him in a hug, squeezing him tightly.

"Haatim," he said. "My son."

Not exactly the greeting he'd expected. It caught him off-guard. He'd avoided his father for months now—not answering his calls and deleting his messages without listening to them. He assumed his father would be furious with him, but he seemed the opposite.

"Oh, how I've missed you," Aram said.

"I've missed you, as well," Haatim said. "I'm sorry I've been out of touch. I've been extremely busy."

Aram waved the concern away. "Think nothing of it," he said. "I appreciate how difficult things must have been for you since your time at Raven's Peak. Everyone has their way of dealing with things, and yours has always been internal."

They stared at each other for a moment, and Aram rubbed his son's shoulder and smiled at him.

"Your mother misses you, too," he said, finally.

"She's here?"

"In Lausanne." Aram separated and released his son. "I've put her up in a hotel nearby for a couple of weeks. After you left, she didn't want to be alone, so when I had to go to work, she came with me. She's had an excellent vacation."

"I'm sure she has," Haatim said.

He missed her. He'd spoken with her a few times in the last couple of months, but they hadn't had a lot they could talk about. His mother remained unaware of this world, and he didn't like lying to her.

Unlike his father, apparently.

Still, it felt nice that she stayed close by. It would be good to visit her.

"How have things been with Frieda?" Aram asked.

"Busy," Haatim said. "Thirteen countries. I've seen more of the world in the last few months than the rest of my life."

"Her life is rather hectic." Aram nodded. "She likes to oversee things and micromanage. Has she been kind to you?"

"She has," Haatim said. "And she's told me ... a lot of things. We met some of the operatives out in the world."

"That's good," Aram said. "It's good that you're learning about this world."

"The trial has her concerned," Haatim said. "She doesn't think there's a good reason to have it at all, and I tend to agree with her. That's why I came here to speak with you today."

Aram frowned. "Haatim, I don't wish to talk about—"

"Abigail saved my life," Haatim said.

"After putting you at risk."

"Through no fault of her own," Haatim said. "They were after me, whether or not she got involved."

"That's debatable," Aram said. "And, I'm still looking into just what happened in Arizona. You nearly died, son."

"I remember," Haatim said, his voice sharper than intended. "I promise you that she had nothing to do with it."

Aram looked as if about to object, but then his expression cleared. "I understand your position, but things happened for which she cannot be forgiven. At least, not without a trial."

"Why are you pushing so hard to have her punished? What has she done to you?"

"It's not about her or me," Aram said. "It's about the *law* and upholding our values. You've been with Frieda. You've seen the sorry state of what we've become."

"What do you mean?"

"How many operatives did you visit? Ten? Twenty? There aren't many of us left, and the ones we do have, feel afraid to act. Our Order has grown weak, and gets weaker by the day because we refuse to uphold the values that made us great."

"What values?"

"Truth, strength, and obedience." Aram held up a finger to enunciate each point. "We need to unite behind one goal. Not many."

"How does Abigail fit into that?"

"What she did ... it goes against everything we stand for."

"She saved thousands of innocent people, including your son, *multiple* times, and stood against and defeated a horrible demon. How can that go against what you stand for?"

"You don't understand." Aram squeezed Haatim's shoulder once more. "This isn't your world. One day, you will, but for now, you need to trust that I know what is best. I have things in hand, and what I am doing is right."

Haatim took a deep and steadying breath, desperately trying to keep his anger and emotions under control. He hated when his father became patronizing and demeaning, and part of him wanted to storm out of the room in frustration.

When younger, he would have done just that. And, now, he'd done with taking his father at his word. "I intend to testify on Abigail's behalf."

"Absolutely not. I forbid it."

"You cannot stop me. I know the laws and what rights I have. I am allowed to testify and am both willing and able."

"A mistake. We should stand united."

"I survived Raven's Peak. I know what transpired and what Abigail did. She risked her life. She is a selfless and *good* person, Father, and if you are too ignorant to see it, then I pity you."

"Did Frieda put you up to this?"

"No," Haatim said. "The decision is mine alone."

Clearly, Aram didn't believe him. "My son, you need to take more time learning and finding out about this world before jumping in with both feet."

"I don't have that luxury," Haatim said. "Considering everything that happened, I'm certain I'm submerged already."

"I don't want you to end up on the wrong side of this," Aram said. "We have forces at play here that you don't understand. Perhaps it would be best if you remained an impartial bystander."

"No," Haatim said. "I've made up my mind, and I know enough about the rules to know you can't keep me away. I wanted to do you the courtesy of telling you myself rather than you hearing it secondhand."

Aram frowned. "You cannot be persuaded?"

Haatim just stared at him.

"Very well," Aram said with a deep sigh. "When the trial begins, you will, of course, be allowed to testify on Abigail's behalf."

"Good."

An awkward moment passed, and Haatim couldn't think of anything to say to break the silence.

Finally, his father spoke. "I missed you. And I can see that you aren't a little boy anymore. I'm proud of everything you've done and the man you've become."

"Thank you," Haatim said.

"When this trial is over, and things settle back down, we need to spend more time together. I can show you things that Frieda never will."

Haatim didn't respond, not sure if his father wanted to create doubt in his mind about Frieda or if he simply wanted an excuse to spend time with his son.

Not that it mattered. He did miss his father, and maybe once they had put Abigail's trial behind them, they would be able to move forward without disagreeing about everything.

Not likely, but worth hoping for.

"Of course," he said. "Once the trial is over. I should head up to my room now and unpack. Good seeing you."

"Goodbye," his father said, giving him another hug.

Haatim headed for the door. As he opened it, his father said, "Oh, and make sure to go visit your mother as soon as the weather gets better. She misses you."

Chapter 2

Abigail paced back and forth across her makeshift prison cell, clenching and unclenching her fists. She would have preferred it if they'd locked her in an actual prison, surrounded by concrete walls and metal bars, rather than the clean and monotonous place that she now occupied.

The hotel room completely lacked personality and style; the sort of place vacationing families stayed during long trips away from home. Though full of amenities, it felt like the walls had shrunk, just a little bit more each day, as she paced the gap between the bed and bathroom, caged like a wild animal.

The entire situation left her frustrated and annoyed. She should be out doing her job rather than stuck in here. She should be hunting for the person she'd seen in the tunnels at Raven's Peak. She should not be trapped by the Council in a hotel in Lausanne, Switzerland.

The Council didn't have an official location or citadel anywhere in the world, preferring to relocate every few months to throw off their enemies. Right now, they rented an old hotel in the mountains, which they'd converted into a temporary hideout, from which they could conduct their business and hold Abigail's trial.

Built in a seventeenth-century style, it stood five stories tall. Due to the nearly impassable roads, while the snow fell, it had closed for the winter. Several kilometers of difficult terrain hid the hotel away from any nearby towns. Visitors would have to travel up and down switchback roads through the mountains to get here. All of this meant that they wouldn't have to worry about people stumbling into their hideout.

A converted and reinforced guest room on the first floor made Abigail's holding cell. They had barred shut the windows, and two armed guards stood outside at all times to keep an eye on her.

She'd tested the effectiveness of her prison during her first weeks in here and found it lacking. To break through the walls and slip free wouldn't have been difficult, given enough time, which meant that they assumed she wouldn't attempt any escape due to her morals.

Unfortunately for her, they had it right. Abigail had no intention of running away. If she left now, her guilt would solidify in the eyes of the Council, and they would most assuredly find her guilty.

Her patience wore thin. She'd been tucked away in this hotel room for four months now—much longer than she'd anticipated when they first arrested her. The Council hadn't even begun hearing her case. They were, allegedly, gathering evidence and giving Frieda and Aram time to build their cases for and against her defense. All that meant, in reality, was that the Council members sat on their hands and refused to do anything.

Business as usual.

The trail of the person from Raven's Peak had long since grown cold: finding him should be the Council's priority, not deciding if Abigail had broken some of their stupid rules. Whatever artifact the thief had stolen from that cave had importance, and the culprit didn't plan on using it to slice vegetables.

Abigail had tried explaining to the Council how dangerous the situation was months ago, but they hadn't taken her seriously. The problem lay in the fact that Aram Malhotra provided her only point of contact outside this prison. He had charge of the Council's temporary mountain citadel, and so they'd assigned him to keep watch over her until the trial commenced. He hadn't even come to speak to her once during her imprisonment.

To be honest, that was probably for the best. After everything that had taken place with Haatim and The Ninth Circle, Abigail didn't trust Aram as far as she could throw him. As soon as they cleared her name, after this stupid trial, and let her back out into the world, she intended to look into all of Aram's shady dealings and find out exactly what was going on and the nature of his involvement.

A knock came on the door, causing Abigail to pause midstride. She turned just as the door opened. Dominick stood there. In his late thirties with brown hair and brown eyes, he looked a handsome man. One of her few friends, he never treated her poorly or treated her like an outcast as many of the other members did.

"Don't take too long," one of the guards said from outside the room. She recognized the voice as Jim Fronson, one of her least favorite people and a Hunter who hated her. Dominick didn't respond, but instead, closed the door behind him and shook his head.

"What a jerk," he said.

Abigail felt certain that he'd said it loud enough that Jim could hear him through the door, which, knowing Dominick, was his exact intention. He walked across the room toward her, stopping a few feet away and sizing her up.

"You look terrible," he said, smirking at her. "Confinement doesn't suit you."

"Great to see you too, Dom," she said. "I thought you were in Germany?"

"I was," he said. "But I had enough schnitzel, so I asked for another assignment. Did you know they drink beer warm there? Tastes like piss when it isn't cold."

"Are you here to guard me?" she asked.

"Jim's got that covered," Dominick said. "Along with some mercenaries."

"We're hiring mercenaries now?" Abigail raised her eyes.

Dominick shrugged. "Dark times. Only twenty-three Hunters left and no recruitment to speak of."

"Twenty-three?" Abigail chewed her lip. "I thought we had twenty-five."

Dominick frowned. "You haven't heard? James Scott and Louis Lamoure got killed about a month ago."

"How?"

"No idea. Someone found them, and it wasn't pretty."

Abigail had liked James and Louis, and it saddened her to hear that they had died. It also surprised her because it wasn't that common for one of their own to get killed.

"How long are you here?"

"Not sure yet," Dominick said. "Got back into town last night."

"Here to keep an eye on me? Make sure I don't try to escape?"

"I'm supposed to shoot you if you do," he said.

"You'd miss anyway. Never were much of a shot."

"Hey, I resemble that remark." He grinned. The smile disappeared almost as soon as it came, however, as he sobered up. Dominick hesitated, and then said, "I should have gotten here sooner. When I heard they had you locked up, I wanted to come, but things have been so busy, and I always found an excuse not to make the trip."

"It's fine."

"No, it isn't. I owe more than that to Arthur, and I definitely owe it to you. I should have reached out sooner, and I'm sorry."

Abigail fell silent for a moment. "You're here now."

"Yeah," he said, nodding. "How are you holding up?"

"Not too bad. Everyone treats me like I'm some kind of animal, and no one will tell me a damn thing about what's going on, but at least I get fresh towels."

"That's rough."

"I don't even know when my trial is supposed to start."

"Next week," Dominick said. "That's what I heard. Frieda is on her way, and then the trial will get underway."

"I thought Aram was overseeing things?" Abigail asked. "The trial is supposed to be remote."

"It is, and only Frieda is coming. She pulled some strings and got an exception. Aram is pretty pissed about it, but the Council already approved her coming to stay."

"What about security?"

Dominick shrugged. "More mercenaries, I guess."

"How do you know about that?" Abigail asked. "That kind of information is above our pay grade and doesn't trickle down to our level."

"I'm the one who flew Frieda in," Dominick said. "Her train came into Lausanne yesterday, and I brought her out here."

"Fly?"

"Snows started early this year, and we've had a rough couple of days. All of the roads have closed until they can get trucks out here. Should open by next week, but for now, we're just flying. I brought in her and Haatim."

"Haatim? He's with Frieda?"

"Yeah," Dominick said. "She's filled him in on the Council and Order."

"Not his father?"

Dominick shrugged. "Rumor has it they don't talk much anymore, but I guess that'll change while Haatim is living here. Only met him the once myself, when I flew them in. From everything I've heard, he's clueless."

Abigail chuckled softly. "You're telling me."

"Frieda asked me to come so I could train him."

"Is she training him to be a Hunter?"

"I don't think so. Just teaching him how to survive. I'm supposed to give him the basics and a couple of advanced lessons."

"Go easy on him," Abigail said. "He's sensitive."

Dominick burst out laughing. "I used to have a dog that was sensitive. Peed on the carpet all the time."

"I don't think you'll have to worry about that from Haatim," Abigail said.

"Don't worry, if there's any iron in that kid," Dominick said. "I'll find it."

Abigail nodded. If anyone could help Haatim get a crash course in the world he'd stumbled into, Dominick could. He could be brutal and harsh, and Haatim would be in for a rough couple of weeks, but by the time he'd done, Haatim would be a completely different person.

Dominick's expression grew pensive, and it felt like the air grew heavier around her. He folded his arms across his chest and looked away.

"This isn't good, Abi."

He'd shifted the conversation and talked about her trial now.

"I know," she said.

"Aram wants to charge you with treason. He wants to dismiss you from the Order and have you executed. This is serious."

"I *know*," she said. "But, after everything that happened in Raven's Peak, he won't be able to, will he?"

"No one is quite sure what happened out there. Reports are still coming in, but they're conflicting. Other things have come up, though, and it won't just be about Raven's Peak. These things won't help in your defense."

"Things like what?"

Dominick hesitated. "Did you speak with a demon without Council consent?"

"What do you mean?"

"We found Delaphene at Arthur's cabin. She'd been there for weeks and was rambling, but she remembered talking to *you* quite clearly."

Abigail's stomach dropped. "I ..."

Dominick frowned and shook his head. "Abi ..."

"I needed to know ..."

"Needed to know what?" Dominick narrowed his eyes. "What could possibly be so important that you would break the Council's laws to find out?"

"How to find Arthur." She hung her head. "I can't leave him there with those demons, Dom. It's my fault they have him in the first place. I can't just abandon him, can I?"

He sighed. "No, but it looks awful, Abigail. Frieda thinks she can make the charge go away. Delaphene isn't exactly a reliable witness, but they also have a lot of little things. You know you weren't supposed to go near Sara or *any* of the girls that Arthur rescued. It was a direct Council order."

"I didn't have a choice," Abigail said. "And, I helped Sara. Her scar is gone, and the link is closed. She's safe now."

"That doesn't matter," Dominick said. "The order came from the Council, not from Frieda. If they find out, then they won't take it lightly."

"What do you mean?" Abigail asked. "You said 'if they find out.'"

"A report came to me from Richard Abernathy about what you did at the park, and I passed it along to Frieda. Right now, it's need-to-know, and we haven't told anyone else."

"You mean they don't know?"

"I mean they don't know *right now*. Richard is loyal, but who knows if the Council could find out some other way. If they do, it'll look bad."

"I know," Abigail said. "But I had to discover the truth."

"They'll try to use it all as evidence that you've turned. A sort of roadmap for your fall from grace."

"What do you mean? They want to say I'm going to end up like Arthur?"

"Worse," he said. "Aram and some of his cronies want to blame *you* for what happened to Arthur."

The words hit her like a truck. Shocked, a light breeze could have blown her over in that moment. "What the hell does that mean?"

"It's just Aram blowing smoke." Dominick put a hand up, palm outward. "But it's a hefty accusation. A lot of the Council respected Arthur, and they want an excuse for why he turned."

"I loved Arthur like a father. How the hell do they think *I* could have had something to do with—?"

"I know, Abi." Dominick reached out and squeezed her shoulder. "I know, and you know, and everyone who matters knows what's in your heart. They're just saying anything they can to try to discredit you. It's only a few people who support Aram, and the rest of the Council will see right through his lies."

Abigail sighed, forcing herself to calm down. "You're right."

"Frieda isn't having any of it. The Council keeps overreaching and overstepping. She's supposed to be in charge of the Hunters, yet they keep challenging her authority and trying to micromanage. She'll not rest until your name is cleared."

Abigail hesitated. "Or, until I'm dead."

Dominick frowned. "Don't think that way. Everything is going to work out. Have faith."

"I haven't had much of that these last months," she said. "But I'll try."

He checked his watch, and then glanced back up at her. "I have to go. I have a meeting with Aram in a couple of minutes, and then I'm heading back to the city to wait for Frieda and Haatim. Do you need me to bring you anything?"

"No," she said. "I'm fine."

"All right. Keep your chin up and stay positive. I'll come back as soon as I'm free and make sure you're okay. We'll take care of all of this, and you'll be back in business in a couple of weeks. You'll see."

Abigail nodded, but she didn't believe his words. She doubted he believed them either. They had such devastating evidence against her, and so many Hunters and Council members disliked her.

Dominick gave her a quick hug, and then headed toward the door. He flashed her one last smile before leaving. Abigail found herself in the cell alone once more, suffocating under the weight of everything and powerless to influence anything.

She stood there, thinking about what her friend had said, and trying to convince herself that all of this could have a happy ending. Unfortunately, she couldn't stop thinking about the idea that people blamed her for what had happened to Arthur.

How could they possibly think she'd had anything to do with what he did? Only a child when he'd taken her in, an orphan with no one to turn to for help, he'd raised and trained her. Abigail hadn't even been with him when he had his breakdown. Hadn't seen him for months before that fateful day.

How could they possibly hold her responsible for something she had no control over?

A few minutes later, she found herself pacing back and forth across the room, trying to clear her head and get rid of the emotions raging inside. She clenched and unclenched her fists, glancing down at the wrist she'd broken when the demon had possessed her body all those months ago.

When she'd killed Arthur.

It didn't hurt anymore. It had, in fact, almost fully recovered since that day in the Church. Even the scars had disappeared. She'd expected to have those cuts for the rest of her life, a constant reminder of when she had failed and lost her mentor, but they had healed far better than expected.

A miraculous recovery, but one that meant little in the greater scheme of things. Not for the first time, she wondered if these would be her last weeks on Earth.

Chapter 3

Both confused and hopeful, Haatim left the meeting with his father. The meeting hadn't been what he'd expected, but it had gone quite well. He looked forward to spending time in the hotel and seeing more of his father.

Haatim also felt gladdened that he'd gotten to state his position about the trial. He'd known his father would disagree but didn't want it to turn into something more. His father had it wrong about her—about everything. Old-fashioned about a lot of things, his father, but it pleased Haatim that they could have a disagreement without it devolving into a screaming match.

The problem was, however, that his father's opinion influenced Abigail's future directly. The idea that a Council of people prepared to make a decision about whether or not someone lived or died seemed unfathomable to Haatim.

Very dark-age, to be honest. He could understand their desire for secrecy and the need to punish disobedience. They battled against creatures that wanted to kill and possess people, and so, mistakes could wind up costly.

But the idea that Abigail would be put to death if the Council decided it was ...

Insane. The only good word Haatim could think of that fit. He found it hard to wrap his head around just how high the stakes of this trial rose.

When he made it up to his room, his breaths came heavy. The building had so many stairs, and the idea that he would need to walk up them every day seemed ridiculous. Especially when a perfectly good elevator lay only a short ways away.

However, he didn't want to get on Dominick's bad side, at least not this early in the relationship. Dominick seemed like a fun-loving and slightly wild person, and completely different from Frieda's strict attention to practice and routine. What, exactly, would his "training" entail?

Certainly, Frieda had never ordered him to walk up the stairs instead of using the elevator.

Haatim dropped off his stuff, and then headed back out. Exhausted, he wanted to take a nap, but still had one more stop to make before he could rest. He walked down the stairs and through the hall toward Abigail's holding cell.

He admired the surrounding decorations. Tapestries hung on the walls in muted earth-tones, detailing a regional history that he knew nothing about. The artwork looked intricate and clean, and everything felt ancient but cared for immaculately.

It felt as though he'd stepped back in time a few hundred years. The entire place had an almost gothic feel to it that appealed to his sensibilities.

Two guards stood in the hallway outside the room that held Abigail. One seemed a short man with greasy hair and rough features, and the other, tall and lanky with a baby face that only a mother could love.

Both of them stood armed with assault rifles and wore bored expressions. The short one looked Haatim over while he approached, dismissing him completely as a threat. Haatim couldn't decide if he should feel offended, and then decided not to.

"Yes? Name and business?" The guy held his rifle in a non-threatening manner, but his eyes said he would shoot Haatim in a second without even the slightest regret.

"I'm Haatim Arison. Just got here a few hours ago."

The guy stuck out his hand, and Haatim grasped it.

"I'm Jim; this is Mike. We haven't met, have we?"

Jim had an iron grip and, unlike Dominick, seemed the kind of guy that made it clear he was trying to inflict pain with how hard he squeezed. Haatim's grimace elicited a grin from his partner.

"Not yet," Haatim said. "A pleasure."

"Aram's son," the guy said with a nod. "Heard a lot about you."

Haatim frowned. Over the last several months, it seemed like everyone he met recognized him, but he'd never been introduced to any of them. It made him uncomfortable, but he couldn't say much about it. "It seems everyone has."

"We don't get a lot of outsiders turning into a Councilman's son, you know?" Jim said. "And you're friends with Abigail, so the rumors say."

"Yeah," he said. "She saved my life."

"Did she, now?" Jim said.

Haatim couldn't be sure, but the tone sounded sarcastic.

"So ... can I go in and talk to her?"

Jim stared at him. "The thing is, kid, you might be Aram's son, but that doesn't mean squat down here. Got it?"

Haatim felt unsure what to say, so he kept his mouth shut.

"You might think you're something special, but you're just some dumb kid with an important father. So, how about we start this conversation over, and this time show a little respect?"

Haatim bit back a disgusted sigh, and then forced himself to nod. He could bite back his pride. The other guy, the lanky one, just watched with an amused expression.

"Hello, my name is Haatim Arison. May I, please, go in and speak with Abigail?"

"You mean the prisoner?"

Haatim frowned. "May I, please, go speak with the prisoner?"

"Yeah, kid, you may," Jim said. "And, I'm gonna let it pass this time. But, if I were you, I'd show a little more respect to the people that can whoop your ass."

"I apologize," Haatim said. "It won't happen again."

His words seemed to mollify Jim, and the guy nodded at him. "I'm going to pat you down now. There isn't anything sharp in your pockets I could hurt myself on, is there? If you lie to me, and I cut myself, I won't be happy."

"Nothing," Haatim said. "Just my wallet and phone."

Jim handed his rifle to Mike, who just kept staring at Haatim in a way that felt supremely uncomfortable, and then stepped up behind Haatim. He patted Haatim's sides and legs, hitting every conceivable area where he might have a concealed weapon. He made it considerably rougher than he needed to, especially in tender places.

Fortunately, Haatim hadn't thought to wear his gun or carry a knife. A few weeks back, Frieda had taught him how to shoot and given him a pistol, but he still hadn't grown used to keeping it with him. Decent at shooting targets now—at least the ones that didn't move—he still didn't feel right having a weapon on hand.

"All right," Jim said, finally. "Just knock when you're ready to come out."

Mike opened the door and gestured Haatim through. He stepped into the hotel room, and the door slammed behind him. The lock clunked a second later.

Inside, he found a decently sized abode with an attached bathroom and a bed set against the leftmost wall. The lights glowed dim, and it took a few seconds for his eyes to adjust. Abigail had the drapes pulled shut, which left the room gloomy and unwelcoming.

Old trays and half-eaten food covered a dining area with a bar and stools. A bed sat along the left wall, messy and unmade, and several chairs sat covered in dirty clothes and other items next to a table by the window.

Abigail paced back and forth between the bed and television, muttering to herself and lost in thought. So distracted that she didn't even notice his entrance. The woman clenched and unclenched her fists, bristling with energy like a caged animal.

"Abigail?" he asked.

She froze, tensing up. Slowly, she turned to him, a muted expression on her face. They stared at each other from across the room, neither one moving. The seconds ticked past as she stared, expression unchanging.

Suddenly, she rushed forward and wrapped him in a tight hug. Abigail squeezed him a lot harder than someone her size should have been able to, and he gasped for air.

"Jesus," she said, finally, letting him go and stepping back. "I've worried so much about you. Where the hell have you been?"

"Out of the country," Haatim said, a little defensive. "And we only just now got back."

"We?"

"Frieda and myself. I traveled with her for the last few months. It's why we couldn't come because my father had already come here."

"With Frieda? Why?"

"She filled me in about the world my father kept secret from me."

Abigail frowned. "No one tells me anything that happens outside these walls. I've had no idea what happened to you. I didn't know if you'd died or anything."

"I've been fine," he said. "I tried calling several times, but they told me you aren't allowed to receive any outside communication. My father wouldn't allow Frieda to come until the Council overruled him, and I didn't want to see him, so we had to stay away."

"It's fine. I understand. It's just that I've been stuck here with no one to talk to for months," she said with a chuckle. It sounded forced. "I'm going a little stir-crazy."

"I can imagine." Haatim nodded.

"You mentioned your father. Have you spoken to him? Did he

send you?" Abigail crossed her arms.

"No." Haatim shook his head. "I talked to him a little while ago. He said I shouldn't visit you, and he doesn't want me testifying in your defense."

"Of course not," she said with a sigh. "I'll understand if you ..."

He shook his head, this time with vehemence. "No way. I am definitely going to help defend you. You saved my life."

"You've already repaid that debt," Abigail said.

"I'll never repay that debt," Haatim said. "Besides, we're friends, and what kind of friend would I be if I didn't stick up for you?"

She smiled. "A crappy one."

"Exactly. You talked to Frieda earlier, right?"

"Briefly." Abigail nodded. "She's trying to put together my defense. Apparently, Aram has found more evidence to use against me, and she feels worried that some of it will stick. She told me you might testify, but she wasn't sure. Aram is your father, after all."

"I'll tell them what happened in Raven's Peak. They don't know the full truth, and when they hear what you did to save all those innocent people, they'll have no choice but to side with Frieda and let you go free."

"What *you* did," she said. "Not me. I tried to face Belphegor and failed."

"We did it," Haatim said. "Teamwork. I just provided the distraction."

"True," Abigail said with a laugh. "You can be quite distracting at times."

"This whole thing is stupid," Haatim said. "I can't believe they're having this trial at all."

"I know. This shouldn't even be an issue; the entire situation is stupid. There are *real* threats out there that we should be dealing with, but no one is even talking about them."

"Like the person who tried to set us on fire," Haatim said.

"Exactly," Abigail said. "They are still out there, and we should be looking for them, not talking about whether or not I broke a couple of stupid rules."

He heard bitterness as she said the last part, and he could sympathize.

"They are only doing this because they hate me."

"Why?" He blurted the question out before he could stop himself. "Why do so many people dislike you?"

"I don't know." Abigail sat on her bed. "Maybe it's my sunny disposition. I don't know. I wish I did. It isn't just your father, either. A *lot* of the Council hate me, and they have since I was a little girl."

"It doesn't make sense. Does it have something to do with Arthur?"

"They ..." She looked away.

"They what?" Haatim said.

"They blame me for what happened to him."

"The thing that happened at the Church?" Haatim asked. "When you were ..."

He couldn't bring himself to say "possessed." He'd heard bits and pieces of the events from Frieda and a few other people. Everyone seemed to have conflicting accounts about exactly what had happened in that Church in the forest.

Haatim didn't know what to believe. Everyone agreed that Arthur had confronted a demon that had possessed Abigail, and yes, he lost his life in the conflict. But, Haatim doubted Abigail had any control over the situation.

From what he'd heard, the Council screwed up by sending her there in the first place, underestimating the threat. If anyone were to blame, it was them. They shouldn't hold her responsible for something out of her control.

At the very least, he wouldn't hold it against her. Haatim cared much more about his interactions with people than any stories he heard. Abigail had a good heart. She was a kind and honorable person—more than he could say for many of the other people he'd met, especially the ones who disliked her.

"Frieda told me about it," he said. "But I don't think you were responsible for any of it."

"That, yes, but also so much more," Abigail said, shaking her head. "They blame me for *everything* that happened to him."

"What do you mean?"

"It doesn't matter. I'm not even sure what I mean," she said, then changed the subject. "What have you been doing with Frieda?"

"She's teaching me about what the Hunters and Council do," Haatim said. "And training me how to fight. Now that I'm ... now that I know what's going on, she's afraid more things like what happened in Raven's Peak could happen to me, and I should be prepared."

"Good idea," Abigail said. "Are you getting any better?"

"I know which end of the knife to hold and how to squeeze the trigger of a gun. I can even hit things, you know, as long as they don't move. But I'm not ready to take on anything more than a loaf of bread.”

“Stick with it,” Abigail said. “You’ll get good enough in no time.”

“People who are good enough are usually the ones who get beat up or murdered. I’d rather be either awesome at fighting or never fight at all.”

Abigail smiled. “Touché.”

“Frieda said she’s going to have you train me once you get out of here,” Haatim said.

Abigail’s smile soured. “*If* I get out of here. That’s still up in the air.”

“I’m not done talking to my father about it. He’s a good man, just misguided. I’ll make him understand what kind of a person you are, and then he’ll move to our side.”

Abigail chewed her lip, looking away. “You should probably get going.”

Haatim frowned. “All right,” he said. “I’ll come back and keep you company, though. As often as they let me.”

“Thanks,” she said.

“Do you want me to bring you some books or other reading material?”

Abigail burst out laughing. “No,” she said. “Books aren’t really my thing.”

“You sure?” he said. “They can distract you. Take your mind off what’s going on.”

“I’m sure,” she said. “The company would be nice, though.”

“Definitely.”

She turned away, and Haatim took that to mean she had dismissed him.

“I’ll come back soon.” Haatim walked toward the exit. “We’ll get through this.”

Abigail didn’t respond. Haatim knocked on the door, and Mike opened it to let him out. Jim had gone.

“Where’s Jim?” Haatim asked.

Mike closed the door and gave Haatim a look that told him he wouldn’t get an answer. Time to get moving. Haatim headed down the hall and toward the lobby.

He would need to find Frieda and let her know he’d spoken with Abigail. He agreed with Dominick: she wasn’t doing well in her captivity, though he seriously doubted he’d do any better after four months locked in a cage. All things considered, she seemed relatively calm and held it all together.

As he approached the lobby, hushed voices spilled out of a side room. One sounded like the voice of Jim, and the other, he recognized as his father.

Haatim drew closer to that room, and then hesitated, not sure if he should make his presence known or eavesdrop. He didn't much care for listening to people without their knowledge, but he also knew his father wouldn't speak honestly with his son around. This might be a good opportunity to find out the truth about everything going on.

He waited at the corner of the doorway, out of sight, and listened. His father spoke, "... don't care what it takes. Find her and bring her here."

"Frieda will want to know what we're doing. What am I supposed to tell her?" Jim asked.

"You're not on assignment," Aram said. "You can do whatever you want. I'll cover your tracks for you. Just bring her back to me as soon as you locate her."

"Where is she?"

"Last report put her in Paris ten hours ago."

"We'll leave in the morning."

"You'll leave tonight," Aram said. "This is of the *utmost* importance."

"What about Abigail?"

"Mercenaries will guard her now. Frieda doesn't want you here, which works just fine with me. Dominick will fly you out to the airport, and a jet is already waiting."

"All right. I'll grab Mike, and we'll go."

"No mistakes this time."

"Yes, sir."

Footsteps came toward the door. Haatim slipped back and ducked into a side alcove behind a statue, out of sight. A moment later, Jim walked past, headed back down the hall toward Abigail's cell. Another pair of footsteps went in the opposite direction, into the lobby.

Who was his father talking about? Why would he try to keep this a secret from Frieda?

Part of him wanted to go tell Frieda about the conversation. She had charge of the Hunters, and his father meant to circumvent her control. Frieda had behaved nothing but kindly to him during these last few months, and he owed it to her.

However, this was his father he was thinking about, and even as much as he didn't trust Aram right now, they were still kin. Whatever

Aram planned, it seemed to have nothing to do with Abigail's trial. For all Haatim knew, the conversation held nothing untoward, and his father just wanted to locate someone.

Still…

He didn't like the fact that his father worked against Frieda willfully. After his speech to Haatim about following the rules, this felt hypocritical. He would look into it on his own and try to find out what Aram planned, and if it proved something he felt Frieda should know about, he would tell her.

✳✳✳

The next morning found Haatim sprawled out on his bed with someone knocking on the door. Still dark out, his clock informed him that he'd woken just before five.

Whoever stood at the door knocked again. Haatim rolled off of his bed and onto the floor, letting out a groan, and staggered to his feet. Bleary eyed, he yawned.

"Hang on," he said, rubbing his eyes. "I'm coming."

When he opened up, Dominick stood there, wide awake and chipper. Already smiling, his grin widened when he saw what Haatim wore.

"Superman pajamas?"

"Don't mock me," Haatim said, stepping back into the room. "It's too early."

"Never too early," Dominick said. "The morning is the best time of the day when you can accomplish the most. We have a lot to do, so hurry up and get dressed. Meet me in conference room 'A' in five minutes."

Then Dominick disappeared from the room, closing the door behind him. Haatim yawned and headed to the bathroom to splash water on his face. He'd gotten up early since he started spending time with Frieda, but never *this* early.

He threw some clothes on, mussed his hair, and then headed out toward the conference room on the other side of the hotel. It felt completely and eerily quiet walking through the halls. It had seemed empty yesterday, but nothing like how it seemed today.

When he went into the conference room, he found Dominick standing next to the table. He had on a pair of ugly glasses and was looking at one of the chairs and talking, but no one else occupied the room.

Haatim hesitated, but Dominick waved him in, still looking at the chair. "Hey, hang on a couple of minutes, and then we'll get some breakfast."

"Uh ..." Haatim said. "Sure."

Dominick looked at him, frowning, and then laughed. He picked up another pair of glasses from the table, flipped a switch on the side, and tossed them to Haatim.

"I'm not crazy," Dominick said, turning back to the chair.

Haatim slipped the glasses on and, suddenly, saw someone sitting in the chair. A small and pretty Asian woman with her hands folded in her lap.

"Wow," he said, flipping the glasses up to see the chair again."

"Augmented reality," Dominick said. "She's in Brazil right now."

The image looked imperfect, and on closer inspection, it became obvious that she wasn't sitting *on* the chair, but rather a part of her stuck out of it. Still impressive, though.

"That's so cool," he said.

Dominick shrugged. "It beats television screens, but not by much. Anong, this is Haatim. Haatim, Anong. He's Aram's son."

She bowed her head toward him. "Nice to meet you."

"You as well," he said.

Dominick turned back to her. "You said Aram wanted you to come?"

"He spoke with Colton yesterday," she said. Her voice came through little speakers on the glasses next to Haatim's ears. "We'll be there Friday."

"Why?"

"Security," Anong said. "He wants more of us on hand."

"And more mercenaries." Dominick leaned against the table. "It's like he's afraid of something. Has he spoken to you about any real concerns?"

She shook her head. "He only speaks with Colton. Do you think I should mention it to Frieda?"

"No," Dominick said. "I will. Just keep doing what Colton said and keep me updated."

"Will do." She reached up and touched the glasses, and then disappeared in a blink.

Dominick removed his glasses, frowning.

"Frieda never showed me these," Haatim said, holding up his pair. "I've seen her wearing them once in a while, but I just assumed her nearsighted."

Dominick chuckled. They put their glasses back on the table and headed for the door.

"More Hunters are coming?" Haatim asked.

Dominick nodded. "Yes, but I have no idea why."

"Is it because both Aram and Frieda are here?"

Frieda had told him about their security policies and how they rarely met in person. They always sought to avoid needless risk and expense whenever necessary.

"No," Dominick said. "Aram called them here, not Frieda. He's in charge of this outpost, so technically, he's allowed to, but it still seems shady."

"Shouldn't he tell Frieda?"

"Definitely should, but he's doing all kinds of stuff behind her back. Just last night, I had to fly Jim and Mike back to the Airport. I have no idea where they were heading."

Haatim hesitated. "Paris," he said after a moment. "They are looking for someone."

Dominick scrunched up his face. "How do you know?"

"I might have overheard my father talking to Jim about it," Haatim said.

"Did he say who they were looking for?"

"Some woman," Haatim said, shaking his head. "I don't know. My father just wanted her brought here."

"Because of the trial?"

"Didn't sound like it," Haatim said.

Dominick fell silent for a moment. "What game is he playing at?" He scratched his chin.

"Should we tell Frieda?"

"You said it wasn't about the case," Dominick said. "Right now, that's all she cares about. We'll take care of Aram in a few weeks when all of this is over with, but in the short term, I think it's best if we just keep our heads down. Besides, we have plenty of other stuff to do today."

"Like what?" Haatim asked.

Dominick grinned. "Hiking. Come on, let's get breakfast."

Hiking, it turned out, meant a multiple-kilometer slog through knee-deep snow. They did a circle around the hotel, spending about two hours walking.

Dominick spoke with Haatim the entire time, asking him questions about his life and telling him things about his own. He liked to tell stories, Haatim discovered, and half of them seemed completely fictional; of that, he felt certain.

"What about the Council?" Haatim asked while they walked. He felt cold and miserable, but determined to put up a tough front.

"What do you mean?"

"When did it start?"

Dominick shrugged. "I have no idea. Not much for history. Somewhere in Europe, I think."

"It's multi-religious?"

"Yep," Dominick said. "No true God, but there definitely is something strange out there. I used to be an atheist."

"Not anymore?"

"I know there's something out there; I'm just not quite sure it needs a label, you know?"

Haatim nodded. "Yeah, I know what you mean. I was a theology major, so I know a lot about world religions. They share a lot of stuff in common, and most of it can be broken down by psychology."

"What do you mean?"

"Well, you know how writing developed independently in different parts of the world but still shares some things in common? That's basically the same thing with religion. It fills a need for answers in all of us."

"You think everyone just wants answers?"

"And hope," Haatim said. "It's biological. You know how you walk into a dark house late at night, and a chair with a blanket on it suddenly looks like a bear? There's a part of your brain that lights up, and it helps keep you alive by exaggerating threats and filling in explanations for things that aren't quite true.

"The same part of your brain handles religion. We have a biological need to believe in things like that, and it only makes sense that different cultures would fill that need in different ways."

"I see what you mean," Dominick said. "There's more than one way to skin a cat."

"Sort of," Haatim said. "I used to think it was just a form of comfort. Something to keep people happy and content and fill that need. Now, though, I think there's something out there, it just doesn't fit the labels we try to put on it."

44

Dominick nodded. "We're almost back."

"Good," Haatim said. "I'm starving."

They walked in silence for a couple of minutes. "Is the Council the only one like it?"

"Nope," Dominick said. "Hundreds of them exist. Thousands, maybe. We aren't even the oldest one. We work with a few of them, but some seem more interested in serving their own purposes than helping people."

"You chase down cults?"

"And other things."

"Like vampires?"

"Haven't heard about anything like that in ages. I guess they used to be a lot more common. Now, they just keep to themselves."

"Most mythology is rooted partially in fact," Haatim said. "I just never imagined stuff like this would be real. Who funds the Council?"

"Governments. Organizations. If you can think of them, they probably fund us. They just might not know it."

The hotel appeared ahead of them, and after a few minutes, they returned to the warmth. Haatim let out a sigh of relief, finding an air vent pumping out warm air and standing by it.

"Let's get some lunch," Dominick said. "And then we'll spar. Don't worry; we won't spend any more time outside today."

"Good," Haatim said. "That felt terrible."

Dominick chuckled. "Just a short jaunt. We'll do a lot of hiking, and it'll usually be a lot farther than that. You better get used to it."

Haatim didn't like that idea, but maybe Dominick exaggerated it or wanted to scare him. "Should we go get changed first and put on dry clothes?"

"Yeah," Dominick said. They walked toward the stairs. "You were able to overhear your father earlier, and he might trust you. If you hear anything important, make sure to let me know, okay?"

"Sure," Haatim said.

"I hate asking you to spy on your father ..."

"No, it's cool, I get it," Haatim said. "I'm not sure how much I trust him right now, anyway."

They climbed the stairs. By the second staircase, Haatim felt exhausted, and he panted, barely able to keep his legs going.

"Why so many stairs?" he asked, gasping.

"It'll get easier," Dominick said. "And there's no better way to train your body. This is my stop."

They stood on the landing of the third flight. Haatim, still panting, had grown sweaty, and Dominick didn't even breathe hard.

"I think I hate you," Haatim mumbled, resting his hands on his knees.

"Everything is to make you stronger," Dominick said with a grin.

"If it doesn't kill me."

"Don't be so melodramatic. It won't kill you."

"Can I get Frieda back and have her train me again? That seemed way easier."

"She's busy," Dominick said.

"Doing what?"

Dominick frowned. "Trying to keep Abigail alive."

Chapter 4

Frieda sat across the conference room table from the digital representations of Jun Lee and Deborah Cofield. Neither of them occupied the room with her, but rather, their 3D creations came through her glasses in similarly organized spaces around the world.

Currently, Jun lived in Japan with his family, and Deborah was out on assignment in Southeastern Georgia.

This pair made for two of the more important and undecided voters in the upcoming trial for Abigail Dressler. Right now, Frieda felt fairly certain that she had six votes on her side, and that another five wouldn't vote on her side, no matter how hard she pleaded.

She'd lobbied hard for support during these last few weeks, and now the trial loomed only a few days away. Jun and Deborah might be the last supporters she needed to solidify Abigail's freedom.

She had two weeks left to convince at least one of them of Abigail's trustworthiness. Aram worked just as hard to swing them to his side, but Abigail felt mostly certain that he wouldn't manage to get both of them.

Jun, a small man in his seventies, had a balding head with leathery skin and a kind face. When younger, he'd become known for his loud boisterousness, and notorious for partying and living life to the fullest. Those years had passed him by, but he still celebrated life.

He'd always been honorable and treated Frieda in a fatherly way, having been close friends with her real father, who'd died some twenty years earlier.

For all intents and purposes, he gave a solid vote in her corner on most decisions. The problem was, he also knew about Abigail's past. He'd been there when Arthur's family got murdered. He'd been there when Arthur first rescued Abigail from the cult.

Jun remembered the days when she had helped Arthur work against the Council, undermining their authority to keep her alive. He'd forgiven Abigail, but it still made a sore spot between them.

Obstinate in his belief that Abigail offered a threat to their security, he believed that she should have been dealt with swiftly and completely during those first days after her rescue.

He'd softened his opinion of her over time, as she proved herself, but not much. Now, he had a second chance to vote to end Abigail's life. Frieda had to pray that, this time, he would vote differently.

Deborah, on the other hand, a quiet and withdrawn Southern woman, felt unwilling to make waves and stand up for what's right. A Baptist, and in her forties, she had fiery red hair and a big smile full of pearly whites.

And, although incredibly smart with an agile mind, Frieda didn't hold her in high regard. The woman seemed indecisive and weak and would vote with whichever side she felt likeliest to win.

Frieda's job was to convince Deborah that she'd already won. Hard to do when the trial hadn't even started.

Both wore virtual glasses to create the facsimile that they were in the same meeting place. The specs looked especially awkward on Deborah's face.

"Thank you, both, for speaking with me." Frieda nodded to each in turn.

"Of course," Jun said. "I trust you've arrived safely in Lausanne, and your trip went well?"

"I have," Frieda said. "The snow is packed down tight but looks beautiful."

"Send us pictures!" Deborah said.

Frieda smiled pleasantly at her, careful not to let out a sigh of annoyance. Martha monitored this call and would take care of such a trivial detail. With important things to discuss, it proved hard to take someone like Deborah seriously.

"Of course. I'm sure you both understand the nature of this conversation?" Frieda said.

"We do." Deborah nodded. "It deals with the upcoming trial of Abigail Dressler and her dismissal from the Order of Hunters."

Frieda bit back her anger at the characterization. This wasn't about Abigail's dismissal, but about her execution, and talking about it any other way came from Aram's propaganda. He'd attempted to mask his true intentions. Make it sound less threatening, and people won't consider it so important.

She forced herself to nod, however, wanting to keep the conversation on track and not get into an argument with the Southern belle.

"Yes. It is about the trial."

"These are serious accusations," Jun said. "Do you want us to believe that they are *all* lies?"

Frieda had to be careful with what she said because Jun knew as well as she did that much of what had been said was true. Abigail, a firebrand, broke rules all the time. The trick lay in downplaying the minor ones and skating around anything more serious.

"Many of them are exaggerated charges, as well as some that are completely unsubstantiated," Frieda said. "Abigail has been a member of the Order for seven years, and Arthur himself trained her. She's one of our best."

"She was the one who killed Arthur, was she not?" Deborah asked.

This comment felt harder to let slide. Frieda wanted nothing more than to dive through the satellite connection and strangle Deborah where she sat.

"Relax," Martha's voice said through the speakers. Her voice sounded soothing. "Take a moment."

"There were underlying circumstances outside anyone's control," Frieda said through gritted teeth. "The Council's inaction put Arthur into the situation that cost him his life, and we can see from hindsight that the decisions *we* made in the matter proved sorely inadequate for the events that transpired."

Deborah frowned. "We had no way to know something like *that* would happen."

"If you had listened—"

"These events have passed." Jun held up his hand and spoke softly. "What's done is done, and it isn't worth regretting our mistakes. All we can do is look forward."

Frieda took a deep breath. "Agreed. Abigail risked her life to save the people of Raven's Peak."

"And disobeyed direct orders at the same time," Deborah said. "An order *you* gave her."

"Her disobedience saved us from murdering thousands of innocents," Jun said, this time directing his statements at Deborah. "I, for one, feel grateful not to have that blood on my hands."

Deborah cast him a glance, and then nodded. She admitted, "True. We do owe Abigail for her quick decisions in Raven's Peak."

"Yet, these other accusations cannot be dismissed so lightly." Jun turned back to Frieda.

"Many of the accusations stem from unverifiable sources," Frieda said.

"Delaphene claims Abigail made a deal with her," Jun said.

Frieda had expected this because the rumor flew all through the Council. Though true, she didn't feel terribly concerned with it because no one else could prove it. Delaphene made for a loose cannon, and if Aram tried to use her as a witness, it could backfire in his face.

"You would trust the word of a demon and notorious liar?"

"What reason could she have to lie?"

"What reason would she have to tell the truth?" Frieda asked. "Other than discrediting one of our own and sowing dissent in our ranks."

"I admit, it is only hearsay," Jun said. "Not verifiable."

"So, I trust you won't give it much weight in the coming trial?"

"None," Deborah said. "Delaphene's tried things like this before. I, for one, won't take her seriously."

"Nor I," Jun said. "Such an accusation, without verification, is useless."

"Good," Frieda said. "I'm glad that is settled."

"Do you have anything else you wish to discuss?" Jun asked. "More accusations you wish to dispel before the trial?"

Frieda fell silent for a moment, pondering her best approach to deal with the situation. She had other things she could bring up to discuss, but felt unsure if it would be her best move.

For example, Abigail had gone to see Sara and communicated with the young girl. That made a much more serious crime than speaking with Delaphene or many of the others because it *was* verifiable *and* in direct disobedience of an order from the Council.

However, no one talked about it, so it didn't seem that word of the communication had made it past Frieda's reports. To bring it up now could turn it into a topic of discussion in the trial, and Frieda might inadvertently doom Abigail.

However, not bringing it up here, and then having Aram raise it during the trial, would prove devastating as well. If she warned them that such a transgression had occurred, she might be able to smooth things over and convince them that it wasn't nearly as big a deal as it seemed. After all, Sara was safe, and Abigail had helped her by healing the scar on her forehead.

Still, it would be a gamble.

Frieda elected not to bring it up. Not yet, at least. If it became a rumor, she would contact them again and face the problem head on.

For now, she would hope that it didn't show up.

She took another tack in the conversation instead by addressing the elephant in the room, "You know what it will mean if Aram is successful in discrediting Abigail, correct?"

The other two Council members exchanged a glance.

"Abigail will be put to death," Jun said. "She knows too much about the structure and membership of the Council."

"I assure you," Deborah said. "That we do not take our responsibility in this matter lightly."

"It's been hundreds of years since such a decision got passed down," Frieda said. "And, in that case, it was clear betrayal from one of our own. Abigail would never betray us, and though she acts selfishly and makes mistakes, she *is* loyal."

"What is loyalty apart from following orders?" Deborah asked. "Her job isn't to question or second guess our decisions. Her job is to protect us."

"And she will continue to do so," Frieda said. "Arthur sacrificed everything to protect Abigail and keep her safe."

"She isn't Arthur." A hint of coldness crept into Deborah's tone. "If memory serves, Abigail had already gotten slated for execution once before in her life."

"That happened years ago," Frieda said. "And that decision got revoked."

"Out of fear and respect for Arthur."

"Arthur saved all of our lives on countless occasions," Frieda said. "He protected our families and did everything we ever asked of him, bar one decision to save the life of a little girl. All I ask is that Abigail be given the same opportunity to prove herself that we gave Arthur."

They all stayed silent for a long moment, and then Jun met Frieda's gaze. "I will take your words under advisement. I cannot speak for Deborah, but I owe Arthur and Abigail many debts. I fear, however, that her actions may be shown to be inexcusable, and if the evidence borne against her is incontrovertible, I will have no choice but to side with Aram."

"The evidence won't be," Frieda said. "I can promise you that."

"Then, I pray for her sake that you are right," Jun said. "I would greatly appreciate having a clean conscience at the end of this trial."

"That's all I ask," Frieda said.

He nodded at her and said his goodbyes, and then he terminated the connection. His image flickered out of existence, leaving only an empty chair in the conference room.

Frieda turned to Deborah. "What do you say? Will you vote to absolve Abigail of these crimes and give her a second chance?"

Deborah stayed silent for a long minute, staring at Frieda and pursing her lips. By the time she spoke, Frieda already knew that she'd lost her vote. "I fear you all made a grave error all those years ago," Deborah said. "In allowing Abigail to live. This would be considerably easier if you'd dealt with her as a child when the Council ordered it, and if I were a member the first time, things would have been handled considerably better."

And then she, too, terminated the connection before Frieda had time to respond. Frieda let out a growl, alone in the conference room once more, and tossed the digital glasses onto the table. They skidded and bounced to the center. She pushed her chair back and climbed to her feet, wanting to hit something.

A moment later, the door opened. Martha padded silently into the room carrying a tray of tea. The assistant set the tray on the conference table and collected the glasses, sliding them into her pocket.

Frieda took a cup and poured a small amount of the hot liquid, hands trembling in frustration. She took a sip, and then set the cup back onto the tray.

"What am I supposed to do?" Frieda asked. "The Council is full of cowards and liars, and I'm supposed to convince them that Abigail proves no threat."

"She *did* capture and make a deal with Delaphene," Martha said in soft tones. "And torture, if you believe what the demon says."

Frieda frowned. She felt furious with Abigail, not only for kidnapping a demon but doing it behind her back. She was forced to find out from the Hunters weeks later what Abigail had done when they found Delaphene raving in Arthur's cabin in the woods.

Worse, if Delaphene was to be believed, then Abigail had treated and bargained with her—an executable offense on its own. Very few members of the Council, and certainly no Hunters, had permission to converse with demons.

Luckily, Frieda could dismiss those charges by pointing out the manipulative nature of demons. Delaphene wasn't to be trusted, and no one would give her testimony any weight. It could even hurt Aram if he tried to push too hard because the Council stood firmly against *ever* dealing with demons, even in a case like this.

"Thirteen votes," she said. "I need one more."

"We will get it," Martha said. "Do you think Jun or Deborah will side with us?"

"We have to convince Jun. Aram got to Deborah already, and I don't like the idea of her having the swing vote. Are there any others we initially dismissed that I could reach out to?"

"You could entreat Victor," Martha said.

Frieda hated the idea. She'd known Victor for a long time, and he was a strong advocate for revoking her command over the Hunters. He wanted to have them serve the Council directly, and didn't like her having any autonomy with how she used her soldiers.

Still, he wasn't a friend of Aram's either. Maybe she could promise him some future favor to get him on her side. Frieda would even relinquish some control if it would win him to her side.

It had to be worth the attempt if nothing else.

"Try to contact him," Frieda said. "And set up a meeting."

"Of course."

"Let's just pray—" Frieda said. "—that nothing else comes up in the trial. Did you find anything else about what evidence Aram intends to use?"

"Only Delaphene and the disobeying of your orders," Martha said. "He hasn't given a notion about anything else."

Frieda nodded. "Let's just hope that's all there is. With any luck, all of this will be behind us in a month or two."

Chapter 5

"Did you find her?" Jim Fronson asked when Michael made it back to the Paris safe house. They'd rented a room in a two-story outdoor motel with a clear view of the street. It seemed a pleasant room with a lot of amenities and quick access to the city, though they didn't expect to stay the night if everything went according to plan.

They'd landed earlier this morning, and it proved rainy and dreary in the city. Already, Jim looked forward to leaving: he'd always found Paris a dreary place, full of pretentious people trying too hard to impress outsiders.

He'd arrived at the motel a few hours earlier, after acquiring a pair of illegal pistols. Michael had gone out searching for their target at all of her known haunts. He'd expected it to take several more hours for his partner to return, and it surprised him to see him back so quickly.

She must have no idea she was being hunted.

And why should she? They were damn good at their jobs, keeping a low profile and maintaining distance until it came time to strike.

Luckily for Jim, that time had come.

"Yeah," Michael said. "I found her. At a bookstore, browsing."

"On her way out?"

"Settling in. She'll probably be there a couple of hours."

"Good."

"Do you know who she is?"

Jim shook his head. "No clue," he said. "And I don't care. It isn't our place to ask. You know that."

Michael shrugged. "I know, just wondering. I like to know what I'm getting myself into."

"Probably the Ninth Circle."

"You think she's a cultist? Too cute to be one if you ask me."

"Aram told us that this job was need-to-know, and we sure as hell don't *need* to know who she is. We're just grabbing her and taking her back."

Michael shrugged. "I don't care that much."

"Well, drop the curiosity and get your game face on. It's time to get to work. Did she spot you?"

"No," his partner said. "She's completely unaware that we're following her."

"Good," Jim said. "This'll be easy."

"She's small too," Michael said. "Won't put up much of a fight."

"You ready?" Jim handed one of the pistols to his friend.

Michael checked the clip, made sure a bullet sat in the chamber, and then nodded. "Definitely."

***

Jim Fronson and Michael Epplinger strode through Paris on opposite sides of the street, keeping an eye on their prey, as she walked down the right-hand sidewalk. She didn't seem to have any clue that they tailed her, but they kept their distance anyway. They didn't want to take any chances.

Michael had it right, she did look cute; at least as much of her face as Jim could see. She had a wide-brimmed hat pulled low over her face and never seemed to glance in his direction.

That suited him fine, though. Only her body interested him, anyhow, and he could see how nice that was. She wore loose-fitting clothes and had a long coat over her shoulders to avoid the rain, but just the way she moved gave him enough to know her to be well-built and athletic: his kind of woman.

The rain sprinkled, but not enough to worry about an umbrella. She'd been in that bookshop for almost two hours while they kept watch, waiting for an opportunity to grab her. They couldn't risk coming in guns blazing and causing a scene because they couldn't risk her getting injured. It was important that they capture her alive and get her back to Aram in one piece: he wouldn't accept anything less.

She turned a corner into an alleyway shortcut behind a few buildings. Off the beaten path. They'd found their opening. He signaled for Michael, and then he followed her in, picking up his pace. The woman walked at a leisurely rate, carrying her stack of books and with her head down to avoid the wind and rain.

Jim slipped a bottle of chloroform out of his pocket and a rag, soaking the chemicals into the cloth. He didn't know why Aram wanted this particular girl—and to be honest, he *was* a little curious—but it wouldn't be difficult getting her back to the motel once he'd knocked her out. From there they could get her onto the private jet and fly her to Switzerland.

He glanced back, making sure Michael remained behind him. His partner strolled casually into the alley. Most people stayed inside this late in the day, avoiding the rough weather, and so they didn't have to worry about anyone noticing them while they captured the young woman.

They moved deeper into the alley, completely out of sight of any bystanders. Mike walked backward and made sure that no one followed them. Jim had his opening.

But when he turned back to look for the girl, she had gone.

"What the hell?" he muttered, stopping. A chill ran up his spine, but he brushed the concern away. He looked around and tried to figure out where she might have hidden.

No doors broke the wall near where she'd been walking, and the only access points into the shops would be closed and locked this late. Even if one *wasn't* locked, he hadn't heard a door open or close, so she hadn't taken that route.

A large dumpster sat up ahead, the huge monstrosities that apartment and industrial complexes used. That's where she would be. She must have realized she had someone following her and ducked behind it to try and hide. It was the only place she could have gotten to while he hadn't actually stood looking at her.

Still ... it looked far up ahead, and he, probably, would have heard her running if she made it all the way up there.

The realization that he felt unsure what had happened left him unnerved. He'd only looked away for a few seconds. Jim liked to be in control of the situation, and he had the terrible feeling that something wasn't quite right.

No reason to panic, though. Maybe he hadn't heard her running because of the rain, and he had no doubt he would find her cowering behind the huge dumpster. No sense adding in monsters where there weren't any.

He moved forward, toward the huge green box, drawing his nine-millimeter just in case. Aram didn't want him to injure the girl, but he wouldn't risk his life without good reason. He crept slowly, controlling his breathing, and stepped around the side to where the girl should be hiding.

Nothing.

Empty.

"What the hell?" he muttered again, shaking his head. He looked further down the alley to anywhere else the girl might have hidden, but could see nowhere else that she could have reached in the few seconds he'd looked away. "Mike, are you seeing this?"

No response.

"Mike?" He turned around.

His breath caught in his throat.

Mike hung from a noose in the alley, maybe ten meters behind him, swinging to and fro. Someone had tied the rope to a balcony a few levels down from the roof.

His stomach cut open, entrails flopped down, but he hadn't died yet. He clutched at the rope around his throat with one hand and tried to hold his stomach in with the other. His legs kicked in the air, trying unsuccessfully to find something to stand on.

A chill ran down Jim's spine when he saw his friend dangling there; something had gone terribly, horribly wrong. He'd seen Mike maybe thirty seconds ago, and his friend was fine. He'd heard *nothing* ...

None of this made sense.

Mike just dangled there, slowly dying before his eyes. Jim stood, watching with his mouth hanging open and trying to get his body to move. He felt frozen. He had no idea what was going on but he knew they'd come *drastically* unprepared for this situation.

"Hang on," he mumbled, looking for some way to get his friend down.

Mike swung five meters up in the air, too high to cut loose. He could try shooting the rope down like they did in the movies, but it was way harder to shoot a swinging line than Hollywood made it seem. Most likely, Mike would die before he managed to hit his target and free him.

Still, he didn't see any better options. He raised his gun and aimed up above his friend's head. "Hang on," he said. Maybe he would get lucky.

"Convenient, isn't it?" a voice said from behind him.

He spun, panicking, and saw the girl they'd followed standing in the center of the alley behind him. She looked calm, her hat pulled low over her face so that he would only see her lips.

"I don't need to go hunting for *you* when you come to me. Isn't this just a stroke of good luck?"

"Who are you?" Jim asked.

"I'm the person who is going to kill you," she said. "But not just yet. Take a moment to say goodbye to your friend if you like. He has a few moments left."

Jim raised the pistol to fire at her, but she moved even faster than he could have imagined. She spun, flinging her overcoat into the air between them. It billowed in the wind, spreading out and obscuring his sight. Jim pulled the trigger over and over, spreading his shots in a wide pattern and hoping that one of the bullets would hit her. He aimed low, figuring she would stay close to the ground, and kept firing.

The gunshots barked in the alley, echoing back at him. He emptied half the clip as the coat settled to the ground.

She wasn't there.

A scuffling sound came from his left, and he looked up to see her crawling across the wall toward him. Her body contorted unnaturally, and she moved at an incredible speed. He turned to fire at her, but she leaped out from the wall before he could pull the trigger.

She kicked the gun, and when he fired, the bullet went wide. She landed on his chest, staggering him and knocking him to the ground. He landed with a thud, the back of his head bouncing on the pavement. It dazed and disoriented him, and he couldn't quite get his bearings.

She ripped the gun from his grasp, and her other hand grabbed his hair. Then she slammed his head against the pavement again.

"Wha ...?" he muttered, struggling to stay conscious.

"Are you asking what I am?" she asked, climbing to her feet. "Or why I'm doing this?"

He tried to stand, and she kicked him in the stomach, knocking him back down. He had to find a way to stand and fight back, or he would end up dead.

"I am exactly what I was made to be. I was fine resting away, but *you* and your kind had to bring me back. As for why I am doing this? That's simple. It's the job I was given. I am nothing if not efficient in taking care of my responsibilities."

The woman drew a knife from her boot. An ornate and beautiful dagger, curved and covered in gems and rubies. Jim moaned and crawled away, trying to make it back to the street to maybe find help.

A heel pressed into his lower back, digging painfully into the bone and tender muscle there.

"But I sincerely mean it when I say thank you. Thank you so much for coming to me and making my job a *lot* easier. I mean, the more of you I kill *now,* the easier my job will become."

She dug the heel in deeper, and her breath came warm on his neck when she leaned down to whisper in his ear.

"Enjoy hell."

And then he felt a knife press against his throat and slice across the soft skin, opening his jugular. Blood spilled out, hot and sticky, as he tried to hold his throat closed. The wound went deep, and he grew weaker each time his heart pumped.

"Ah," she said, walking away down the alley. "I love the smell of fresh blood in the evening."

And then he knew nothing more.

Chapter 6

By the time Haatim finished speaking, his throat felt dry and exhaustion drained him. He'd talked for almost four hours, recounting the events that had taken place in Raven's Peak, leading up to the showdown with Belphegor.

The Council members sat around the conference table, staring at him and listening to his story. Occasionally, one of them chimed in with a question or asked for clarification on a point, but for the most part, they allowed him to speak uninterrupted.

He had, originally, planned to tell the entire series of events from when Abigail had found him, hoping it would serve in her favor to have the Council know how she'd rescued him.

Frieda had counseled him against it, however, because those events included the kidnap and meeting with Delaphene, as well as meeting with Sara. Neither of which would help Abigail at all. Haatim didn't feel comfortable lying about that or trying to dance around the truth, so he'd elected to start with them arriving at the city.

So, he answered things as well as he could, telling the truth about everything. The showdown with Belphegor the only part he did modify slightly. The last few moments of the fight when he'd entered the factory. Instead, he said that he'd stood in the doorway and watched while Abigail took down the demon, and that fear had paralyzed him.

Not so far from the truth.

Silence enveloped the room once he had stopped talking. The other thirteen people stared at him, expressions ranging from annoyed to pensive. A long few minutes passed, and then one of his father's supporters spoke up.

"Is any of your account verifiable by another source?" Ferris Kollam asked.

Frieda had warned him about Ferris. The old man had brown skin and an owl-like face. He always looked angry about something, and during Haatim's story, he had asked the most pointed and least useful questions, trying to discredit everything Abigail did and cast a negative light on her actions.

"No one else who would be allowed to give testimony at this trial was present," Frieda said. "Haatim is our best and only eyewitness."

"So, we don't know if any of this is true?"

"We know that it was recounted as faithfully as possible by our only eyewitness," Frieda said. "The son of a Council member."

"Eyewitnesses are notoriously bad evidence in a trial," Ferris said. "And, he himself claims that he felt afraid much of the time. Does not fear sour memories?"

"Yet, when there is no alternative method for acquiring evidence, we would be wise to take the word of an actual witness to the events that transpired rather than mere speculation."

"Speculation, at least, would not have self-interest. How do we know he isn't making things up or withholding information for his own purposes?"

"What purposes? What reason could he have for lying about what happened at Raven's Peak?" Frieda asked.

"Perhaps, he is being coerced, or he simply wants to tell a fantastical story about—"

"Enough," Aram said, his voice low. "No one in this room will call my son a liar."

The room fell silent while exchanging glances. Haatim found himself a little surprised and gratified to hear his father defend him, even if they sat on opposite sides.

"All right, then," Frieda said, after a pause. "Haatim's testimony has been submitted into evidence. If there are no further objections, we shall move on."

No one spoke up. Frieda nodded at Haatim, signaling he could leave his place at the table. He stood, stifling a groan, and walked to his corner of the room, from where he could observe. His entire body felt sore, and he couldn't remember a time when constant pain hadn't plagued him.

Every day, he woke early, went on a long hike, sparred, did more exercises, and then went to bed. Not given enough time to rest or think or recover. Just a steady and grueling process that felt physically and mentally draining.

His body had grown stronger, but it seemed an incredibly slow process. Dominick focused mostly on low-impact tasks to minimize injuries, and Haatim just did tons of them. Still, it felt like every time he took one step forward, he ended up taking two steps back.

Then again, he'd never slept so well in his entire life.

Luckily, because he had to participate in the trial, held early in the morning, they had skipped out on their hike. At least he had one day to relax.

Haatim, the only outsider allowed into the trial room, had a special dispensation because he also acted as a witness. They hadn't even allowed Dominick inside, and Haatim wasn't supposed to share any details outside of the room.

The hotel had filled up with more mercenaries over the last two weeks. They patrolled the outside and surrounding areas and carried heavy weapons, giving it the feel of a military complex. It all had a dystopian feel for Haatim, locked away from civilization.

Add to that the purpose of this trial, deciding life or death for Abigail in, essentially, a space for a corporate gathering, and the image became complete. The weight of what the Council was doing in a hotel conference room felt hard to wrap his head around.

This made the third day of the trial. The first two, they hadn't allowed him to watch, but Frieda told him they'd gone well. The discussions leaned heavily toward forgiveness and reprimand, and now that he'd given his testimony, he hoped that most people still on the fence would side with Frieda.

After all, Abigail was a hero. No matter how else they described her, she had saved the lives of countless people in Raven's Peak. He didn't even need to embellish to prove just how amazing and selfless Abigail was.

"Who is your next witness?" Frieda asked, directing the question at Aram. Apart from Frieda, he made for the only other person actually in the room. The rest had connected remotely through the AR glasses.

"My next witness against Abigail," Aram said. "Is Delaphene."

Frieda spoke up immediately, "I move to strike this witness."

A look of anger flashed across his father's face. Everyone had heard about what testimony Delaphene would give, but unless they logged it in as evidence, it would serve no purpose.

"She has testimony to give about actions taken prior to Abigail's entrance to Raven's Peak."

"She is a demon," Frieda said. "On that fact alone, we cannot give her testimony any weight. It is in their nature to lie."

"I second the motion," Jun Lee said from across the room. "I have no wish to hear the lies and half-truths of a demon. Even if she did speak the truth, she would have an ulterior purpose."

"She has damning evidence," Aram said. "She claims deals were made and could give specifics."

"Then, are we to make deals with her ourselves to find out what she knows?" Jun asked coolly, meeting Aram's gaze.

Aram hesitated for a second, just long enough to show his apprehension about this testimony. "She has no reason to lie, and we should allow her to speak."

"If you cannot prove Abigail's guilt without this witness, then your case is a smokescreen," Jun said.

"It will be brought to a vote," Frieda said. "Those who do not wish to treat with a demon should, at least, be allowed to voice their objections."

Aram, clearly, didn't like the proposition, but he also didn't have any alternatives. He nodded. "Very well. All who would like to hear the testimony of Delaphene about the actions Abigail took against the Council, vote yea."

A flash came in the middle of the table, and a counter appeared, showing the votes as they poured in from all over the world. It didn't differentiate who cast the votes but did track them as the voters cast them.

It only took a few seconds to realize that Aram wouldn't have his way. Overwhelmingly, they voted to dismiss Delaphene's testimony as evidence.

"The nays have it," Frieda said, a note of smugness in her tone. "Delaphene and all of her testimony will be struck from the record."

"Very well," Aram said. "The Council has spoken."

"I believe that is all of the evidence that is to be submitted today," Frieda said. "We will break and pick up in the morning to have more discussions and cast our final vote—"

"One moment," Aram said. "I have one more piece of evidence I would like to submit, with the Council's approval."

Frieda frowned, dismayed with where this had headed.

"You made no mention of this before?"

"It only just came to my attention," Aram said. "I apologize for the unusual request but feel this evidence necessary to our final deliberations."

"It was not submitted earlier in the trial," Frieda said. "So, I do not believe it should be submitted."

"It is even more important to the nature of this case than Delaphene."

"What is it?" Frieda said with a cold grin. "Another demon?"

She said it in jest, but it didn't go over well in the room. At best, she got a few half-smiles, but no one laughed, and one red-headed woman even coughed.

"May we vote to hear the evidence?" Aram said. "With Delaphene removed, I feel it even more important that we show equality in our considerations of each item. I assure you, what I have to show is completely necessary to this trial, and quite compelling."

"Seconded," the woman with red hair said, raising her hand. She had a distinct Southern accent and wore a dress that matched her hair. It made her freckles stand out and gave her an unattractive ruddy appearance. Haatim thought that maybe her name was Deborah, but he couldn't be sure.

"Very well," Frieda said, wary. Aram had backed her into a corner with no easy way out. "We should vote."

A second later, the tally began flashing. This one a mirror image of the last, with eleven votes tallied in favor for presenting this new evidence.

Aram smiled at Frieda after the vote finished.

"All of the evidence to this point has included Abigail's willing opposition to orders from her leader. This evidence will show her complete disregard for her place in the Order and her willingness to disrespect the Council."

"Please, get to the evidence," Frieda said, an edge of annoyance in her tone. "Spare us the theatrics."

Aram ignored her, still addressing the other members of the Council.

"The Council, after the original events of Raven's Peak when Arthur lost his life, gave Abigail an explicit directive. One of them, to stay away from the children whom Arthur saved that day. We didn't know what role she might have played in their capture while under demonic possession, and we didn't want her presence to cause issues with their recovery. Was this not so?"

"It was," the red-haired woman said. "We all voted for it."

"Unanimously," Aram said, now turning to Frieda. "Was it not?"

Frieda hesitated. "Yes, everyone agreed that until we had further information about those events, we should keep Abigail away. But only because we *didn't* face the original problem correctly—"

"So." Aram turned toward the Council. "It would be a direct violation of a Council order if she went to one of those girls, would it not?"

Everyone stared at him, waiting for him to continue. He paused, gloating, and then said, "I have incontrovertible evidence that she ignored such a Council order. Further, she not only visited, but directly interacted with, Sara Heinelman."

He moved to a table on the side of the room where a laptop sat. As it came to life, so did a television in the corner of the room, showing the screen. Aram tapped a few times and played a video. Haatim recognized it instantly, and his heart sank.

It showed the park he'd gone to with Abigail to see Sara. The view came from up high with a wide-angle lens, and on the screen, he could make out Abigail walking down a park sidewalk.

She stopped in front of a little girl. The image looked unclear, but he knew Sara immediately. On screen, Abigail knelt in front of her, handed her something, and then touched her thumb to the little girl's forehead.

When she did this, the image on the screen flickered, going out of focus from a disruption. Haatim heard drawn breaths when this happened and knew how damning the evidence would look to someone not there.

Hell, it didn't look good to him, and he had been distracting children at that time.

It only lasted a few seconds. When the image came back into focus, Abigail looked exhausted and drained, kneeling in front of the little girl and struggling just to keep her balance. Sara felt her forehead and ran off, disappearing out of the frame.

Another few moments passed before Abigail found her feet and staggered off in the other direction, disappearing off-screen as well. When she disappeared from view, Aram stopped the video and turned off the laptop.

A blanket of silence wrapped the entire room as its occupants tried to absorb what they'd just seen. Haatim supposed the only saving grace for him was that it didn't show him too. At least they didn't get to see his pathetic and creepy attempt to distract the children so Abigail could have that moment alone with Sara.

Finally, Jun spoke up, "This action is clearly in direct violation of our orders." He addressed Frieda. "Did you know of this?"

Frieda hesitated, which Haatim knew further damned her. She looked about to lie but changed her mind. "One of my Hunters, monitoring the children, informed me," Frieda muttered. "However, when that report came in, we also noted that the link had severed and the scar on her forehead healed. Our doctors proved unable to achieve such a result after months of work."

"It doesn't matter what our doctors were or were not able to do," Aram said, savoring the moment. "This was not her decision to make. Nor *yours* in keeping it from the Council."

Frieda didn't respond, keeping her face passive, but Haatim could see the cauldron of emotions raging. He thought to bring up the fact that his father had known about this as well, so why did he withhold the information until now except to get as much impact out of it as possible?

However, that wouldn't help Frieda or Abigail. The damage done, their only hope now lay in the fact that this new evidence wouldn't make too much to overcome in a final vote.

Surely, even with this new information, it wouldn't offer enough to punish someone with death, right?

"That is the last of my evidence," Aram said. "Do you have anything else to present for the defense?"

Frieda didn't respond except to stare at him. Haatim just felt glad that she aimed her look at his father and not himself.

Aram seemed to have a similar feeling. His smile faded, and he looked a little uncomfortable.

"Very well," he said. "We will reconvene in the morning for our final vote on the matter. Thank you, everyone."

✳✳✳

"She just stormed out?" Abigail asked.

"As soon as my father finished speaking and dismissed everyone, she ran out of the room. I've never seen her so angry."

"I have," Abigail said. "But usually directed at me."

Haatim smiled. They sat in Abigail's room, him in an armchair, and her on the edge of her bed. He came by every day, at least for a little while, filling her in on what happened outside the walls of her little prison. Continually, she asked him about how the trial went, but this made the first time he could give her an actual answer.

The Council would be angry if they knew he'd told her about it, but he didn't care.

"You seem to be doing well," he said. "How are you feeling?"

"Better," she said. "It's nice having the trial underway. For better or worse, at least I'll have an answer."

67

"Tomorrow," he said. "I can't believe it's here already."

"I know."

"It must have been a nightmare just waiting around like this. People making such a huge decision about your future, and you can't even be involved in it."

"You have no idea," Abigail said. "Don't get me wrong; I definitely would prefer getting good news tomorrow."

"Unless they find you guilty," Haatim said.

"Yeah. Unless that."

"They won't," Haatim said. "You don't have anything to worry about."

"How can you be sure?"

"I met several of the Council members today. They seem like genuinely good people, who want to help others, not hurt them. I'm confident that they will realize we live in a more beautiful world with you in it than if you weren't."

As soon as he spoke the words, he realized how sappy and romantic they sounded. Abigail, however, either didn't notice or chose not to point it out.

"I hope you're right," she said. "I knew going to see Sara was a bad idea, but I don't regret doing it. I needed to know."

"I get it," Haatim said, unsure if he agreed with her—not in a million years would he have acted against the Council the way she did—but, at the very least, he could respect her decisions. Beyond impressed by her willingness to stand up for what she believed in, he would have liked that trait in himself.

But, he had enough honesty to know that he wasn't made of the same stuff. He worried too much about what people thought of him to act so unilaterally.

"Thank you," Abigail said. "For coming to visit and keeping me company. It's miserable not knowing what's going on, and I'm grateful that you're willing to put up with me."

"Always," Haatim said. "Only one more day to worry, and then you'll be free once again."

"You'll be back tomorrow?"

"Of course," he said. "As soon as the trial is over. I can't wait for the opportunity to come and tell you that you're innocent!"

She smiled at him, but a sad smile. They sat in comfortable silence until a knock came at the door. A few seconds later, Dominick poked his head into the room.

"Ready to go?" he asked Haatim.

"Go where?"

"Hiking," Dominick said.

Haatim groaned. "Now?"

Dominick grinned. "Oh, buddy, do I have something special in store for you," he said. "Meet me outside in two minutes."

Then he disappeared. Haatim sighed.

"Sounds fun," Abigail said, chuckling. "Wish I could go."

"I wish you could, too," he said. "Instead of me."

"Oh, come on, it can't be that bad?"

"I've never felt so tired in my entire life. I feel like one of those stuffed chew toys you give to your dog and it flails around with it."

"Yeah, that sounds like Dominick."

"It's freezing outside," he said. "Snow isn't my thing."

"Mine either," she said. "At least, I get to stay inside where it's nice and toasty."

Haatim laughed. "You're mean."

Abigail smiled. "You might hate it now, but Dominick is one of the best people I've ever met. If anyone can help you learn how to take care of yourself, it's him."

"Yeah," Haatim said. "That's what Frieda keeps telling me. In fact, every time I have to do something crappy, everyone tells me that, one day, I'll look back on it as a learning experience and feel grateful it happened."

Abigail shrugged. "It builds character?"

"Why can't sitting around and eating a tub of ice cream build character?"

"It does," Abigail said. "But only if you're lactose intolerant."

Haatim chuckled. "True. I better not keep Dominick waiting. I'll be back tomorrow as soon as the trial is over."

"Okay," Abigail said. "I look forward to it."

"It'll be good news." Haatim headed for the door. "I promise."

Abigail smiled again but still didn't believe him completely. "Sounds good," she said.

He headed out into the hall to meet Dominick, praying he had it right about the trial. He didn't know what he would do if they found her guilty.

"How much farther?"

"Only a little," Dominick said. "Stick with it."

Every time they crested one hill, another waited for him on the other side. Haatim felt convinced that Dominick was just leading them in circles, always pretending like they were on their way back to the Council hotel but secretly leading him further away.

Probably to kill him. By now, he couldn't feel sure of anything. They'd stayed out here for hours, at least twice as long as their normal forays.

Light snow fell, which meant he couldn't prove or disprove his theory by using their tracks. Everywhere he looked, a fresh dusting of snow covered everything, and it all looked the same. Mountains, hills, and valleys all around.

These mountains aren't beautiful, he decided, revoking his earlier opinion on the matter. *They are evil and terrible.*

His lips had frozen, his cheeks felt like he could scrape them off, and his eyes as if they'd iced into his skull. Cloudy and dark one moment, the sun would peek through the clouds and threaten to blind him the next. It reflected off the snow and made it impossible to see until it went away once more.

Dominick had a pair of sunglasses but hadn't brought any for Haatim. The lesson, he'd informed Haatim a few hours earlier, was always prepare for anything.

Right now, Haatim felt sure the lesson was never to trust Dominick.

"How much farther?"

"Two kilometers," Dominick said. "It's getting late, so this time, I mean it."

If Haatim could have run forward and punched Dominick, he would have. The problem was, he didn't have enough energy.

"I don't think I can go any more," Haatim said, stumbling down to his knees. His winter clothing hung heavy, and drenched in sweat now, it froze solid when the temperature dropped. It felt like he carried an extra kilo of body weight.

"Sure you can," Dominick said. "The alternatives are either stop here and build an igloo or die."

"You could carry me."

"This is about teaching you how to survive," Dominick said. "If you can't make it on your own, then it defeats the entire purpose."

"That's why we form into cultures," Haatim said. "So people can survive as groups."

"Your group is yourself for today. The only person you can ever count on is the same one that looks you in the mirror each and every morning. You need to test your limits and push past them. That's what we're doing. Trial by fire."

Haatim grumbled, "I don't see any fire. Quite the opposite."

"Would you like me to add fire to this exercise?" Dominick asked.

Haatim tried to imagine the myriad of terrible ways in which Dominick could torture him further using a torch.

"No," he said. "I'm fine."

"We're almost back. I won't push you more than you can go. Think about something else. Distract your mind and let your muscles do the work."

"What else is there to think about?"

"How beautiful it is out here."

"It's just hills, mountains, and trees," Haatim said. "It stopped being beautiful hours ago."

"Think about a beach in Tahiti."

"Escapism has never been my thing," Haatim said. "I can imagine the beach, sure, but I imagine it being just as cold as these stupid mountains."

"Then focus on Abigail," Dominick said. "Tell me about her trial. They allowed you to observe today. Give me some clues about what's going on."

"Frieda hasn't told you?"

"I'm not in the loop," Dominick said. "She's too busy."

He couldn't imagine how it would help, but he'd try regardless. It couldn't make things worse.

"They talked for about an hour, and then I gave testimony," Haatim said. "Told them about Raven's Peak."

"Oh? What'd they think?"

Haatim shrugged. "No clue. They aren't exactly the most responsive crowd."

Dominick burst out laughing. "You can say that again," he said. "It's like talking to a brick wall, except the brick wall might get more done."

"The meeting didn't end well, though," Haatim said, and then told him about the video. "It didn't look good."

Dominick fell quiet for a minute. They walked through the snow for a while, plodding along. The only sound came from Haatim's heavy breathing as he tried to keep pace with Dominick.

"Abigail has always been impulsive," Dominick said. "She decides to do something, and then she does it before she can stop and realize how foolish her plan is. It's one of the things that makes her so good at her job. She's confident."

Haatim chuckled. "Boy, do I know that."

"And reckless. The Council has had it out for her for a long time. This is just the culmination of years of work from Aram. I just wish she hadn't given them the impetus to actually do it."

They walked for a while longer, cresting another hill and climbing down into another valley. More trees, more hills. Haatim bit back his desperation, not sure how much farther his body could go. He'd never experienced so much exhaustion in his entire life or felt so broken.

"I used to be jealous of her," Dominick said.

"Why?"

"Arthur trained her."

"I've heard about him," Haatim said. "But I don't know much. He was Abigail's mentor?"

"That, and a lot more. It's hard to explain just how influential he proved to the Council. I'm a normal guy. In better shape than most, tough, and I can handle my own. But Arthur, he was something else."

"What do you mean?"

"He would charge headlong into a building full of enemies and win. He always stood up for the right, even going toe to toe with Council members if they got out of line. Hunters never do that because they have the power to turn everything against us. If things hadn't happened as they did, Arthur would have been on the Council in only a few more years."

"What happened?" Haatim asked. "No one will give me a straight answer."

Dominick stopped walking, frowning. He looked at Haatim. "Ever hear the expression that the men with the greatest strengths also have the greatest flaws?"

Haatim shrugged. "Yeah, I suppose."

"Arthur lost it. He lost control. An incident happened, and he killed a lot of innocent people. To this day, I have no idea what happened or why he did it. I think he just ... snapped."

"He murdered people?"

"A lot of them," Dominick said. "That's why they locked him in that black-site prison. A lot of the Council wanted to have him executed instead. I bet you can guess which Council member pushed for that."

"My father," Haatim said.

"Bingo. But they couldn't do it. You don't murder Superman, even when he turns evil."

"But, he trained Abigail?"

"He never trained anyone before her. Kept to himself and did his thing. Abigail proved different, and I always felt jealous that she got trained by the best."

"Did you and she ever ...?"

Dominick glanced over at him. "Date?"

"Yeah," Haatim said. "I'm sorry, that's way too personal."

"Yes, it is," Dominick said. "It's fine, though. Abigail isn't the dating type. Too independent. I guess that's what makes her so appealing."

Haatim hesitated, realizing that Dominick hadn't given him a straight answer. He knew better, however, than to push the issue.

"What's that?" Haatim pointed ahead. Hard to tell, but it looked like smoke.

"I told you," Dominick said. "We're just about here. Top of this hill, and then we're in the final stretch."

They crested the top of the next rise, and the hotel sat in the distance. Only a few hundred meters ahead now, tucked into the mountainside.

Haatim stumbled forward. "Thank God."

"Only a little longer. Don't press. Just focus on keeping up this same pace, and we'll get there."

Haatim ignored him, practically running now. He could imagine the heat pouring over him when he stepped into the lobby. It would feel so good once he made it back to his room and could take a nice hot bath and order room service and ...

His foot slipped on a sheet of ice hidden under the snow. He fell onto his butt and rolled down the hill, bouncing painfully along the ground and getting snow inside his coat and clothing.

He landed deep in a snowdrift on his back, staring up at the sky. Behind and above him, up the rise, Dominick laughed raucously.

His entire body hurt, and he felt too exhausted even to stand. He tried to roll out of the snow, but it had packed tight, and he could barely move.

Dominick appeared overtop him, blocking out the sky and smiling.

"You got yourself nice and stuck, didn't you?"

"Yeah," Haatim said, reaching his hand up. "Can you help me out?"

Dominick laughed. "Nope. I'll see you back at the hotel."

Then he turned and set off walking. Haatim struggled to pull himself loose. More snow found its way into his clothes each time he shifted.

"Trial by fire, Haatim," Dominick called, disappearing from Haatim's view toward the hotel. "Trial by fire."

✳✳✳

It took another thirty minutes for Haatim to make it to the hotel and into the lobby, and by the time he did, his entire body ached and tingled. Never had he felt so cold or weak, and his entire body shook from the chill. He needed to get out of these clothes.

Haatim tracked snow through to the elevator and pressed the button. With no Dominick in the lobby, just this once, he'd ride up. If ever a time had come when he needed to bend the rules and cut a corner, this was it.

He stood there, rubbing his hands and blowing on them. The heat of the room enfolded him. Glorious. He couldn't wait to warm his body with a nice, long bath.

The elevator dinged, and the door slid open. Dominick stood there, leaning against the wall. He'd changed clothes and looked like he'd warmed up already.

"No elevators," Dominick said. "You know the rules."

Haatim groaned. "There have to be exceptions."

"No exceptions." Dominick pointed toward the stairwell.

"It's five flights!"

"Then, you'd better get a move on."

Haatim stared at him for a second, grumbled a few unmentionable words, and walked to the stairs. He trekked up slowly, putting one foot in front of the other, up each flight. His body screamed in agony, and when he finally made it to his room, he felt so exhausted that nausea rolled through him.

By the bed, he peeled off his sodden clothes, letting them fall to the floor around him, and staggered to the restroom. Then he ran water into the tub and dipped himself in, letting out a long sigh.

Haatim lay in the water for almost an hour, soaking his tired muscles and staring up at the ceiling. He couldn't remember any time in his life that he'd ever gotten so beaten down physically.

But, it had a good side, too. Being this tired released endorphins he wasn't used to experiencing, and lying in the warm water gave him one of the most pleasant experiences he'd had in a long time.

After an indeterminate amount of time, a knock sounded on the door. At some point, the sun had set, and the room had grown almost completely dark. Haatim grabbed a towel before checking through the peephole.

Dominick. Of course.

"One second," Haatim called, rushing over and throwing on a shirt and shorts before opening the door.

"Get warmer clothes on. We're off to the city to have dinner. Five minutes, in the lobby."

Then he turned and headed down the hall before Haatim could reply. Quickly, he changed, putting on dry winter clothes. He felt refreshed from the bath, but at the same time, his body was weak, and he staggered everywhere.

Also, however, he felt half-starved, and the idea of getting hot food sounded fantastic.

When he made it to the lobby, Dominick waited for him. He looked chipper and excited as if they hadn't just hiked for hours through knee-deep snow.

"How do you feel?" he asked, as they headed outside.

"Broken," Haatim said. "My legs feel like I'm walking on rubber."

"You'll sleep well tonight," Dominick said.

"I'm sure I will," Haatim said.

They climbed into Dominick's sedan and headed out to the road. The twenty-minute drive, made longer by the packed snow on the roads, took them into late evening, and the city lights came on.

They drove to an expensive restaurant near the center of town, the sort of fine dining establishment that Haatim had only been to a handful of times.

"We're eating here?"

"It's a special occasion," Dominick said. "Come on."

They walked into the establishment. Haatim felt woefully underdressed for this, wearing jeans and a brown overcoat. Dominick went through the restaurant, nodding at the man behind the counter, and headed for a specific table.

"If he asks," Dominick said as they walked. "We work as technical consultants for a company called Central Development Agency."

"What?"

"CDA. Remember it. And, we've been here for two weeks working on a Capital Expense project. We're developing a web application for tracking employee timesheets. Got it?"

"What are you talking about?"

Dominick ignored him, striding ahead just as a man in a business suit stood at a table in the center of the room. He had dark skin and a shaved head with a goatee and brown eyes. Dominick smiled, stepped forward, and embraced the man in an affectionate hug.

"Hey, hun," the man said, squeezing Dominick tight before letting him go. Dominick shifted to the side between the man and Haatim, holding up his hand toward Haatim and glancing back and forth at them.

"Allow me to introduce you two," Dominick said. "Marvin, this is Haatim. We work together. Haatim, this is Marvin. My husband."

✳✳✳

It took Haatim a few seconds to regain his composure before he reached out and accepted Marvin's extended hand. Neither man noticed his pause. Or, at least, they were gracious enough to pretend not to.

"It's a pleasure," Haatim said.

They took their seats at the table, Haatim on one side and Dominick on the other, beside his husband.

"I thought you would make me wait all night," Marvin said to Dominick. "I worried that you'd cancel on me."

"It's been crazy at work," Dominick said, picking up a bottle of wine from an ice bucket and filling his and Haatim's glasses. "Several projects coming due all at once. We can hardly keep up with it, right?"

Haatim, looking at his menu, took a second to realize Dominick sat staring at him. His eyebrow raised as he poured amber liquid into Haatim's glass.

"Oh yeah," Haatim said. "Ridiculous. My boss works me to the bone."

Marvin laughed. He had a full laugh, disarming and pleasant, and Haatim found himself joining in.

"The crazy life of a software developer. I don't envy you guys."

"Marvin, here, is a doctor," Dominick said. "So, he naturally distrusts computers."

"Not the computers," Marvin said. "Just the people trying to use them. He said your name was Haatim, right?"

"Yes," Haatim said. "That's me."

"Dominick has told me so much about you," Marvin said. "It's nice to put a face to the name."

Haatim looked over at Dominick in surprise. "He has?"

"Yes."

"What sort of things?"

"Only good things," Dominick said, grinning. "I don't tell him the whole truth."

Marvin laughed again, shaking his head. The waiter came by and took their orders. Haatim couldn't help himself, he ordered the half-chicken, crab cakes, mussels, and a sharable portion of mashed potatoes just for himself. He also eyed the desserts, figuring he would still have an appetite after his meal.

Once the waiter had disappeared, they engaged in pleasantries. Most of the time, Marvin spoke with Dominick, asking about work and talking about the crazy weather since he'd arrived in Lausanne, but occasionally, one of them would turn and address a question or comment to Haatim.

He tried to follow the conversation as best he could, nodding and answering questions with the shortest and most mundane of answers he could. He knew nothing about writing software or tracking timesheets, but clearly, Dominick knew quite a bit.

The wine made Haatim feel loose and relaxed, and when the food arrived, he ate as fast as he could. He cleaned up his entire plate. Marvin watched him with fascination.

"And I thought only Dominick had such an appetite," Marvin said. Haatim paused, slurping a mussel in one hand and holding a chunk of bread in the other. "Do all software developers eat like the two of you?"

"Only the talented ones." Dominick bit into his steak. He smirked and winked at Haatim.

By the end of it, Haatim declined the dessert. Not because he wasn't still hungry, but because it would have embarrassed him to eat so much food and then finish off an entire dessert alone. Dominick paid for the meal, they said their goodbyes, and then he ushered Haatim to the exit and out to the car.

During the drive back, the exhaustion set in, and a heaviness fell over Haatim. He yawned, glad Dominick drove and not himself.

"Your husband seems nice," he said.

Dominick nodded. "He is. We've been married four years, and I'm usually able to get positions closer to home. It's not every day something crazy comes up like the trial of one of my closest friends."

"Seemed like it was supposed to be a date," Haatim said.

"It was," Dominick said. "Marvin came to visit for the weekend and wanted to do something special."

"That's weird." Haatim shook his head.

"What? That he wanted to see me?" Dominick asked with an amused smile.

"No," Haatim said. "That it's the weekend. I forgot what day it was."

Dominick chuckled. "Hard to keep track when every day is the same."

"Why did you bring me?"

"Backup," Dominick said. "I hate lying to him, but there are some things I just can't tell him. I've been so preoccupied with worrying about Abigail that I needed to add a distraction. He won't ask quite as many questions when we have company. He heads back home tonight."

"He was okay with me coming along?"

"I told him you were lonely, and I felt sorry for you. He was totally fine with it, and I have to say, you played your part perfectly."

"You told him about me?"

"I told him you were a Java developer with an emphasis on full stack integration," Dominick said. "The sort of thing no one understands outside of certain company. This way, he wouldn't ask you any tough questions."

"How do you know so much about computers?"

Dominick shrugged. "A hobby."

They drove the rest of the way in silence, and at some point, Haatim must have dozed off. Dominick tapped him on the shoulder to wake him.

"We're here."

Haatim grunted in response, staggering out of the car. The cold wind felt bracing on his skin, waking him fully. He shivered and headed inside. Halfway to the elevator, he let out a huge sigh and turned, instead, for the stairs.

Dominick chuckled behind him. "Good. You're learning."

"Have I told you yet, today, that I hate you?"

"Nope," Dominick said. "Get some sleep. Big day tomorrow. We'll get exercises in before the trial starts to help limber up your muscles. Helps with the recovery."

"Great," Haatim said. "Just what I wanted."

"Don't worry; that's the big hike. It'll get easier from here."

Haatim didn't know whether or not to believe him.

He leaned toward not.

Haatim sighed again, heading into the stairwell and staggering up the stairs. His body cried out in agony with each step, but somehow, he made it up to his room and inside.

There, he collapsed face first on the bed, fully clothed, and fell asleep in seconds.

"We've heard the testimony from my son about the events that took place at Raven's Peak," Aram addressed the Council members gathered around the table. "I will not dispute that her actions were heroic and that she showed willing to risk her life for the sake of saving others, including my son."

From his corner of the room, Haatim watched his father, nervous about the fact that one of the most important chairs sat empty—well, emptier than normal, considering the AR glasses and digital connection.

Frieda's chair remained conspicuously empty. She hadn't answered her cell phone. Haatim hadn't heard from her all morning, and this on the last day of the trial with them set to cast their final votes.

A task his father seemed in a hurry to do. They'd told Haatim that he wouldn't be allowed to speak during this meeting, but could watch.

"However, we also saw the video of Abigail's indiscretion with Sara Heinelman in which she disobeyed a direct order from the Council. This was not the first time, nor even the second, that she made a mockery of our decisions. Her willful disobedience has gotten out of hand, and the question here today is whether or not we can ever trust her again."

Haatim wanted, desperately, to speak up and remind them that this wasn't a vote about slapping Abigail on the wrist. The vote held much more importance, and his father tried to downplay the responsibility.

"The Council had their concerns about Abigail when she was a child. They worried about what sort of person she might grow into. They wondered what sort of corruption might manifest itself. Many of you were present during those days, and you remember that the machinations that kept her alive were not based on reality or facts.

"We keep giving Abigail more chances to redeem herself, and every time, she throws them back in our faces. This sort of behavior can become infectious and create a cancer in our organization if left unchecked. I, for one, feel it is time we checked this behavior and did the necessary to assure the future of this Council."

"Perhaps, we should await Frieda's presence to cast our votes," Jun Lee said. "This isn't a decision about what sort of takeout we're going to order."

"And where is Frieda?" Aram asked. "Have you spoken with her?"

"I have not," Jun said. "She has not answered any of my messages."

"It seems she is too busy to be bothered with this trial," Aram said.

"An unfair characterization," Jun said. "Perhaps, she has other issues to attend to."

"What issues might these be?" Aram asked. "I know of no other issues more important than this."

"Perhaps, a pressing issue only just presented itself. I feel we should postpone this vote until Frieda is present."

"I can go look for her," Haatim blurted out. Everyone in the room turned to look at him, and many of them wore angry expressions.

"No," the red-headed woman said. "I agree with Aram. We scheduled this meeting, and at an inconvenient time for many of us. If Frieda chooses not to attend, that is her prerogative, but we will not hold back on our vote to accommodate one person. I recommend that we move the vote forward and cast it immediately."

The room fell silent for a minute, and then Jun Lee said, "Your actions feel deliberate."

"Your tone sounds accusatory," Aram said. "I am not the one who chose today to make myself unavailable."

"This isn't justice," Jun Lee said. "I refuse to vote until all Council members are accounted for."

"That is within your rights," Aram said. "But, I am in charge of this meeting. All in favor of casting our final votes now rather than postponing?"

Everyone shifted and cast their votes. A tally flashed up: seven for, five against. Only Frieda's vote remained unaccounted for.

"Wait," Haatim said, standing up. "This isn't fair. A decision so important shouldn't be handled like this!"

"That is the second time you've interrupted," Aram said, staring pointedly at Haatim. "It will not happen again."

Haatim opened his mouth to speak again, and then changed his mind. He sat down and bit back an angry sigh.

Where the hell are you, Frieda? What the hell is so important that you're missing this?

"It is agreed," Aram said, addressing the room. "We will now cast our votes for the future of Abigail Dressler."

✳✳✳

"Who sent them there?" Frieda asked.

"I don't know," Martha said.

"What the hell were they doing in France?"

"I can find no record. Ma'am, you *must* go to the Council meeting."

"I will, as soon as we sort this out," Frieda said. "If this was Aram, I'll finally have what I need to bring him down."

"You think he did this?"

"Who else?"

"We have no evidence."

"Nothing direct," Frieda said. "But, certainly enough to justify looking more closely."

Frieda sat in her room with her assistant. Jim Fronson and Michael Epplinger had been out of contact for the last few days, suspicious on its own, but now she stared at images of their dead bodies in the streets of Paris. Murdered in gruesome fashion and left for the authorities to find.

Jim lay torn apart, and Michael hung from a balcony in an alleyway, his abdomen torn open to spill his intestines. Whoever had done this didn't just want the two men dead; they wanted to send a message.

Neither Jim nor Michael was supposed to be on a mission right now, yet both had drawn from their mission funds and organized a flight to and from Paris on a private jet. The most confusing part was that their flight to Paris listed two passengers, and the flight back added a third. No other information showed as logged about the trip, nor a signoff of approval from any Council member.

Which meant someone had gone behind her back and sent these Hunters on a mission. What worried her the most? The fact that a Council member had acted to control her Hunters without permission? Or the fact that Jim and Michael had gone along with it and disobeyed her?

"You need to get to the meeting," Martha said. "It is the last day of the trial, and Abigail needs your support."

"The trial will need to be postponed," Frieda said. "Or dismissed completely. This is significantly more important. Two Hunters are dead, Martha, and someone is actively working against us. We have a traitor in our midst."

"We still can't prove it."

"Not yet," Frieda said. "But I will still enjoy watching Aram squirm when I bring this information to the Council's attention. His time is nearly through."

She strode out of the room and down the hall. The Council meeting had been scheduled to start twenty minutes ago, but they would, probably, still be discussing and deliberating and waiting for her to show up.

Their deliberations would end, however, when she brought this to their attention. Even if she couldn't find a way to tie it to Aram, it would be enough to turn a lot of his supporters to her side.

But that wasn't the only problem.

Frieda didn't think that Aram would work against the Council. Sure, he was self-centered and prone to manipulating things to serve his agenda, but he'd always been a loyal member. She couldn't imagine him working actively against their interests, and he had someone in Paris he was searching for.

Who, and why?

She needed answers.

Frieda burst into the Council meeting in a rush, determined to take control and get her answers. She knew immediately, however, that something had gone terribly wrong.

Aram, seated at the end of the table, wore a smug expression. Haatim sat in the corner, looking worried and depressed.

Martha appeared beside her, handing her a pair of AR glasses. She put them on, and the rest of the Council appeared around the table. They had various expressions of happiness and anger on their faces.

"Frieda," Aram said. "So good of you to finally show up."

"We have a problem," she said. "Someone is acting without the authority of the Council."

"What do you mean?" Jun Lee asked.

"Two Hunters were sent to Paris a few days ago, and now both are dead."

"Who sent them?"

"It wasn't logged," Frieda said. "So, it could be anyone."

The Council members murmured and looked at each other. Frieda tapped a few times on her tablet and transmitted the images to all of them, showing the brutal images of Jim and Michael. The murmuring intensified.

"What assignment were they on?" a Russian woman named Vasilisa asked. "What were they doing in Paris?"

"Nothing was reported," Frieda said. "Neither of them was on assignment, yet both of them requested a private jet and planned on bringing something back with them."

"Back where?"

"To here," Frieda said.

"The only Council members out there are you and Aram," Jun Lee said.

"Perhaps, a mistake?" Aram said.

Frieda glanced at him. He looked at the images in horror. His face grew pale, and she knew, instantly, that she had it right. He had sent them and hadn't expected this outcome.

"No mistake. Council funds were approved and used, and now two men lay dead. Whoever did this has betrayed us completely and will have to answer for their crimes to the Council."

A hush fell over the room. Frieda wheeled on Aram.

"We must suspend the trial until after *this* is taken care of. Perhaps, it will shed some light on the truth about what's been going on and help in Abigail's defense."

No one responded, and Frieda realized from the silence that events had moved faster than she.

Jun spoke up, "Apologies, Frieda, but we have already cast the vote. Abigail's fate has been decided."

"Decided?" She looked around at the Council in bewilderment. "What has been decided?"

Another hesitation, and then Jun said, "She is to be executed."

"Then, it needs to be stopped!" she said. "Is it scheduled for the morning? We can cast a vote to revert the decision until all of this is sorted out."

This time, Aram spoke up, cowering meekly in his chair and tugging at the collar of his shirt. He cleared his throat. "I've already dispatched Hunters to carry out the sentence."

Frieda froze, completely shocked by the information. She stared at Aram for a few seconds, and then said, "You pathetic coward."

Then, she took off the glasses and threw them onto the table. Next, Frieda sprinted out of the room and down the hall. Haatim ran behind her, as they dashed for Abigail's room.

"You won't make it in time," Aram shouted from behind.

Frieda prayed he had it wrong.

Chapter 7

Abigail waited to hear the decision of the Council, as nervous as she'd ever been in her entire life. She'd tried exercising to take her mind from worrying, but it hadn't helped, and she found herself pacing in the center of her room once more.

It felt like it had taken forever but it hadn't been that long. Either it would be a quick vote, or they would take a long time deliberating, and she didn't know which one worked better in her favor. Seconds dragged by at a snail's pace, and Abigail felt sick, she was so scared.

She kept her body moving, focusing on breathing and relaxing. Should she try to escape? That might be her best option at this point, and the more time that passed, the better that option seemed. Her hearing nothing probably meant things had gone poorly, and they were trying to decide the best way to kill her. The most humane.

At least, that's how she imagined it.

The thick walls held no other openings leading into and out of her room other than the door. The bars on the windows offered gaps too small to slip through, but maybe she could jar one loose and slip out.

Or, maybe, she could make a run for it as soon as the door opened. She could push past the guards and try to escape down the hall before they could put a bullet in her back.

None of those options, however, made her feel any better. Neither of them would work. Abigail had left it too late to try and escape now. If that had been her plan, she should have done it months ago.

Now, she was stuck with whatever fate the Council handed down. Haatim had assured her it would go in her favor and that they had all the votes they needed to find her innocent of these crimes, but she still couldn't help but imagine he might be wrong.

If this were to be her end, then she wouldn't beg or plead. Arthur had taught her to remain strong and independent and to face death bravely. Sure, she hadn't planned to go out, but at the very least, she could take control of the situation and go out on her terms.

After what felt like an eternity, the door opened. Four men stood just outside the room.

Two of them, the mercenaries posted as guards, and the other two, Hunters she'd known for years. Colton Depardieu and Anong Sao.

The pleased expression on Colton's face told her what decision they'd passed down. They hadn't come to set her free.

Anong, a small woman and pretty and nimble, came from Southeast Asian descent. Colton, a burly and ugly man, had blonde hair and blue eyes. He loved attention and behaved like a complete jerk in his treatment of women. That formed part of why she'd never gotten along with him. The other reason came down to him just being an asshole.

They all stepped into the room, leaving the door open behind them.

Colton looked thrilled to be here now that he would get to murder her. He'd always hated Abigail, and Arthur too. An unrepentant bully, he didn't like that Arthur always proved quick to put bullies in their place. Anong, carrying a pistol and frowning, looked worried and a little disconcerted by the situation.

"It's time, then?" Abigail tried to sound brave. Her voice came out a lot weaker than she would have liked, and her pretense felt all too obvious.

"Yes," Anong said. "Abigail, I am so sorry about all of this. I know you—"

"Oh, shut up," Colton said. "It's long past time we did this. She's been a problem since the Council first rescued her, and if not for Arthur, I would've put a bullet in her a long time ago."

"She's one of us." Anong shook her head. "She deserves our respect."

"She'll *never* be one of us," Colton said. "She's one of them: a cultist. They should have killed her when she was a little girl. But, at least we get to rectify that mistake now."

Abigail's muscles tensed as he spoke. Her hands clenched, and she forced them to relax. Her nails dug into her flesh.

"Wait!" someone shouted from down the hall. Footsteps approached. The four turned and aimed their rifles back at the door.

A second later, Dominick appeared. He skidded to a halt, holding up his hands, and they all lowered their guns.

"Don't do this," he said, speaking to Anong and Colton. "Let's think this through."

"We're past thinking," Colton said. "The Council ruled that she's to be executed for her crimes, and I, for one, am thankful that I get to be the one who does it."

Dominick pulled out his gun and aimed it at Colton. "I'm warning you. I won't let you do this."

The two guards and Anong raised their guns as well, aiming them at Dominick. A tense moment passed.

"You aren't thinking straight," Colton said. Casually, he walked toward Dominick. "You don't want us to have to kill you, too, right?"

"Dominick, it's okay," Abigail said. "Stay out of it."

Dominick glanced at her but didn't lower the gun. "I'm warning you to stop."

"Or what?" Colton asked. "You'll shoot one of your own?"

"You seem ready to."

"Abigail isn't one of ours." Colton stepped closer, hands up, and Dominick jerked back. His hands shook. "She never will be, and you'd do well to remember that."

Then Colton reached out and grabbed Dominick's gun, yanking it from his grasp. Dominick stood there, hands still shaking.

"See? That wasn't too bad," Colton said. Then he flipped the gun over and pistol-whipped Dominick on the face, knocking him to the ground. He hit hard, dazed.

"Hey!" Anong shouted.

"Don't worry," Colton said. "He'll be fine."

"You didn't have to hit him so hard."

"He's just getting what's coming to him. Like Abigail, and Arthur before her. You know, I'm glad Arthur is dead. Such a pretentious jackass all the time, always thinking he was better than the rest of us."

Abigail felt in a daze, barely breathing. Her muscles clenched tighter, and she could only see red as rage washed over her. Colton's words infuriated her, but also so much more than that.

"Everyone thought he was great, but I knew better. I knew he was just an uppity—"

Abigail moved before she realized it, charging forward at Anong, who spun with a shout, raising her pistol. However, Abigail was already on her. She pushed the barrel away, and the shots went wide over her shoulder. Then Abigail stepped in and punched Anong in the chest, knocking her back and to the ground.

Abigail kept moving while the other three tried to react. The two guards with assault rifles raised to fire at her. She dove to the side, sprinting in an arc toward one of them. The other fired, but she slipped past his partner and used him as a body shield. The bullets thudded into his chest, rocking him as Abigail held him up.

Two bullets went through his unarmored body and out the other side, but they didn't have enough force to pierce Abigail's skin. They hit and bounced off, thudding to the floor.

The other man stopped firing and let out a gasp, realizing he'd shot his friend. Abigail took the opportunity to throw the man at him. She threw a lot harder than she expected, and the body collided with the other guard, knocking him to the floor.

Abigail charged in after, pushing the guns away and kicking the unhurt guard in the face repeatedly.

Colton had spun back to the fight and now aimed at Abigail, who ducked and dove just as he pulled the trigger. Bullets flew close to her body. She closed the distance to him, dodging and weaving to narrowly avoid the shots, and then tackled him.

Though a big and strong man, she thought she might manage to wrestle him to the ground if she got hold of his legs. It surprised her at how easy it proved to lift him from the ground. Abigail slammed him into the wall hard, and the drywall collapsed under his weight.

Colton groaned, barely conscious, and Abigail let him sink to the floor. She raised her foot to stomp him in the face, and then noticed Dominick standing a few meters away.

A deep gash ran down the side of his face, and he'd picked up his gun, which he aimed at her. However, his hands continued to shake, and he wore a horrified expression.

"What ... what the hell?" he muttered.

Abigail took a menacing step toward him, and then realized what she was doing. Instead, she took a deep and calming breath and forced her heart rate to slow.

"Sorry," she said. "I just sort of lost it there—"

"Stay back." Dominick took a step backward, toward the hall. His hands, if anything, shook even worse now.

"Dominick, it's okay. I don't want to hurt you."

He didn't seem convinced and took another step into the hallway.

Loud footsteps approached and, suddenly, Haatim and Frieda rounded the corner to the room. Both of them glanced inside. Haatim took a sharp intake of breath.

At first, Abigail put it down to a response to the four people on the ground, one of whom lay dead.

And then she realized that his gaze had fixed on her.

Frieda stepped into the room, a concerned look on her face. She pushed Dominick's gun down, and he looked at her with an expression of fear.

"It's okay," she said, gently taking the gun from him.

"What ...?" Clearly, he didn't know how to finish the question.

"What?" Abigail asked. "What is it? Why are you all looking at me like that?"

None of them answered. Into the silence, an alarm blared overhead.

"Come on," Frieda said, gesturing for Abigail to come with her. She walked at speed down the hall. Abigail followed, and Haatim and Dominick moved back, getting out of her way. She cast them each a glance, but then simply went after Frieda.

"Where are we going?"

"Your identities won't work," Frieda said. "But you'll find two new ones in the glove box that should hold you over for a while. Stay out of sight and don't make yourself conspicuous."

"What are you talking about?"

"You'll need to lay low for at least a few months, but eventually, they'll stop searching for you. In the trunk, you'll find a suitcase with enough cash to last you a few years. Euros."

"Frieda, what are you talking about?" Abigail asked. They stood near a side exit. "They came to execute me."

"I know." Frieda pulled out a pair of keys and handed them to Abigail, and then pushed open the door. Outside, snow met them in the pitch black, and the moon lay hidden behind the clouds. Wind whistled around them, bitingly cold. "Remember this address."

Then Frieda rattled off a location. Abigail committed it to memory. "Where is it?"

"Ohio," Frieda said. "You'll need to find out for yourself. Now go."

Then Frieda turned and headed back into the building. Abigail stood in the doorway, thoroughly disoriented and confused by everything that had gone on.

Frieda disappeared around the corner, leaving Abigail alone with only the sound of the alarms around her.

She hesitated, and then headed out into the snow. It took her a few minutes to find Frieda's car, and only moments after that, she drove toward town and away from the hotel.

$$* * *$$

"What the hell just happened?" Shocked, Dominick stared at the carnage of the room where they'd held Abigail. Haatim stood beside him.

The destroyed room had bullet holes littering the walls, broken furniture, and a man lay dead. Anong had found her feet, but still felt dazed and out of breath. Colton remained unconscious, as did the other guard.

Abigail had done this ...

Dominick remembered the way she'd looked when she slammed Colton into the wall. The feral look on her face; eyes red. Not like bloodshot red, but like demonic and angry red.

"I wish I knew," Haatim said. On the floor, Colton groaned, returning to consciousness.

A few moments later, Frieda reappeared. Despite everything that had just happened, she appeared calm and collected. She stood next to them for a second, staring at the room around them.

"Arrest me," she said, turning to Dominick.

"What?"

"Arrest me. Handcuff me and bring me before the Council."

"Why?"

"I just freed Abigail," she said.

"You did what?"

Frieda eyed him for a long second. "She's gone. I understand your duty now, so I won't put up any fight. Now, arrest me."

Dominick rubbed his eyes, trying to understand. "All right," he said. "Frieda, you're under arrest. Let's go."

Chapter 8

When a knock sounded on the door to her makeshift cell, Frieda looked up from the book she sat reading. In the last few days, she hadn't had many visitors and enjoyed the chance to relax and not have a million concerns about which to worry.

Her cell occupied a separate floor from where they had kept Abigail, and Frieda had no doubt that she had a larger room and more luxuries. And yet, it felt more confining. They hadn't bothered to reinforce the window and had posted only one guard at the door.

Should that offend her or not? Abigail had two guards. Frieda liked to think of herself as dangerous, under the right circumstances. Or, at least, conniving. Before making any decisions, she planned things out carefully so that everything went smoothly. She didn't like surprises.

Surprises like what had happened a few days ago.

Everything had spiraled out of control since she'd first let Abigail escape. Dominick had brought her before the Council to explain what had happened, and she'd told them, in the most uncertain terms as she could, that she'd freed Abigail because *this* was not how they were supposed to operate.

Naturally, they'd been furious. Immediately, Aram had demanded a trial for Frieda for letting a sentenced woman go free, and all of his cronies had jumped on board. Some had supported Frieda, of course, but even they appeared reluctant to stand by her with an open admission of guilt.

The thing was, Frieda felt sick of all of the manipulation and lies. She was done putting up with it, and the time had come to take a stand. The Council had become fragmented and corrupted in the last several years, divided against itself, and Frieda had grown tired of fighting shadow battles against her fellow members. Everything happening with Abigail had simply shone a light on how deep the corruption went, and shown her that she needed to take a stand.

Frieda set her book down and walked to the door. Jun Lee stood there. Not the Augmented Reality avatar of Jun Lee she'd grown used to seeing over the years, but the man himself.

He looked even more vibrant in person, though he carried a decorated hickory cane.

"Frieda," he said, leaning on the cane and smiling. "It's good to see the real you."

"You as well," she said. "It's been what, twenty years?"

"Longer," he said. "The last time I saw you in person, you were a little girl."

Frieda laughed. "I haven't been a little girl in a *really* long time."

"Nor I a young man," he said. "And yet, here we are."

"Here you surely are," she said. "Pulled some strings to come visit me while I'm locked up?"

She expected him to perhaps chuckle, or at least smile. Instead, he sobered up, and his expression became grim.

"I'm only the first to arrive."

"What do you mean?"

"The Council is gathering. All of us."

"Everyone?" Frieda asked. "That hasn't happened in …"

She shook her head. She didn't even know how long ago something like that had happened. Even hundreds of years ago, the Council was reluctant to bring everyone to the same location at the same time because of security.

"Not in my lifetime," Jun said, just above a murmur.

"Should I feel flattered?"

"The Council has stripped you of your command of the Hunters. They plan to start the trial as soon as everyone arrives because of the security risks. Some have called for your removal from the Council."

"They couldn't do that." Frieda shook her head. "My forefathers *founded* the Council."

"Exactly why many of them don't trust you," Jun said. "They feel like you got handed your position and didn't have to earn it. They want you out.

"Also, we've looked into the two dead Hunters. Their deaths have been added to your crimes."

"What?" Frieda asked. "Aram did that."

"The Hunters answer to you," Jun said. "Aram is making a case that you acted unilaterally in sending them and are withholding things from the Council. It's a compelling case."

"But I didn't do it," she said. "*He*'s the one who betrayed us."

"I know," Jun said. "We have no real evidence that you had

anything to do with it, but unfortunately, there isn't evidence against him, either."

Frieda sighed, rubbing her brow. She'd landed in the precise position Abigail had, though with higher stakes.

"Still, this needed to happen in person?"

"Any decision on this level must be made by all of us in person. We can't take the risk of anyone outside hacking into our systems and being able to watch the events that take place. It's too personal and important. We will remove all technology from the meetings."

"It's risky," Frieda said.

Jun nodded. "Incredibly. I voted against it, even for something so important as this, but I lost, and so the trial will take place soon. Aram feels confident that we will all be protected."

"Mercenaries?"

"Many got hired just this morning, with more being sought in the coming weeks. They erected an electric fence and have regular patrols. We should be safe."

"It's still an ignorant decision," Frieda said.

"Yes," Jun said.

"I guess our goal isn't to hide anymore," Frieda said. "Aram is turning this place into a fortress."

"Indeed," Jun said. "Impractical and quite expensive. With operating costs this high, however, it won't be long before the trial commences. Everyone is preparing their travel plans now, and we will vote within a month."

"How will they vote?"

"Things will work out in your favor," Jun said. "People have had time to think about it, and sentencing Abigail to death was a poor decision. Aram will seek to have you stripped of your command, but not from the Council. It'll be an easy feat, considering all the evidence against you."

"You hope," Frieda said.

Jun stood in silence for a long moment. "Yes," he said. "I hope. Execution for treason *is* on the table."

Frieda sighed. "What else did you find out about Jim and Michael? Do we know who killed them or why?"

"No," Jun said. "No one has taken responsibility. We have people looking into it, but it isn't encouraging. A Hunter's life is a risky life. We ask much of them."

Frieda shook her head. "Not in this case. They went somewhere without approval and weren't even on assignment. I don't know who sent them, but they didn't act under my orders."

Jun scratched his chin. "You're certain that Aram sent them?"

"As certain as I can be," Frieda said. "This past year, he's acted erratically. If he has betrayed us, we need to find out why. A lot of things have gone on that the Council hasn't received notification about. Something strange is going on, and we need to get a handle on it before it gets out of hand."

Jun nodded. "I agree. As soon as the trial is sorted out, I will assist you in investigating this issue."

"Thank you, Jun."

"We'll sort this out, Frieda," Jun said. "I shall return to discuss things with you in preparation for the trial."

Jun stood and gave her a hug, and then headed out into the hall. Frieda sat alone in her room once more, trying to figure out her best move.

From in here, she wouldn't be able to investigate Aram. She had limited communication with her assistant, and Martha could only do certain things while Frieda remained locked up anyway.

No, she would need to be patient and let things run their course. Aram would strip her of her command, which would give him control of the Hunters. Frieda felt confident, however, that once they set her free, she would manage to find all the evidence she needed to bring him down.

It had gone past the time that they should begin reorganizing the Council and remove some of the most egregious blemishes. Frieda sat on the bed and picked up her book, hoping to distract herself. Not being in control felt so difficult.

Had Abigail gotten away? Had she found the house? Though a difficult decision for Frieda, Abigail should learn the truth about Arthur and herself now. Tough times drew near for the young woman, and Frieda didn't envy her position.

Chapter 9

Abigail's attempts to stay one step ahead of the Hunters in pursuit of her had left her rundown and exhausted. Almost two weeks had passed since Frieda had rushed her out of imprisonment. At least six members of her Order hunted for her, and she'd even had a few close calls on her way out of Europe and back to the United States.

The closest of those calls had taken place in Frankfurt while she booked her flight to New York. She'd planned to take a tram to get to the airport but felt that something was off. At the last second, she changed her mind and found a hiding place, from where she could watch the passengers load onto the tram instead.

Her caution paid off; Colton and Anong showed up and lurked in a nearby café, watching the passengers enter the tram. They must have realized the route she'd most likely take to get off the continent and tracked her to the location.

Luck had kept her from getting caught then. That happened a week ago and had forced her always to look over her shoulder and second-guess every decision she made. Intentionally, she did things erratically and made poor choices, not wanting to back herself into a corner.

It wore on her, though, and she couldn't keep it up for much longer. Eventually, she would make a mistake, get spotted, and they would fall upon her.

Abigail had managed to make it to the States this morning, flying in to New York and then to the airport in Columbus, Ohio. Under one of the false identities that Frieda had set up for her, she'd made it across the ocean.

The airport terminals had proved a nail-biting experience: people thronged the area, and Abigail found it hard to keep track of everyone. If the Hunters had learned her destination from Frieda, they might be able to move against her.

But no one had approached her, and she'd slipped easily through customs. At the airport, she'd rented a car—an ugly little blue thing, but cheap—and now she drove through the Amish country of Ohio on her way to the address that Frieda had given her.

The drive through the countryside felt like a blast from the past: she'd been to this part of the country on many occasions when a little girl. Arthur liked to visit this part of the world, and they'd spent countless hours exploring Amish Country and relaxing when they had downtime between missions.

As a kid, Abigail had hated it. Endless fields of corn and beans and old farmhouses. Boring. She craved excitement and had argued with Arthur every time he brought her out here, telling him it wasn't fair and that she wanted to be somewhere else, where she could have fun.

Now, it brought back painful memories and nostalgia. Abigail found something calming about driving down the two-lane highways in these rural areas. It reminded her of good times spent with Arthur, and she felt like the sheer weight of his loss would suffocate her.

By the time she reached the location that Frieda had given her, night had fallen. Out in the middle of nowhere, with only sporadic farmhouses decorating the landscape, endless fields of corn and beans and sorghum wafted in the breeze.

The address belonged to a gravel driveway at least a kilometer long. Abigail passed through several copses of trees and across an old wooden bridge before arriving at an old house on the top of a hill.

A two-story blue structure, the paint had faded with time. It looked to have been abandoned many years earlier. Abigail pulled the car up in front of the garage and climbed out.

Why had Frieda given her this address? She'd never been here before and didn't recognize the area. With pursed lips and a slight frown, she went up the stairs and onto the porch, boards creaking underfoot, and listened at the door. All quiet. Next, she tested the knob. Unlocked.

With a shrug, Abigail stepped into the house. The entrance opened into a foyer covered in dust and cobwebs. A staircase ahead of her climbed to the second-floor landing. To her left lay a living room, and to the right, a dining room and connected kitchen.

Plastic sheets and dust covered every piece of furniture. Abigail headed into the living room. An old fireplace, built into the far wall, sat filled with ash. On top of the shelf stood lines of old pictures, also covered in dust and faded. She went over and brushed one off.

The picture of Arthur, from many years ago, showed him in his

96

mid-twenties (or thereabouts), earlier than she'd ever known him. A woman stood with him, beautiful with black hair and a bright smile, as well as a little girl in a yellow dress.

This must have been his home before they died. Abigail had known about his cabin in the forest of Colorado since they had spent much of their time there training, but this house proved entirely unexpected. Arthur had never told her about this place.

While Abigail had known about the murder of his family, he refused ever to speak about this part of his life. It made sense that he would have had a home before she lived with him, but she'd never thought to bring it up.

Also, she'd never before seen any photos of his wife or daughter. It looked like Arthur had abandoned this not long after they had died.

Was that why he always brought me out here? she wondered. Abigail had never realized what connection he would have to this part of Ohio and, suddenly, it all made sense.

Had Arthur come here to visit this home without telling her while the two of them traveled in the area? Maybe during the times he left her in a hotel while he went out on a job?

Questions and emotions flooded into Abigail when she thought back to those days. Part of her felt surprised that Arthur had kept this from her, but another part knew it was exactly like Arthur. He didn't like to talk about his past or dwell on things, and he certainly wouldn't have wanted to explain this to her.

Abigail kept moving through the house, looking at all the broken-down furniture and family items that had deteriorated through the years. Age had not been kind to them. A little girl's room matched the age of the girl she'd seen in the photos. Pink walls, pictures of princesses, and the usual stuff.

As a child, Abigail had never had any interest in princesses. If anything, she always associated more with the knights and heroes of the stories. She knew, all too well, what being helpless felt like, and determined never to be that way again.

When Abigail went into the basement, she found a safe built into one of the back walls. The lock had an alphanumeric digital input and looked like it didn't belong with any of the other items. Too new and modern and way too much security for a white-picket-fence family.

Curious, Abigail glanced it over, guessing it had to weigh a few thousand pounds and lain into a concrete slab to make it even heavier. It would be a nearly impossible task to move it, and breaking it open would prove time-consuming too.

Fingers tapping her chin, she studied the keypad. What might the password be? Frieda, she realized, had sent her here for this. The safe held something that she was supposed to find.

The most confusing part, however, was that she had no idea what the password would be.

First, Abigail tried Arthur's name. Nothing. Then she tried his wife's name, and then his daughter's. Neither combination worked.

Frustrated, Abigail stepped back and stared at the safe. Had Frieda known the password? Or, maybe, she'd never been privy to that detail. Perhaps, Frieda thought Abigail would know the password, and that was why she'd sent her.

Abigail tried a few dozen more options—things she thought Arthur might turn into a password. Details of his life that had seemed important to him; phrases he said all the time; she tried any and every combination that came to mind.

Yet, still, the safe remained locked, and with each failure, it just buzzed to announce the incorrect password.

At least it didn't have a failsafe to lock her out after too many invalid attempts. With a growing headache, Abigail found a chair tucked in the back of the basement and dragged it out in front, staring at the monstrous green safe. Tired from traveling, she needed to rest, but couldn't bring herself to leave.

This belonged to Arthur. It belonged to him and must have had importance to him. Abigail needed to know what it contained. What had Arthur put here?

Abigail felt certain that his sword would be stored here, but what other trinkets or notes might it contain? Information about his family? She'd known of his wife and daughter, but what about his extended family? It was something he'd never talked about.

Abigail stood and punched in a few more combinations at random, but nothing worked. All of the important dates and names she knew, she had now exhausted.

Except ...

She had tried Abigail (and experienced a twinge of sadness when it hadn't worked) but hadn't thought to try her last name.

When they found her with the Ninth Circle, they'd never known her identity. The Council combed through missing person's reports within hundreds of miles to try and find out where she came from. She'd known her first name but never anything else.

Almost five years had passed before they got a hit on the missing person's report associated with her. She'd reached thirteen when she found out that her full name was Abigail Dressler. That she came from Minnesota and had no living relatives. Her grandmother had reported three-year-old Abigail missing but had since passed away.

Arthur had taken her to visit the woman's grave, but it had meant little to her. She'd even felt some guilt on the trip, hoping it wouldn't make Arthur sad to have a reminder that he wasn't actually related to her. Her previous life defied memory, and Abigail had felt disconnected from it.

They were her blood, but Arthur was her family.

Still ...

Abigail typed the name into the safe. *D-R-E-S-S-L-E-R.*

It clicked open.

✳✳✳

The sword, leaning against the inside wall, caught her attention first. It lay in an ornate sheath, about a meter long and curved slightly. Gently, Abigail picked it up and slid out the blade. It had a sheen of oil on it to hold the sharpened edge and looked to have rested here a long time.

Arthur took the blade everywhere with him. He trained her how to fight with it, but swords never became her thing. She preferred guns. If people got in too close, she had knives to deal with them.

Abigail had felt extremely saddened, though, when Arthur went to prison, and the sword had disappeared. She'd never had the guts to visit him while he festered in that cell, and so never asked what had happened to it and just assumed it forever lost.

Now, she held it, testing its balance. It felt comfortable in her hand. Right. She'd never had enough strength to use it effectively, but she'd grown older now.

Abigail set the sword on the chair behind her and looked back into the safe. A bag sat on one of the shelves, filled with money—at least a few hundred thousand dollars—and false identities. Two of them for her.

Abigail also discovered various other weapons and trinkets that Arthur had carried over the years. She recognized some of them, but many more were objects she'd never seen before. Like a shard of glass that looked as though it had been removed from an old stained-glass window, and a small chunk of wood that had hardened over time.

Too much stuff to carry. Abigail would leave it here because it would be more secure in the safe than with her.

The last thing she found was a binder of documents. The pages looked old and dry and had faded somewhat. With much of it written in another language, she couldn't tell what the documents related to, but on the top one lay a post-it note with a phone number.

The sticky-backed paper had aged, and the writing proved difficult to read. Abigail hesitated, and then pulled out her phone and punched in the number. Though late, she couldn't wait.

Someone answered on the fourth ring. "Hello? Who is this?"

Abigail didn't recognize the voice. A man's voice, and he sounded older and a little frantic.

"This is Abigail," she said.

A long moment passed. "Abigail? Jesus. How did you get this number?"

"Arthur Vangeest," she said.

"Arthur is dead."

"I know," Abigail said. "I was his adopted—"

"I know who you are," the voice said. "Why are you calling me?"

"I found your number in Arthur's things," she said. "You knew him?"

"We shouldn't do this over the phone," the man said. "Do you have a pen?"

"No," Abigail said. "But I have an excellent memory."

The man rattled off an address, and she made note of it. It wasn't too far away, still in Ohio, just on the opposite side of the state. "It's my shop," the man said. "Come alone."

"Okay," Abigail said.

"I mean it," the guy said. "No one else."

Abigail didn't even bother to respond, just disconnected and slipped the phone back into her pocket.

Someone she'd never met before who knew Arthur. What sort of connection had they had? And why had Arthur never mentioned him?

One thing at a time. Abigail took the sword but left the other items. She didn't need the money, and it might be best to save the identities for later. On second thought, she took the binder as well, locked the safe, and headed back to her car.

As soon as she stepped outside the house, she knew something was wrong. She no longer stood alone, although she couldn't see anyone else around her in the immediate proximity. How could she know? Nevertheless, she felt certain.

Alert and alarmed, she slipped her gun loose and crept toward her car, scanning the area around the house. Dark and cloudy, she couldn't see anything.

When she drew closer, Abigail noticed that the vehicle rested lower than it should have. Someone had slashed the tires.

Not waiting for the trap to spring on her, she sprinted to the right, running toward a fence leading into an old horse paddock. A shout came from behind, followed by a gunshot. Abigail ducked and dashed to the fence, climbed over it, and dove into the tall grass below.

Years of horses walking over the muddy terrain had made the ground uneven. Luckily, the grass stood several feet tall and disguised her entire body, especially with such little light.

Abigail landed hard and rolled, ducking into the grass as more shots fired behind her. She kept moving, crawling low through the grass and, occasionally, glancing back the way she had come.

Near her car, three people ran toward her. Although Abigail couldn't recognize their faces, she knew them from the way they moved: Colton Depardieu, Jack Wright, and Anong Sao.

It looked like they had come to finish what they had started back in Lausanne. Colton raised his pistol and fired into the grass. The shot fell behind her, but not as far away as she would like.

Abigail flinched, ducked again, and continued crawling. On this breezy night, the grass wafted in the wind and masked her progress. She moved fast, staying low, and went another fifteen or so meters. When she checked again, her pursuers had made it through the gate and into the field. They combed the area slowly, spread out to fan the entire field and worked their way toward her.

Abigail held onto her revolver. At the least, she could drop one of them from her hiding spot. Anong stood closest, oblivious to her. They hadn't prepared for her to retaliate, and she could put a bullet in Anong and still perhaps crawl away without the other two being able to find her immediately.

However, she didn't. These were Hunters, her brothers and sisters, and killing them felt ... wrong.

Though she might well regret it, Abigail slipped her revolver away instead and belly-crawled through the weeds and toward the fence. There, she found an opening that she could crawl under and slid outside the field. Abigail couldn't see any other houses or vehicles in the area, but an old barn sat only fifty meters from her.

It looked like it had burnt up in a fire years ago, probably due to lightning or hooligans, and only half of it remained standing. Still, it gave better cover than nothing.

Abigail moved cautiously, crouching low, and made her way to the barn. Once there, she ducked inside, out of sight of the fields, and let out a quiet sigh.

"Spread out," Colton shouted from somewhere out in the open. "And find her."

Abigail searched around the area. An old four-by-four beam lay on the ground. It felt heavy and looked about three feet long. A rough, splintered edge showed where it had snapped from the roof. Not as sturdy as she would like, but an excellent makeshift club.

Then Abigail located a hiding place near one of the old horse stalls, around the corner, which she slid into with her beam and waited.

After a few minutes, footsteps came into the barn and padded across the old dirt floor. Too heavy to belong to Anong. Probably Jack, but Abigail couldn't be sure.

She ducked low, controlling her breathing. The man moved slowly, checking the area. Her head thudded violently while he checked her stall, glancing in but not checking thoroughly. His breathing came from just outside, and Abigail prayed that he wouldn't notice her hiding spot.

He didn't, but instead, kept walking to the next stall in line. Abigail waited until he moved out of sight and crept out. She left the binder tucked into the back of the hiding place. He'd just looked into the next stall when she stepped up behind him and bashed him with the club.

She hit him hard, and he staggered into a wall and let out a cry. Abigail followed through with another whack to his leg, knocking him off balance. He caught himself and launched a punch at her, but it came feeble and un-centered, and Abigail blocked it with ease.

Then she hit him a third time, knocking him to his knees, and followed up with a knee in the face. He collapsed, groaning and rolling to his side, trying to call for help.

Abigail kicked him again, silencing him, and then once more for good measure. She didn't want to kill them—even if they were trying to kill her—but that didn't mean she didn't want to beat them up a little. She felt pissed as all hell and didn't mind using them to let off steam.

The confrontation had produced a lot of noise, so Abigail wasted no time in heading back toward her hiding spot. She didn't quite make it, though, before Anong rounded the corner and spotted her.

Abigail changed course and charged straight at Anong, throwing her club at the small Asian woman. Anong raised her pistol to fire but was forced to duck back to avoid the beam flying at her head.

Her momentary distraction proved enough for Abigail to close in on her. Anong raised her gun once more, but Abigail drew near enough, now, to make it a difficult shot. When Anong fired, her bullets went wide over Abigail's shoulder.

She stepped in and punched Anong on the right side of her face, following with a kick to her stomach and a punch to her chest. Anong staggered back and tried to raise the weapon again, but Abigail stayed with her. She caught her wrist and knocked the gun out of her grip, and then punched her twice more in the jaw.

Anong staggered away from her, rolling across the ground. The woman managed to find her footing and launched a series of attacks, forcing Abigail to give ground. Abigail backpedaled, blocking attacks and trying to hold her own.

Not easy. Anong had incredible skill and had spent her entire life fighting. She landed quite a few heavy punches and kicks that kept Abigail off-balance.

Anong took an opening in the fight to draw a short blade from her boot and slashed out at Abigail, forcing even more distance between them.

Abigail was running out of time. Colton might be closing in on her now and could appear at any second. She could barely hold her own against Anong, let alone the two of them combined.

Desperate, she drew her gun. Abigail couldn't run the risk of letting Colton enter the fray and tip the scales against her. Anong fought too fast and strong, and Abigail couldn't think of any other ways to end the fight quickly.

Plus, shooting her in the arm might be painful, but it wouldn't kill her.

Anong's eyes went wide when she saw Abigail pulling the revolver loose, and she charged in. Abigail had time to get one shot off, which clipped the Asian woman in the shoulder, but then they stood too close. Anong punched her twice in the stomach, and then swatted the gun out of her grasp.

Abigail grunted in frustration but did manage to draw her knife and stab out, forcing her opponent back. She moved forward, kicking Anong hard in the face, and then she punched the hilt of her blade into the woman's nose.

The bone shattered, and blood poured out. Anong stumbled back, but Abigail stayed with her, kicking her repeatedly in the stomach and legs and hitting her in her broken nose as hard as she could.

Anong staggered, and Abigail finished with a roundhouse kick, knocking her unconscious. She stood there overtop her opponent, panting and trying to catch her breath. Her heart thumped in her ears while she tried to listen for Colton's approach.

Nothing. All quiet. So far. Abigail waited a second. Where had Colton gotten to? Then she moved to retrieve her revolver; she'd come back for the binder later. She left the two unconscious people lying there in the barn and moved slowly outside, scanning the area and looking around for her last opponent.

It seemed clear, but he had to be somewhere out there. Straight up fights weren't his thing, so it came as no surprise that he hadn't joined the fray. Too much of a coward.

It was a cat and mouse game now. Abigail moved toward the house, keeping low and watching for any sign of movement.

Abigail couldn't see that far in front, but at least that meant things wouldn't be any easier for Colton. Hopefully, he had given up. Maybe he would count his blessings and let her go.

She didn't believe that, though it was a nice idea.

He shot at her just as she got up near the car. He hid on the far side of the house, around the corner. The bullet hit her in the side before she heard the gunshot, and it caught her completely off-guard.

Abigail staggered, and instinct kicked in. She dove to the side as he fired more shots, and then rolled to her feet and sprinted toward the house. She ran along the side of the building, moving out of Colton's line of sight, and around the corner. His next move would be to adjust to get a better angle at her, which meant he would come forward.

In anticipation, Abigail sidestepped and ducked just as he came around the corner. Colton fired more shots, but she quick-stepped and weaved, avoiding the bullets and closing the last few steps, and then she fell upon him.

Abigail kicked and punched with a flurry of blows, knocking Colton backward and to the ground. Then she stepped up, hitting him repeatedly with her fists and forcing him to cover his face with his arms.

She slipped a hit through, knocking his head back against the dirt. He tried to raise the gun again, but Abigail knocked it away and kicked him in the stomach. Colton grunted when the blow knocked the oxygen from his lungs.

He rolled, gasping for air, and tried to crawl away. Abigail hit him again and stepped around in front of his prone body, which she rolled over with her foot.

"What ...?" he gasped, a horrified expression on his face.

"You should have left," Abigail said. "When you had the chance."

"What ... are you ...?"

The words came soft, but they froze Abigail in place. It seemed like being drawn from a dream, and she realized that she was making low guttural sounds as she stood over him. Her heart raced, and she could feel the blood pumping through her veins rapidly.

In shock, Abigail realized that she'd been about to kill the man. Without even making a decision. Just a fact of circumstance. She'd been about to kneel down and slice open his throat.

She felt angry, angrier than she'd ever felt in her entire life, and all she wanted was to murder Colton.

Worse, though, she *still* wanted to. Had a nearly overwhelming urge to slice him open and watch the life drain out of his eyes.

The realization terrified her, and her hands shook. Colton stared up at her, eyes wide, and a scared expression on his face.

"What the hell are you?"

Abigail kicked him in the face, knocking him unconscious. Then she stood there, fighting down her urge to end his life. Instead, she forced herself to take a step away, and then another, and then to keep walking until she reached the porch of the house.

Her hands still shook, as she struggled to regain control. She'd experienced anger before, but never something like this. It took a full five minutes before she could regulate her breathing and get her heart rate down. Even then, it took another few minutes to realize how badly her side hurt.

Dampness chilled the area where the gunshot had struck. Abigail checked it and found a hole on her left side where the bullet had passed clean through. Once she saw the wound, she realized that it hurt like hell and doubled over in pain.

What the hell is happening to me?

Something was terribly wrong, and Abigail didn't know what. She felt powerless and out of control—something she wasn't used to. The idea that she'd almost murdered someone without even making the conscious decision to do it seemed insane.

Once she'd regained some modicum of control, she went back over to where Colton lay and checked his pockets. A pair of keys had her guessing that he'd most likely parked further down the driveway.

Quickly, Abigail retrieved the binder and then set off in search of the car. She didn't want to be near him for any longer than she had to be, and needed to be long gone before any of the three awoke. The car sat about a kilometer down the drive, back near the road itself.

In the trunk lay medical supplies, and Abigail made a rush-job of patching up her side. The kit only had alcohol, which burned like dragon fire when she rubbed it around the wound.

Abigail cleaned the hole as well as she could, and then wrapped a bandage around it. She'd lost a lot of blood, but the wound didn't appear too bad. Luckily, the bullet had missed any vital organs. It would hurt like the jeebies, but she would be all right.

At least physically. Mentally, she felt a lot more worried than she ever had. For the first time in her life, she didn't know what the hell was going on. Could she trust herself?

Upset and at a loss, Abigail climbed into the vehicle and pulled out her phone, which she used to find the location the man on the phone had given her. Arthur had thought this person important, and maybe he would have some answers about what was happening to her.

Chapter 10

Colton Depardieu woke up groggy. He blinked and tried to remember where he was. It remained dark outside, but the sun had risen just above the horizon in the distance. He was at a farm, he remembered, and they'd been after Abigail.

They'd found her, in fact, and it had been a simple job of springing their trap and finishing her off. Somehow, she'd known of their presence and had managed to take them down and get away.

But, she'd also confirmed what he already knew to be true: she was a monster.

When she'd attacked him, her eyes had glowed, and her face wore a mask of rage. She was evil, plain and simple, and needed putting down.

Colton had wounded her—had shot her in the side, and even though it hadn't been enough to stop her, it would slow her down. With any luck, they could track her. He checked for his keys. Gone.

Colton cursed. They'd slashed the tires on her vehicle the night before, but if she'd found their car, it would prove harder to find her. They could drive on the rims to get back to the road, and then pick up another vehicle along the way, but it would end up costing them time. They needed to get moving.

He felt pissed at the idea that she'd managed to get the better of him. Of all of them. They'd ambushed her at this stupid house and had every advantage, and yet, somehow, she'd survived and gotten away.

The woman hadn't even had the guts to finish them off.

He'd known her as weak-willed, and this proved it beyond a shadow of a doubt. He would find her, and then he would end her.

Colton rose to his feet, planning to find and wake Jack and Anong. They would need to catch Abigail before she made it too far. With any luck, the bullet wound in her side would make it easy to finish her.

Not looking forward to the call, he pulled out his burner phone and dialed the number saved there. Aram answered on the third ring.

"We found her," Colton said.

"Where?"

"Ohio."

"Is she dead?"

"Not yet," Colton said. "But she's wounded."

"I'm sending backup to your location."

"We won't need it," Colton said. "She'll be dead within the hour."

"I'm not taking any risks," Aram said. "Make sure you don't miss this time." Aram ended the call.

Colton stretched out his body and dragged in a few breaths, trying to clear his head. He had a raging headache as he walked back toward the barn to find the other Hunters.

Not there. He rounded the corner. That, too, proved empty. Broken beams lay scattered about, and the ground looked messed up from where the fight had taken place, but his two friends had gone missing.

"Jack?" he shouted. "Anong?"

No answer. Colton looked around, confused, and then headed back to the house. Maybe they had woken earlier and gone inside?

Still, if that were the case, why hadn't they woken him? They knew the importance of finding Abigail. If they *had* gone in to rest and just left him out there, he would be furious.

Broken windows had teeth of jagged glass, the door hung askew on its hinges, and bullet holes peppered the walls everywhere. It looked like a war zone. Thank God this had happened in the middle of nowhere, or the police would be swarming by now.

They would get here soon, anyway. No doubt, someone had called in about gunshots. They so had to get a move on.

Jack and Anong lay face down in the living room. The bastards had fallen asleep. Colton walked up and kicked Jack's boot. "Come on," he said. "Let's go."

Jack didn't budge. Colton kicked him again, and then went over and tapped Anong on the foot as well.

"Get up, sleepy heads. We have work to do."

Neither moved. He knelt next to them, frowning. And then he eased Anong over onto her side. Her cut throat gaped open in a red mess, but worse still, someone—or something—had cut out her eyes. Two gaping holes were all that remained where her brown orbs should have sparkled with life.

Repulsed and terrified, Colton dropped Anong's body and

stepped back, removing his gun from its holster. Still gasping in shock, he used his foot to roll Jack. He bore the same mutilations.

"What the hell?" Colton muttered, scanning the room. Now that he paid attention, he saw droplets of blood on the floor, leading from the kitchen. Not nearly enough to justify cut throats, but more than a dribble.

They hadn't died in situ. Someone had dragged them here.

Gun wobbling in his trembling hand, Colton followed the small trail around the corner and into the kitchen. Large pools of drying blood congealed on the floor. Four eyes on a cutting board stared at him. The massacre had taken place in this room.

Noise from behind had him spin on his heels. A woman stood there with a cloak pulled over her face. Colton aimed and pulled the trigger.

It clicked but didn't fire.

He pulled it again, but it kept clicking.

"I removed the bullets while you slept," the woman said, walking closer. Not Abigail, though he had no idea who it might be.

"Who are you?" he asked.

"Call me a concerned citizen." She strode toward him. "I'm cleaning up the streets and taking vigilantes out of commission."

Colton dropped the gun and drew his knife, and then fell into a fighting stance.

"You're a demon," he said. "I would recognize the stench anywhere."

"That's not a nice thing to say." She stepped closer. "Especially to a lady."

Colton stepped forward and stabbed. She deflected his arm, stepped inside his reach, and shoved him on the sternum with her palm.

He staggered back, gasping for air when his lungs collapsed. Never in his life had he received such a forceful hit. She stepped in again, knocking the knife out of his grasp and kicking him to the floor. Colton slid on a pool of blood, and when he hit the floor, the crimson mess soaked his clothes. Then the woman lifted a pan from the counter and bashed him in the side of the head with it.

Time passed while he fell in and out of consciousness. He had flashes of awareness, but when he finally came to, she had tied his hands, and he lay in the living room next to the other Hunters.

The woman stood over him, holding a huge butcher's knife, her cowl hiding her face.

He tested the ropes. Too tight to wiggle out of.

"Reinforcements are coming," he said.

"I know."

"You won't get away with this," he said. "You murdered Hunters. They'll never stop looking for you."

"On the contrary," she said. "By the time I'm done, there won't be anyone left to come looking."

She knelt down, pulling up his pants leg and exposing his shin and calf. "Ever been to a butcher shop? Ever watched someone carve up a cow? I've always found it fascinating, the way they strike down and cut right through the bone."

"Please," Colton said, shivering and trying to scoot back.

"But, often," she said, setting down the butcher knife. "They will use other tools as well. Like a meat tenderizer."

She picked up a heavy-looking mallet from the floor and held it up for inspection. It had ridged sides and looked cumbersome.

"Softens up the meat and makes it easier to cut. More tender."

"I'll tell you everything. Don't do this."

She laughed. "So easy to break. If only I *needed* information from you, I'd feel rather disappointed at how easily I shattered you. No, friend, I don't need anything from you. You're just a victim of circumstance."

She slammed the mallet down on his shin.

Bone crunched.

Colton screamed.

Agony roared up his leg.

She slammed it down again, and once more.

He jerked and crawled back. The foot dragged along the ground, attached only by the wrecked skin and muscle.

"Amazing, isn't it? The tools we've created to make tasks easier. We are remarkable creatures at overcoming obstacles."

She hesitated, and then added, "Well, I guess not *we*, right?"

Then she swung the mallet down again, crashing it against his knee.

He didn't quite black out, but his world became pain and confusion after that. She kept talking, but the words no longer made sense. All he could do was plead and beg while she crashed the mallet against his legs and arms.

At some point, she switched to using the butcher's knife and sliced off chunks of his flesh. She did it methodically, patiently, always doing just enough to make sure it gave him excruciating pain but not enough to kill him.

By the time she finished him off, he lay begging for her to kill him. It took what felt like forever before he died.

Chapter 11

Abigail arrived at her destination sometime in the afternoon. Not having eaten in almost twenty-four hours, she felt starved. However, covered in blood, she couldn't risk stopping anywhere for food.

Her side ached and still seeped blood, but she had to admit, it didn't hurt nearly as badly as she had anticipated. She would need to redo the bandages soon, but first, she had to find out the identity of the man who'd answered her call and led her here, and why Arthur had his number.

Abigail climbed out of the car and went to the little storefront. It looked like a poorly cared for incense and antique shop that didn't get a lot of foot traffic. A tiny bell tinkled overhead when she went inside and, immediately, the aroma of marijuana overwhelmed her, masked only partially by other scents.

The counter stood empty, so she wandered through the store and down the aisles. Statues of dragons decorated most of the shelves, along with the occasional animal statue or trinket. Along one wall hung various tapestries and Kimonos, in no particular organizational structure.

"Hello?" Abigail called toward the backroom.

No response. She felt more than a little uneasy at the quietness of the store. Maybe someone had anticipated her arrival here and waited for her in the back. Colton might have awoken and called someone.

Abigail slid her gun free and moved with caution toward the counter, listening intently.

From the back, music played faintly, something slow and melodic. She pushed aside a curtain blocking the doorway and stepped into a storage room.

In the darkness of the back room, the smell of marijuana only intensified. No other noises reached her as she walked on silent feet across the storage room. It stood in complete disarray, and she had to step past and over various items on the floor.

The music came from a side room on the other end of the storage area. The door hung cracked open. Gently, Abigail pushed it the rest of the way, gun ready, expecting to find a dead body.

Instead, she found a forty-something man lying on a beanbag chair with a water bong on his lap. He just stared up at the ceiling, eyes open but not present. At first, she thought he might be dead, and then—when he blinked at her—she realized him to be extremely high.

A few seconds later, he screamed a high-pitched shrill and tried to extricate himself from the chair.

Abigail lowered the gun and held up her hand, attempting to calm him. He flopped onto the floor and jumped to his feet, holding the bong like a club. Water splashed out, and droplets hit her skin.

"Hey!" she said.

"Who are you?"

"I'm Abigail," she said. "You told me to come?"

"I did?" he asked, confused.

"Yes," she said. "Last night. I called you, and you told me to come."

He hesitated for a long minute. "Oh God," he said, finally, a look of horror on his face. "That was real? I thought I dreamed that."

"Nope," she said, annoyed. Abigail brushed the water from her arm. "Completely real."

He settled down and lowered the bong. She slid her gun away. "I just ..." he said. "I never thought I would actually get to meet you."

"What do you mean?"

"Frieda told me to stay away. I was never supposed to make contact because it could get us all in trouble. And now you're here. You look ..."

Abigail fought not to roll her eyes. "Yes? I look?"

"Different than I expected," he said with a shrug. "I guess I just always had this idea of what you would look like in my head, and the reality is nothing like what I imagined. I mean, Arthur told me a lot about you, but it's never quite like the real thing."

"What the hell are you talking about?" Abigail asked. "Who the hell are you? How do you know Arthur?"

"Of course, idiot me," he said. "Sorry. I'm Mitchell. Arthur's brother."

✳✳✳

Abigail stood speechless. *Arthur's brother*? He'd never told her he had a brother, much less that he remained alive, lived nearby, and had contact with Arthur.

"Arthur had a brother?"

"Had?" he echoed. "Has. I'm not dead."

"He is, though," Abigail said.

Mitchell tilted his head to the side, frowning. "Oh ... oh right, that makes sense then."

"You knew about me?"

"Of course," Mitchell said. "He talked about you constantly."

"He never told me about you."

Mitchell's expression turned to one of worry. "No," he said. "I know. But he couldn't. Frieda wouldn't let him."

"Why not?"

"Because the Council would have been furious and it could have gotten all of us killed. I'm not even supposed to be talking to you right now, and if anyone knows you're here, they'll probably kill me."

"Slow down," Abigail said. "Start over. None of this makes sense. You're Arthur's brother?"

He took a deep breath, and then nodded. "I'm Arthur's younger brother. I'm also a fixer for the Council. I help them acquire supplies and equipment; the sort of rare and illegal stuff you don't find at your everyday supermarket, you know?"

"So, Arthur brought you in to the Council?" she asked.

Mitchell shook his head, a sad look on his face. "No," he said. "I brought Arthur in. Worst decision of my life."

"So that's why Arthur had your phone number."

Mitchell nodded. "We weren't supposed to stay in contact, but he would talk to me once in a while, and I got things for him without the Council's knowledge."

Abigail held up the binder. "What's this? I found it locked in a safe in his basement, and I can't read it."

When he saw the documents, Mitchell paled. "I don't know," he said. "I can't read Latin."

"How'd you know it was Latin?" Abigail narrowed her eyes.

He grew even paler. "You're bleeding," he said. "Let me ... uh ... let me take a look at that."

She hesitated. "Fine, but I'm not done asking questions."

Abigail pulled up her shirt, exposing her bandaged side, and gently, he pulled the bandage loose. She turned her head away and winced, expecting it to hurt, but barely noticed when it came off.

A long moment passed. Still looking away, Abigail asked, "Is it bad?"

Mitchell didn't answer. She turned her head, looking down at the bullet hole in her side, expecting to see a painful, seeping wound that needed stitches.

Instead, a short and thin scar looked like it had already healed months earlier.

"What the hell?" she muttered, confused and shocked.

Mitchell glanced up at her, a worried frown on his face. "It's started already."

✳✳✳

"What do you mean?" Abigail asked. "What started?"

"We need to talk to Frieda." Mitchell took the binder of papers from Abigail and flipped through it. He spoke quickly, nearly frantic, "We knew that once Arthur went this would happen, but it wasn't supposed to happen this *fast.*"

"What are you talking about?" Abigail's blood ran cold. "What's happening to me?"

Mitchell ignored her question. "We need to get to Frieda. She'll know what to do."

"Tell me what the hell is going on!"

"Where is she? Do you know where Frieda's at? Oh God, I don't know what to do. We need to find her."

Abigail slid the gun out again but held it at her side rather than aiming it at him. He froze, mouth hanging open.

"Are you calm now?"

He stared at the gun, and then gulped. "Yeah, I'm good."

"Tell me what's going on."

"I can't," he said softly. "Frieda forbade me from telling you. We need to get to her so that *she* can explain it."

"Frieda's not here, and we can't get to her right now. You're going to tell me *everything* you know. Got it?"

Mitchell stayed quiet for a minute, chewing the idea over in his mind. His eyes looked bloodshot, and he seemed to have a hard time focusing.

"Don't make me shoot you."

"All right," he said, finally. "All right ... okay. ... But would you put the gun down? Please?"

Abigail did, sliding it away once more. Mitchell let out an overly dramatic sigh, and then collapsed back into his beanbag chair. He gestured for Abigail to sit on a sofa opposite him, but she didn't budge. Instead, she stood in the doorway and kept her face impassive.

"Start talking."

He rubbed his face. "Where to begin? When you were about ten, Arthur started to notice it happening and—"

"What happening?"

Mitchell frowned. "You were changing."

A chill ran down Abigail's spine. "What do you mean?"

"I mean you were *changing*," Mitchell said. "I can't explain it any better."

"I was turning into something else?"

"Not exactly," he said. "But sort of ... evolving might be a better word. I don't know much about what happened, just what Arthur told me, but it scared him to death. He said he was terrified of you."

"I don't remember ..."

The thing was, she did remember some things. Abigail remembered feeling angry with Arthur, and she remembered inflicting pain; on pets, mostly, but occasionally other children as well.

She enjoyed it but had never understood why. It remained a part of herself that she didn't like to think about. After a while, she'd grown out of it and assumed it had just been a phase she had gone through.

"You were quick to anger," Mitchell said, speaking quietly. "He did tell me that."

"Arthur always told me to control my emotions," Abigail said in a voice lost in recall. "He told me that good soldiers never give in to their anger."

"It's true," Mitchell said. "But that wasn't the case for you. No, for you, it was something else. This amazing healing was there, too. You would cut yourself playing, and the wounds would close in front of Arthur's eyes. You took pleasure in it, intentionally hurting yourself just to watch it heal."

"I broke my wrist a long time ago," she said. "When Arthur died. I thought I would have the scars forever, and then, one day, they just went."

Abigail held up her wrist to show him, which bore no sign that there had ever been a wound there at all.

"When was this?"

"A month or two ago," she said. "I don't know. I didn't notice at the time. You're saying this happened when I was little?"

"Yes," Mitchell said. "It started around your tenth birthday."

Abigail shook her head. "I don't remember much from those years. What are you saying? What was it that was happening to me?"

"I have no idea," Mitchell said. "And neither did Arthur. I think Frieda knew, but she never told us. She was the one that fixed it."

"What do you mean? She stopped me from … changing?"

"She came to me when you were twelve and gave me a list of ingredients and items to get a hold of. Some of them crazy expensive, and most would have gotten me killed if the Council knew what I'd done."

"You mean Frieda didn't tell the Council about it?"

Mitchell nodded. "What we did goes against, basically, every rule and law they have. Once I gathered the stuff, she and Arthur performed some ritual on you. It's written out in that binder. I wasn't there, but when it was over, Arthur slept for a week straight. He looked like he'd been run over by a truck."

"What was the ritual?"

"A binding," Mitchell said. "I think."

"For what?"

"You," Mitchell said. "And Arthur. Frieda bound your souls together."

"Why?" Abigail felt fairly certain that she didn't want to know the answer.

Mitchell sat in silence for a long moment, staring at her. Finally, he spoke, "So that whatever evil had corrupted you went into him instead."

✳✳✳

The words hit Abigail like a ton of bricks. She stood in the doorway, trying to breathe, and slowly shook her head. She wanted to deny it and scream at Mitchell for even suggesting something like this, but couldn't. Part of her knew it as true, and had known all along.

Part of her had known all along that she held evil.

Abigail knew that that part existed, and no matter how hard she tried to dismiss it or pretend it didn't exist, it always seemed ready to rear its ugly head at her.

Another thought wormed its way into her mind, bringing with it a sickening clarity. The gun shook in wobbly fingers, and Abigail dropped it to the floor. Her knees gave out, and Abigail dropped onto the sofa.

"You mean—" She rubbed her hands on her jeans. "—that everything Arthur went through—his fall, killing those people, going to jail, and dying—it all happened because of me?"

Mitchell hesitated for a long time, staring at Abigail with a look of such guilt and sadness that she thought he might cry. When he spoke, the single word filled her entire existence.

"Yes."

✳✳✳

"Arthur never wanted you to know this," Mitchell said a few minutes later. "He wanted to keep it from you. This burden, he took on willingly and never regretted it."

"Even when I killed him," Abigail said with bitterness.

"You didn't have control."

"Apparently, I never had control." She stared at the ground.

Abigail had known that Arthur gave up a lot to protect her, but never something like this. No, this felt too much, an unfathomable burden that she had placed on the man who had rescued her and given her a chance at life.

"Why?" she asked. "Why would he do this?"

"He loved you," Mitchell said. "And, it wasn't your fault. Whatever the cult did to you manifested, and Arthur wanted to spare you from it. He thought he could control it, and he did for many years. He only wanted you to have a normal life."

"A normal life?" she asked.

"If he hadn't done what he did, they would have executed you a lot sooner."

"All the good that did," Abigail said. "They're still going to kill me, and the only difference is that I killed Arthur too."

"Arthur's death isn't on your hands."

"It is," Abigail said. "It would have been better if he'd just let me die."

"Self-pity won't help anything."

"You think this is self-pity?" she asked, angry. "It's pragmatism. You said yourself, it's starting again. Whatever evil lives inside me, it's still here, and it's coming back. Arthur knew he wouldn't live forever, so why the hell would he do this?"

"He wanted to give you a chance at a life."

"He only staved off the inevitable, and it cost him *his* life. Now, I have to carry that burden."

"He loved you."

"Then, why didn't he tell me about this?" she asked. "Why am I only finding out about it now?"

Mitchell stared at her helplessly, not having an answer.

"Arthur has gone, and now I'm turning evil, what I was always meant to be, apparently."

"You can learn to control it," Mitchell said. "It doesn't have to control you."

"Arthur couldn't control it," Abigail said. "What chance do I possibly have?"

"I'm sorry," Mitchell said. "I wish I had a better answer for you."

"Me too."

He held up the binder. "I have no clue what any of this means, but Frieda left it with Arthur. It could be important, and it might have clues as to something we can do to stop this change from happening."

"I don't know Latin," Abigail said.

"I only know a bit," Mitchell said. "Look, Abigail, I know you're confused and upset, but Arthur loved you. He was willing to give up anything to protect you."

"He lost his life because of me."

"A sacrifice he was willing to make."

Abigail didn't know what to say. She'd cost Arthur so much.

"I'll need time alone with this," Mitchell said. "If you want, you can stay in here, and I'll go out to the lobby."

"No," she said. "I'm off for a walk. I need to clear my head."

Chapter 12

"Do you think Abigail's all right?" Haatim asked.

They sat resting in the lobby of the Council Hotel, out of the cold. Haatim felt exhausted and drained after the last several weeks of training with Dominick and wished he could go back to training with Frieda.

Dominick was a lunatic; he'd decided.

They'd continued their daily hikes through the mountains, but those treks had become shorter and on much more treacherous trails. Though bitterly cold, Dominick insisted on always taking the most dangerous routes, climbing up and down cliff faces. Which meant it took less time, but Haatim felt just as sore, as he used more muscles. On top of that, the extra time they gained from shorter hikes meant more time sparring.

What sparring meant, basically, was that Dominick beat the crap out of Haatim while he tried to defend himself. Both mentally and physically draining, constantly he had to recover from one bruise or another.

It had some benefits to it, though; Haatim had never felt this strong in his entire life. The exercise had honed his physical prowess and coordination. He'd spent years playing Cricket and other agile sports, so he had a decent foundation of physical aptitude, but never anything on this scale.

"Abigail is fine." Dominick took a sip of water.

Haatim stared through the lobby windows at the world beyond. It had snowed heavily for quite some time, but the wind had died down and the day had become serene and beautiful. A patrol group of six mercenaries passed about thirty meters away from the fence, each carrying assault rifles.

"Do you think they will find her?"

"Yes," Dominick said. "Eventually. They won't stop looking, and the longer she's out there, the more people they'll send after her."

"Like you?"

He shrugged. "Aram knows we have history. He doesn't trust me. But, if the manhunt goes on long enough, he won't have a choice but to send me out as well."

"If you found her, would you bring her in?"

Dominick fell silent for a long time. "I don't know," he said. "My job description doesn't include disobeying the Council."

"You know she's innocent."

"You saw her eyes," Dominick said. "I've never seen anything like it, but *you* saw it too."

Haatim hesitated. He had seen it, and the look of anger on her face had paralyzed him with fear. She had seemed like a completely different person, and not one he wanted to get on the bad side of.

"I did," he said. "But we don't know what's going on. I shan't condemn her until I have the whole truth. In either case, they're trying to execute her for a crime she didn't commit."

"A lot of people have paid for crimes they didn't commit," Dominick said. "But, if I help her, I'll end up paying for a crime I *did* commit."

"The Council is wrong about her."

"They make tough decisions every day," Dominick said. "And they had compelling reasons to want Abigail dead." After a brief hesitation, he said, "But, I also know they have this wrong. I've known Abigail for a long time, and the only thing she's guilty of is being way too stubborn for her own good. When Aram sends me out after her, I won't look too hard."

Dominick's phone buzzed. He pulled it out and glanced at the screen, reading a text message.

"Hey," he said. "Good news. They cleared us to fly."

"Fly?"

"Yeah," Dominick said. "The weather has cleared, and we have clearance to take the chopper out over the next couple of days. Ready to go up?"

"Up where? Why?"

Dominick only smiled in response. Then he said, "Come on, we need to take advantage of this."

Haatim groaned as he stood and followed Dominick out of the lobby and into the snow. The early afternoon sunshine made it bright outside, but the cold had Haatim shivering in only seconds.

The exterior of the hotel had changed completely since he'd first arrived. After Abigail had left, they'd hired dozens of armed guards to patrol the exterior fences and make sure that no one came in or out without permission. It looked like a prison now, though most of the additions were temporary and prefabricated.

"Why all the extra guards?" Haatim asked.

"All of the Council is gathering here," Dominick said. "At the same time."

"That doesn't happen often?"

"Almost never," Dominick said. "Definitely not in my lifetime. They only gather for vitally important issues."

"Like Frieda's trial."

"Exactly."

"Will they execute her?"

"Not likely," Dominick said. "A lot of members would never vote to kill her because her family is one of the originals. But they could enact other punishments instead that would be just as bad."

"Like what?"

"Take the Hunters away, for starters. Revoke her position on the Council. They might not take her life, but they could take everything else that matters."

They climbed into Dominick's sedan and headed for the gate.

"What happens if they catch Abigail?"

"It depends," Dominick said. "They might just drop the charges against Frieda or give her less of a sentence. Especially if she cooperates in bringing Abigail back."

"She'll never do that."

"Nope," Dominick said.

He pulled up to the gate. Two men bundled in winter clothing and carrying assault rifles walked up to his car door and tapped on the glass. Dominick rolled down his window and held out his credentials. One of the guards took them and scanned them with a small handheld device.

"Where are you guys headed?"

"The airport," Dominick said. "We have clearance to fly today."

The man typed onto his little device. "Reason?"

"Training."

The man nodded. "If you return after seven, we won't allow you admittance until the morning."

"Understood," Dominick said.

The man waved for another guard to open the gate and handed the credentials back to Dominick, who rolled up the window and drove slowly out of the complex.

"A little crazy if you ask me," Haatim said. "Are the rifles necessary?"

"Not really," Dominick said. "Not unless an army attacks us. Paranoia has always been one of the Council's strongest traits. Still, if I had as many enemies as they do, I would have security like this all the time just for me."

They drove in silence toward town, weaving along tight roads up and down the mountains. Haatim couldn't help but feel somewhat nervous while the car drove along sheer cliffs hundreds of meters high.

"What did you want to be when you grew up?" Dominick asked as they drove.

"I'm not sure. I was one of those kids that didn't have any big ambitions. I guess I wanted to be a religious figure like my father. That's why I went to school for theology."

"I've never thought of him as religious."

"Deeply," Haatim said. "He was a pillar of our community, and I always looked up to him. But, when I got to school, I couldn't just stick to one thing. I thought all of the religions had great ideas, and I wanted to pick and choose the ones I liked."

"So, you cherry-picked your own religion."

"I guess you could say that," Haatim said. "What about you? What did you want to be?"

"I always wanted to be a pilot," Dominick said as they passed into the city. Already, street crews worked to clear off the snow. The bustling city looked beautiful and like something out of a fairytale. "Even when I was a little kid."

"How did you end up here?"

"Circumstance," Dominick said. "My uncle worked as a Hunter and recruited me. I didn't have a lot of options."

"He recruited you?"

"More or less. We stayed at his house one winter, and he told us he was heading out to the bar to get a drink. He did that a lot, and—getting older and braver—I followed him. Long story short, he *did* head to the bar, but not to get a drink. He killed four people."

"How old were you?"

"Fourteen. When he found out I'd tailed him, he gave me two choices."

Haatim felt shocked. "Your uncle would have killed you if you didn't join the Order?"

"No," Dominick said with a laugh. "Vodka or Whiskey. A few months later, they taught me how to fly planes and helicopters, so I guess my dream came true."

They pulled into the old airport and navigated across the grounds to the helicopter pads, which stood quiet today with most people staying inside to avoid the cold. Exactly where Haatim would have liked to have been instead of out here.

They drove out to where Spinner rested, and Dominick parked. "Ready to go up?"

"Do I have a choice?"

"What do you think?"

"Then, I suppose I'm ready," Haatim said. "Ready as I'll ever be."

They climbed out of the car and walked toward the helicopter. Snow crunched underfoot as they went.

"They'll have all of this snow cleared by morning, and we don't expect any more for a couple of days," Dominick said. "But a massive storm front's coming through before too long. We'll want to batten down the hatches for that, which is why we're going up today."

"I never experienced that much snow when I was younger," Haatim said. "And now I know all about it."

"I'm from Quebec, myself," Dominick said. "So I know all about the stuff. This is just a light dusting."

"Why are we going up?"

"To see the area around here." Dominick gestured with a hand to indicate a vague circumference.

"With you, there is *always* an ulterior motive. Why are we *really* going up?"

Dominick slid open the door. "No motives. I promise."

Haatim eyed him warily, and then, after another moment's hesitation, he climbed in. He went up to the copilot's seat and put on the headgear. Dominick climbed in next to him and turned on everything.

"You won't find a better helicopter than this," Dominick said. "It even has automatic flying built in so that it can take off and land by itself."

"Is that legal?"

"Depends on who you ask," Dominick said with a shrug. "I make it a habit never to ask. First things first, safety. See that cord right there in the back? That's a drop cable. You can run the line out, and you've got eighty feet of slack. You can use it as a zip line for quick exits, and I can reel it in manually if need be."

"Okay," Haatim said.

"Second, parachutes. We have four of them stuffed under the

seats in the back. I check and repack them weekly to make sure they stay good to go. One strap through your legs, two over your chest, and then your shoulders. Got it?”

“Got it.”

“All right. Let’s take this puppy up.”

***

Haatim had to admit that the flight proved a lot more fun than he’d anticipated. Heights scared him, but not to an uncontrollable degree, and the longer they stayed up in the air, the more confident he grew.

Though loud noise wrapped around him from the wind resistance and rotor blades, the headphones did a good job of muffling the sound. Dominick gave him a tour of the surrounding area, flying over the mountains and around the hotel.

How amazing being up so high and having a commanding view of the world below. It had a surreal appearance with the fresh snow covering everything and seemed even more beautiful than the first time he’d flown out.

It felt like being in a different world. The helicopter had an internal heating system, so it ended up quite toasty inside. Haatim took off his gloves and just enjoyed the trip.

After everything that Dominick had put him through for these past weeks, to see this side of him made a refreshing change. Just a nice and simple trip to enjoy the countryside. A little reward for all the hard work.

“Probably never did something like this before the Council, did you?” Dominick asked, as they flew. They passed overtop a flat area several kilometers away from the hotel and flew increasingly higher.

“Never,” Haatim said. “I’ve been in quite a few planes in my life because we traveled a lot, but helicopters are completely new.”

“I think you would make a great pilot if you wanted me to teach you how to fly.”

“Maybe,” Haatim said, glancing out the side window. “Should we be this high?”

Dominick ignored the question. “My uncle taught me how to skydive when I was eleven. He told me that, if I expected to be a pilot one day, I had better learn how to get out of a plane fast in case of an accident. He taught me everything through ‘trial by fire’, and I guess it just stuck. He believed that people learn best when their lives depend on it.”

“I’m serious, Dominick. I think we’re going too high.”

“He was a harsh man,” Dominick said. “But the world needs men like that.”

The helicopter kept rising, passing through the clouds and even higher.

“Where are we going?”

“Up,” Dominick said. “I love being up here. It makes the world look small and everything insignificant. Puts everything into perspective, you know?”

“No, I don’t know.” Haatim felt uncomfortable. They could barely see the ground now, through the clouds. He didn’t know how high a helicopter could go, but this seemed way dangerous. “Why so high?”

“I have a confession to make,” Dominick said. “I *do* have an ulterior motive.”

A sinking feeling pulled at the pit of his stomach. “What?”

“I want to show you something.”

Dominick pressed a few buttons on the dashboard and let go of the controls. Then he climbed out of his seat and into the back of the helicopter.

“Where are you going?”

“Autopilot, remember?” Dominick said, grinning. “Come on.”

Reluctant, Haatim followed him into the back. Dominick reached under one of the seats and pulled out a parachute. Haatim had the worst feeling about what might be about to happen. He felt as though in a dream. “What’s that for?”

Dominick didn’t answer, but instead, donned the chute. He put the straps over his shoulders, and then hooked them over his chest. He looped the final one up through his legs and connected it as well, and then cinched them all tight.

“What are you doing?” Haatim asked. “I can’t fly this helicopter. Are you planning to jump?”

“Six hundred meters is the *minimum* distance to pull your chute,” Dominick said. “But one thousand is better.”

“I’ve never jumped out of a plane before,” Haatim said, heart fluttering in terror.

Dominick continued to ignore him, opening the side door of the helicopter. The wind whipped in, chilling Haatim’s skin in seconds. He scooted as far from the door as possible, shivering.

“Please ...” he muttered.

“The helicopter will fly down to the ground and find us,”

Dominick said. "It's tracking my parachute and will find us."

He grabbed another parachute from under the next seat and checked the latches. "Remember. All four straps, and then pull them tight before you pull the cord."

"Please, don't make me do this!"

Dominick grabbed Haatim's arm and dragged him away from the corner. Haatim tried to struggle, but fear weakened his muscles. His breathing came in short and ragged gasps.

"Breathe deep and don't panic," Dominick said. "You have to be in complete control. Always remember, in *this* life, one mistake can get you killed."

"I don't want *this* life." Haatim jerked back. No use, though, as Dominick had an iron grip on his arm. "I didn't choose this life."

Dominick shrugged. "It chose you."

And then he threw the parachute out of the helicopter. Haatim watched in horror while it disappeared, whipping underneath the craft. He looked back at Dominick, who smiled.

"Trial by fire."

Then Dominick jerked on Haatim's arms and dove backward out of the chopper, pulling Haatim out with him. Haatim screamed while he fell without a parachute.

✳✳✳

"Amazing, isn't it?" Dominick yelled over the headset while they plummeted. "You can keep screaming and never run out of breath while you fall. The pressure just keeps refilling your lungs."

Haatim couldn't stop screaming and flailing. He focused on closing his mouth and ended up making gasping sounds instead. Dominick pushed Haatim away and created separation between them as they dropped. The wind whistled past, freezing lips and throat.

"Quick lesson," Dominick said. "Aim your body straight like a torpedo, and you'll fall faster. Spread out and create more wind resistance, and you'll fall slower."

While he spoke, he performed both actions. First, falling faster, and then slowing down. Not a huge difference but noticeable.

"Try it."

"I can't," Haatim said, still flailing.

"You need to get control. Aim your body where you want to go."

Haatim closed his eyes and took a deep breath, and then

tightened his body and forced his legs up over his head. The wind shifted around him, but he couldn't tell if he changed course at all.

He looked back at Dominick a few seconds later. They'd moved farther apart. "Good," Dominick said. "Now, spread out and slow down."

Haatim did, and the wind picked up against his body when he flattened it out.

"We're at fourteen hundred meters," Dominick said, moving closer to him. He pointed down. "There's your chute. You better get moving."

It dropped, maybe twenty meters below him. Haatim pushed the terror out of his mind and focused. He angled his body straight like an arrow and went for it. His speed picked up while he plummeted, and he felt certain he'd nearly reached terminal velocity.

He overshot the bag and had to correct course, rolling onto his back and spreading out his body to catch as much wind as possible. It took another few seconds, but finally, the bag came close enough that he could reach out and grab it.

Relieved, he pulled it to his chest and clutched it like a mother holding her infant. "Good job," Dominick's voice came over the headset. "Eleven hundred meters. Hurry up and put it on."

Haatim scrambled to pull the chute over his shoulder. Just then, he passed through the clouds. The ground loomed huge below with features and mountains coming into full view.

It proved insanely difficult to manipulate the parachute. Each time he tried to roll the other strap toward him to pull it over his shoulder, his body rolled instead, and the strap stayed too far away.

"Better focus, Haatim."

At last, at long, long last, he got a grip and pulled both straps over his shoulder. He snapped the first two over his chest, and then reached for the one under his lower back.

"You're doing great," Dominick said. "Nine hundred meters. We're still in the green, but you're running out of time."

Haatim looked down, and the ground loomed twice as big as before and approached fast. He twisted his body, pulling the strap up under his crotch and snapping it to the ones across his chest.

"Remember to pull them tight," Dominick said. "You've got about ten seconds before you're in the red."

"Would you shut the hell up?" Haatim screamed, grabbing the straps and yanking them.

They slid easily, and he let out a gasp when the ones over his chest crushed his lungs. Suddenly, it felt difficult to breathe.

Still, he decided, hard to breathe had to be better than sliding out of the parachute.

"All right, all right," Dominick said. "You don't have to be a jerk about it. I won't help anymore."

Haatim reached for his shoulder, where he thought the strap cord should be to release the chute, but found nothing there. He fumbled, frantically trying to find it.

"Where's the cord?"

"Not there," Dominick said.

"Where?!"

"Oh, *now* you want my help? It's by your right hip."

Haatim reached down and felt a clasp. He yanked on it and, all at once, a loud whooshing sound erupted when the parachute flew out of the backpack. His entire body yanked upward, and then he spun.

"Over your head, you have two handles. Grab hold and use them to steer," Dominick said.

Haatim grew dizzy from the spinning, but could see the handles. He reached up and grabbed the left one, and then managed to pull it far enough down to get the other in his right hand.

After a few seconds, the chute stabilized, and Haatim fell more smoothly. He looked to the side. Dominick glided down next to him.

"Just enjoy the rest of the trip," Dominick said, swooping away and heading for a plateau.

Haatim looked around at the mountains, but couldn't enjoy it anymore. His body ached, and he felt sick to his stomach. He didn't think he would ever fly again, and most definitely wouldn't go skydiving after today.

He couldn't think of anything more terrifying in his entire life, not even counting everything that he'd gone through with Abigail in Raven's Peak.

Haatim landed hard, bouncing through the snow, and finally came to rest about ten meters from where he'd first hit. He just lay there on his back, staring up at the sky and taking deep breaths.

After a few minutes, Dominick approached, and then he leaned over Haatim, staring down at him. "You good?"

"No," Haatim said, sitting up. "I'm not good at all. Why the hell would you do that to me?"

"Ah, you'll get over it," Dominick said, extending his hand to help him up.

With a sigh, Haatim accepted and raised from the ground.

"Think of it this way; you've experienced the worst possible method of skydiving ever. Next time, it can't possibly be as bad."

"There won't be a next time."

"In this line of work, you can't know something like that. And, hey, now you've earned my respect."

"I didn't before?"

Dominick shrugged. "It ebbs and flows. I'm not a huge fan of Council members, and Aram in particular. Why should his son get a free pass? Now, though, you've completely earned it."

Dominick helped Haatim take off the backpack and fold up the parachutes. They finished just as the helicopter landed on the ground nearby. It touched down gently, but the rotors kept spinning.

Haatim looked at it with skepticism.

"The other option is to walk back," Dominick said. "But it's about fifteen kilometers."

Reluctantly, Haatim climbed into the helicopter and then the copilot's seat. Dominick flipped off the automatic controls, and then took them back into the sky.

"You might hate me today," Dominick said. "And for about a week, or maybe a month. But after a while, you'll look back and think, 'Man, that was actually pretty awesome.'"

"I doubt it."

"Trust me," Dominick said. "My job is to prepare you for the real world and the threats you'll have to face. I wouldn't do you any favors by taking it easy on you."

Haatim didn't respond. They flew in silence for another fifteen minutes, heading back toward the airport.

"You know," Dominick said, finally. "We only used two parachutes. How about round two?"

Haatim shot him a look of terror. "Hell, no."

Dominick just laughed in response. Then he said, "Don't worry. We need to keep the others for a real emergency. You're safe ... this time."

"You're cruel."

"Only sometimes," Dominick said, smiling.

They traveled in silence for a couple more minutes, and then Dominick spoke again, "You said you lived in Arizona? Scorching hot out there."

"Believe me, I know. Still beats the cold, though."

"How did your dad like it when he came to visit?"

Haatim shrugged. "He never did," he said. "The entire time I went to college out there, he didn't come to see me once."

"Yeah, he did," Dominick said. "After your sister died. He said he was flying out to visit you."

"What?" Haatim asked. "When?"

"A few days after she died. Before the funeral."

Haatim did some quick math in his head, counting up the days.

That meant it must've been weeks before he'd moved back out to Arizona and everything crazy had happened. He would have been in India, and there would have been no one in Arizona his father would have known.

"You're sure?"

"Yeah," Dominick said. "I'm the one that flew him in."

"In a helicopter?"

"No, private jet," Dominick said. "He spent two days there visiting you, and then I flew him back to Europe. What are you saying? Are you telling me he didn't come see you?"

Haatim didn't reply immediately. The information caught him off-guard, and he needed to process it.

He lied, "No, yeah." He shook his head. "I remember. He came for a couple of days. Must have slipped my mind."

"Grief will do that," Dominick said with a nod. "I was so sorry to hear about your sister. It must have been rough."

Haatim didn't reply. Truthfully, he barely listened. Then, after a few more seconds, he said, "I'll need some time when we get back to visit my mom," he said.

"No problem." Dominick nodded. "The rest of the Council members will fly in over the next couple of days, so I'll be super busy, anyways. We can spar in the morning, but you'll have most of the day to yourself."

"Sounds good," Haatim said.

Right now, though, things appeared anything but good.

What the hell had his father done in Arizona after his sister died?

Chapter 13

Haatim walked down the hall on the third floor of the hotel, headed to the room where they held Frieda. He hadn't gotten to see her much since her arrest but felt that the time had come to try and get some answers about what was going on. He should have a sparring session with Dominick right now, but this couldn't wait.

One armed guard stood posted outside her room, as well as one at each stairwell and by the elevators.

Distracted, Haatim only noticed the footsteps coming up behind him a split second before the attack came. Dominick stood right behind him, carrying a long cane and grinning wildly. He swung it down, aiming at Haatim's head.

Haatim ducked and threw himself back, landing on the carpet. He rolled to the side, as Dominick kicked out at him, and then he caught Dominick's leg and threw him back.

Dominick laughed. "Need to be ready at all times." He moved forward and swung the cane in a downward arc. "Why didn't you show up for sparring?"

"I need to talk to Frieda."

"About what?"

Haatim lied, "Abigail."

Dominick frowned. "Fine, don't tell me. But you won't get out of your lesson that easily."

Then he waded in and swung the cane at Haatim's shoulder. Haatim sidestepped, and then attacked, punching Dominick in the chest and grabbing his arm. He tried to yank Dominick off balance and knock the weapon out of his hand.

Although he might as well have punched a brick wall for all the good it did him. Dominick jerked free and hit Haatim hard in the shoulder, knocking him off balance instead. He dropped the cane—thankfully—and then hit Haatim with a series of heavy blows aimed at Haatim's face and chest.

Haatim ducked under an attack and countered, falling into a boxer's stance and landing a few hits. He even gave a solid blow on Dominick's left cheek, bloodying his lip.

But that proved the extent of his good luck. Dominick had had enough and came back in hard. He kicked out at Haatim's knee, and then punched him in the stomach.

Haatim scrambled backward, hands up and trying to defend himself. Dominick kept throwing punches. About half of the hits landed, staggering Haatim and backing him up against the wall. Dominick finished with a right hook that put Haatim on the ground.

"Not bad," Dominick said, backing up and giving Haatim space.

"What fight were you watching?" Haatim asked, climbing shakily to his feet. "I just got my ass kicked."

"You're way better at defending yourself than a month ago," Dominick said. "In time, you might even make a respectable fighter."

Haatim wiped his mouth and saw blood. "I think I'd rather be a scholar."

"No longer an option," Dominick said. "Why do you need to see Frieda?"

"I just do," Haatim said. "I need to talk to her about some stuff."

"And you don't want me there?"

"Nothing personal," Haatim said. "It involved my dad."

"No, look, it's cool," Dominick said, but Haatim could tell he'd hurt his feelings. "I guess you still don't trust me. I get it."

Haatim joked, "You did throw me out of a helicopter."

Dominick didn't even crack a smile. "See you later."

Then he turned on his heel and headed back for the stairwell. Haatim watched him go. Had he just seriously damaged their friendship?

It wasn't that he didn't want to tell Dominick about his suspicions, but that he didn't know what to say. Alarm bells went off in his mind, and he knew something was wrong, he just wasn't quite sure what.

When Haatim turned back toward Frieda's room, he saw the guard looking at him. He hadn't moved from his position, but he wore an amused expression. Haatim dabbed the blood from his mouth, stuck his chin up, and walked over to Frieda's room.

"I am here to see the prisoner," Haatim said.

One of the guards picked up a clipboard. "Name?"

"Haatim Arison."

He checked. "Not on the list."

"What do you mean?" Haatim asked. "I'm allowed to see her."

"You're not on the list of approved visitors," the man said. "We can't let you in."

"I need to talk to her," he said. "It's important."

"I'm sure it is, but if your name isn't on this list, then you can't go in."

Haatim grimaced. "Fine," he said.

He turned and headed for the stairs. The man chuckled behind him as he went, but he didn't care. He felt mad that they'd blocked him from seeing Frieda and knew precisely who'd done it.

He went to his father's office. Three guards sat posted in front of this room, but this time, Haatim didn't even bother talking to them before storming in.

"Wait!" one of them said, moving to stop him. Haatim pushed open the door. His father sat at the long table with documents spread out in front of him.

The guard caught Haatim's arm, but he jerked free. The other two had stood by this point and raised their rifles, aiming them at the back of Haatim's head. He heard them but refused to acknowledge the threat. His father looked up, surprise on his face.

"We need to talk," Haatim said.

Aram stared at his son for a second, and then nodded. He waved the guards away. They backed up and closed the door, leaving Haatim alone in the room with his father.

"What is it?"

"Did you go to Arizona?"

A look of shock flashed across his father's face, but it vanished just as quickly. "What do you mean?"

"You *know* what I mean," Haatim said. "Before I went there, did you go to Arizona?"

Aram composed himself, folding his hands on the table in front of him. "Yes."

"Why?"

"Business."

"What business?"

"It doesn't concern you."

"It sure as hell does," Haatim said. "Why would you go there right after my sister died? You should have been with her and us."

"This job that I do doesn't just wait around until I'm ready," his father said. "There are matters that must be attended to."

"Someone else could have handled it," Haatim said.

"No one I trust as much as myself. It was a delicate matter."

"What was?"

"It is irrelevant to you," Aram said.

Haatim knew his father had lied. He hesitated, and then said, "When they captured me and tried to take over my body, someone said something that didn't make any sense at the time. I had no idea what he was talking about, but now I think I do. He said that when I died, they would send my head back to you."

Aram sat in silence.

"I wondered what he meant. Why would he say that?" Haatim asked. "Only now, it makes sense. You went there and made a deal with them, didn't you?"

"Haatim ..."

"What was the deal? Did you have anything to do with me getting captured?"

"No," Aram said firmly, shaking his head. "No. I had nothing to do with that."

"Then, what was it? What deal did you make? Did you betray them?"

"It ... it's not what you think."

"Is that why you blocked me from seeing Frieda? Afraid I would find out and tell her?"

"No. Only Council members have approval to visit her," Aram said. "I have no power over that."

"She's locked up, awaiting trial, and *you're* the one who betrayed the Council."

"I made a mistake, Haatim. A terrible, foolish mistake. But I did it all for the greater good."

"How can you say that? You're a hypocrite."

"I'm not," Aram said. "Haatim, you don't understand."

"Then, help me understand! Tell me what the hell is going on."

"Okay," Aram said, collapsing back into his chair. "You're right. I made a deal."

"Why?"

"It isn't important. I made a terrible mistake. I thought I could control them and get what I wanted, but I failed. I'm taking care of it, and I promise you, it has *nothing* to do with Frieda."

"I need to speak with her."

"She's dangerous," Aram said. "She is manipulative and dishonest."

"Why don't you want me to see her?" Haatim asked. "What are

you keeping from me?"

"It isn't about *you*," Aram said. "It is protocol. Until the trial is over, *no one* is allowed to see Frieda except Council members. No exceptions."

Haatim let out a sigh. "Fine."

"Haatim, I love you, and I wish you would trust me."

"You have lied to me for my entire life." Bitterness settled behind his eyes and dropped into his voice. "And you lied to my mother and sister as well. How on Earth do you expect me to trust you?"

"I didn't have a choice," Aram said. "I had to protect you. Everything I've done, every decision I've made, was for *you*."

"You say that, but you're trying to execute a woman who saved my life and that I care about deeply, and you're ruining the life of another person who has been nothing but good to me."

"Haatim you don't understand—"

"Stop saying that!" Haatim yelled. "As far as I can tell, *you* are the only one keeping secrets from me. Why do you hate Abigail so much?"

"She is a monster." Aram stood. "As was her mentor. Arthur was no hero, but a predator and tool and nothing more. Abigail is no different."

"She rescued me from a situation *you* got me into."

"She did it for her own purposes. The things she did, consorting with demons and acting against the Council, are things for which we must punish her."

"I accompanied her during all of those things," Haatim said. "I am just as guilty as she. Will you execute me too?"

"You were forced and coerced," Aram said. "You had no choice. This is not your world, and you are not guilty simply by association."

"She isn't guilty either. The rules are what's wrong."

"These are the rules we live by. You don't understand because this isn't your world."

"I don't know it because you've kept it from me my entire life!" Haatim shouted.

The door opened behind him, and a guard peeked his head in. Aram signaled to him that things remained all right, and the door slipped closed once more.

"Haatim, you don't know what Abigail is. She can't be trusted."

"I disagree," Haatim said. "Right now, I think she's one of the few people that I can trust. You nearly got me killed in Arizona."

Aram seemed to realize that the conversation wasn't going well.

His face fell, and he looked much older than Haatim ever remembered seeing him.

"Please, Haatim. If you tell anyone about that, anyone at all, they will kill me."

"Maybe that's what you deserve."

He turned before his father could respond and left the conference room. He stormed past the guards and headed back to his fifth-floor room.

He felt furious with his father, but also worried about Abigail and Frieda. Especially Abigail. It killed him not knowing where she was and whether or not she'd reached safety.

He also didn't know what was happening to her. The change she had undergone when she escaped sent chills down his spine every time he thought of it. Not a side of her he wanted to learn more about.

Still, he prayed that she was okay.

Chapter 14

"Did you find anything useful?" Abigail asked.

"Not yet," Mitchell said. He reclined on his beanbag chair with his water bong and stared at the ceiling.

Abigail had been here for two days, and as yet, hadn't seen a single customer come into his shop. He alternated time smoking his product and looking through the binder and making notes.

Luckily, the store had a fully stocked fridge and a microwave, probably in case Mitchell got the munchies. She waited as patiently as she could, under the circumstances, but any more time spent lazing around grated on her nerves.

"What have you found?"

"Just bits and pieces," Mitchell said. "But, most of the words don't make sense. I ordered a dictionary, and it should get here in a couple of days."

"More days?"

"Things like this take time," Mitchell said.

Abigail groaned in frustration, rubbing her face with her hands. "You need to stop smoking so much."

"It helps me think."

"No, it doesn't. It helps you get high."

"And that's when I do my best thinking."

"I'm getting impatient, and that's not a good thing for you."

Mitchell sighed, and then held out the bong toward her. "You want a hit?"

"No," she said. "I don't smoke."

"It'll help you settle. You need to step back and relax for a minute."

"How can I relax? I have people hunting for me and just found out I'm turning into some demonic creature bent on killing people.

"In fact," she added after a short pause. "I'm not sure how *you* can relax. You said yourself that I'll get worse over time. What happens when I decide I need to kill again?"

He froze in his chair, staring at her with his mouth hanging open.

"Is that like ... are you feeling ... I mean, is it something ...?"

"No," she said. "Jesus, relax. I'm not going to kill you."

The tenseness rolled out of his muscles, and he chuckled. It sounded forced. "Yeah, of course not ... why would you? I'm the one that knows Latin."

"Exactly," she said. "I still need you. For now."

He coughed and set the bong aside. "You know, now that you mention it, I did find something interesting when I looked through all the stuff."

"Oh?"

"I translated some things and realized, after a while, that it had nothing to do with what's going on with you. Turns out that the binder has *way* more stuff in it than just the ritual that Frieda did."

"What do you mean? What did you find?"

"Some sort of an elixir you can make. It doesn't bring people back from the dead, exactly, but it can help them stay."

"Stay how?"

"No idea. But, maybe like if a demon wanted to take over a body and preserve it, it might use this."

"How does that help me?"

Mitchell shrugged. "No idea. I said I found it interesting. Not useful."

Suddenly, a beeping and buzzing sounded. Abigail jumped up, hand shooting to the gun on her hip.

"Hey, relax, it's just my phone," Mitchell said.

"What the hell was that sound?"

"My ringtone? R2D2."

"You're kidding?"

"I know, right? I didn't think it was in the store, either, but when I found it, I knew I had to download it. Do you want me to show you where it is?"

Abigail just stared at him.

"I'll take that as a no."

He read over the message, and then put his phone away.

"What is it?" Abigail asked.

"Nothing." Mitchell looked at the floor, and his voice rose a notch. "Just a funny post from one of my friends. You know, a cute cat meme."

"Give me your phone."

"Hey, you know, I think it's time that I get back to work. Do you mind hanging out up front in case I get a customer?"

Abigail narrowed her eyes at him. "Don't make me ask again."

With a sigh, Mitchell retrieved the phone and handed it to her. She glanced it over, frowning. "What is this?"

"A notice from a friend," Mitchell said. "He sent one for your trial as well, letting me know why I hadn't had any business."

"This says they're holding Frieda?"

He nodded. "They arrested her."

"On what charges?"

"Conspiring against the Council. Freeing you. A couple of others, I think, but those are the big ones."

"It says she's charged with treason," Abigail said, reading further down the page. "And that carries a death sentence."

Mitchell took longer in responding this time. "Yeah, it does."

"You mean they will kill her for helping me escape?"

"It is a possibility," Mitchell said.

Abigail stood and headed toward the door.

"Where are you going?"

"Back," she said. "I have to turn myself in."

"She risked her life getting you out of there. Why would you go back?"

"Arthur already lost his life because of me. I won't let the same thing happen to Frieda."

"Most likely, they won't stick the treason charge. Frieda is super important. She'll get off with a slap on the wrist."

"Like I did?" Abigail said. "No way. I can't take that chance. The thing is, I am exactly what the Council thinks I am. A monster."

"No."

"Yes," she said. "I can't stick around here and let Frieda die on my behalf. No one else will lose their life for me."

"What about the binder?" Mitchell pointed to the papers.

Abigail shrugged. "Keep looking and let me know if you find anything."

She slipped out through the doorway before he could respond, and then headed toward her car. She would need to book a flight back to Lausanne.

Hopefully, Colton and his team wouldn't be anywhere nearby. Abigail might be willing to turn herself in to the Council and face their judgment, but she had no intention of letting her pursuers get anywhere near her.

Chapter 15

Haatim rested in his room, reading a book. A knock sounded at the door. He assumed it must be Dominick, coming to spar some more, and didn't feel in the mood. Not after everything that had happened earlier in the day.

He considered just hiding in the dark and pretending like he wasn't inside at the moment, but then dismissed that idea. Dominick was nothing if not persistent, and Haatim had no doubt that he would pick his lock or something to find him.

Plus, he owed it to Dominick to try and explain what had happened before. He felt unsure how much he felt willing to talk about right now, but still wanted to talk to him.

With a sigh, Haatim got up from the chair and tried to stretch out his sore body. The knock came again.

"Hang on, I'm coming," he said, striding across the room and opening the door.

Rather than Dominick, his father stood there. Aram carried a folder under his arm and a pair of cokes in the other hand. They stood for a moment, just staring at each other, and then Aram held up the beverages.

"A peace offering," he said, offering one to Haatim.

He considered leaving his father out in the hall and slamming the door in his face. Right now, he didn't want to talk to Aram about anything, much less accept a peace offering from the man. He remained furious about everything.

Haatim decided not to, though. His father had betrayed his trust, and maybe done worse than that, but was still Haatim's father. He'd reached out, and it wouldn't be fair of Haatim to refuse to hear him out.

He stepped aside, unsure if he would regret this decision, and gestured for his father to come in.

"All right," he said, accepting the beverage. "We can talk."

Aram crossed the threshold, and Haatim cleared dirty clothes and trash from the two chairs next to the table. They took seats, facing each other in silence. The only sound came from each of them taking sips from their cans.

Finally, Aram said, "I wanted to apologize for lying for all these years. I couldn't speak about this life, but I should have brought you into it sooner."

"Why didn't you?"

"Too afraid of losing you," Aram said. "I felt that if I told you about this part of my life, then it would put you at risk."

"Clearly, it put me at risk anyhow," Haatim said.

Aram frowned and nodded. "Yes. I got it wrong and nearly lost you."

"What happened?"

"I attempted to make a deal with the Ninth Circle. At the last minute, I got cold feet and tried to back out. When the Ninth Circle found out that I had betrayed them, they grew furious. They went after you to get back at me."

"What was the deal?"

"Something I'd planned to build a long-term peace," Aram said.

"I thought the Council refused to make deals with demons?"

"We don't," Aram said. "These are desperate times. Our numbers have dwindled, and we don't have many of us left. We need a chance to catch our breath and rebuild before we're ready to confront the Ninth Circle again."

"So, when you went to Arizona, you weren't there working for the Council?"

Aram hesitated. "No. I went of my own accord, and it proved a tremendous mistake. I never imagined that something like that might happen to you, though. You have to understand, Haatim, that every single choice I've made, I did to protect you and your sister. You must know that I would do anything to keep the two of you safe."

"The Council doesn't know?"

"They don't know any of this," Aram said. "I've worked to remedy my mistake, and I believe things are over with. But, you must understand, if they find out what I tried to do, they will kill me."

"What you did ... you are a hypocrite."

"I know," Aram said, bowing his head. "But I've only made decisions for the benefit of my family and the Council."

"I'm the only person who knows?"

Aram nodded. "You hold my life in your hands."

Haatim rubbed his face in his hands and shook his head, unsure what to do.

"I will protect your secret," Haatim said after a while. He remained furious, but a part of him could understand his father's motivations. To make peace—even with the devil—to save lives couldn't be such a terrible thing, right? "But, I do want something in return."

"Anything," Aram said, visibly relieved.

"I still think you have it wrong about Abigail. I spent a lot of time with her, and she never struck me as the kind of person you seem to think she is. She saved my life."

"And I owe her for that," Aram said. "However, I've seen the truth of what she is."

"She isn't a murderer," Haatim said.

Aram handed Haatim the envelope he'd left on the table. Haatim set his drink down and opened the manila sleeve.

He closed it quickly, seeing the gruesome images from a crime scene. Body parts lay strewn about, and blood covered everything. He hesitated a second, steadied himself, and then opened it again.

Dozens of images that showed multiple body parts cut to pieces. He recognized two of the victims as Colton and Anong, the Hunters assigned to execute Abigail by the Council. Anong's eyes had been removed and her throat cut, and the expression on Colton's face ... a mixture of terror and agony that made Haatim sick to his stomach.

"Why are you showing me this?"

"Those were taken two days ago," Aram said. "Three Hunters went after Abigail to bring her back, and she murdered them all."

"They were trying to kill her. She only defended herself."

"Does this look like self-defense?" Aram asked.

Haatim glanced again at the images and couldn't help but admit how horrible they looked. He could hardly believe Abigail would do something like this, even to protect herself.

"Why are you showing me this?" he said.

"Because I want you to understand," Aram said. "When Abigail was a child, something happened to her. The Cult she's been trying so hard to destroy did terrible things and changed her. I believe that she tries to do good, but an evil lives inside her that she will never escape."

"You don't know that."

"I do," Aram said. "When we first found her, as a little girl, the Council voted to execute her because of what she might grow into. Only narrowly did we decide that she be allowed to live, and even then, only because Frieda and Arthur blackmailed and coerced the

Council to vote in their favor. I will *never* condone such actions."

"Why tell me any of this?"

"I want you to understand the truth," Aram said. "I want you to help me fix all these problems. I have made mistakes, I admit, but everything I've done was in service to the Council. Abigail is dangerous, but she trusts you. I want you to help me bring her in safely and without further incident."

Haatim hesitated, trying to sort through what his father had told him. If true, it changed everything. He couldn't detect any hint of a lie from his father.

The images in his hand felt compelling. "You're certain that Abigail did this?"

"Colton called me and said he was on her trail, and then this happened. I don't know what other conclusions to draw from this."

"I'll need some time to think about it," Haatim said.

"I've lied to you in the past," Aram said. "And put you at risk, but never again. I want Abigail to be brought in safely."

"So you can execute her."

"Look at the people she's *murdered*, Haatim, and tell me their lives are worth less than hers?"

Haatim couldn't think of a good reply. Those images had burned into his memory now and made him sick to his stomach. If Abigail had caused them—and that remained a huge if—then no way could he trust her again.

However, he couldn't take things at Aram's word, either. The truth would lay somewhere in the middle, and it would be up to him to find it.

"I'll think about it," Haatim said. "But, I won't be a part of her execution."

"I promise you that she will receive full consideration and justice for everything that has happened. If we find her guilty, we will punish her, and if we find her innocent, we will find the truth. That's the best I can offer. Is justice enough?"

Haatim nodded. "All right," he said. "No more lies."

"Never again," Aram said. "I have suspended the hunt for Abigail until after Frieda's trial. We've recalled all our resources until after we decide everything regarding Frieda."

"This trial is a terrible idea," Haatim said.

"She's a loose cannon prone to rash actions and acting against the best interests of the Council. But, even then, I do have great respect for her. No one lives above our laws, and sometimes, people simply need reminding of that."

"Like you," Haatim said. "You've broken far worse rules than anything she did, and yet you want me to give you a second chance. Shouldn't she get the same?"

Aram stayed silent for a moment, head bowed, and then he nodded. "You are right. What do you want from me?"

"Give her that second chance."

"I can't call off the trial," Aram said. "Too many things are already in motion."

"But, you're the one pressing for her punishment. Just back off."

"I can request a lower reprimand. Perhaps, simple removal of her position as head of the Hunters."

"Temporarily," Haatim said. "I've seen her interacting with many of them, and she does an excellent job."

"Is that what you think fair? I can ask that she be placed on probation for a few years. It would be little more than a slap on the wrist, but would still serve to send a strong message to the other members of the Council."

Haatim thought about it, and then nodded. "Yes, that seems reasonable."

"Very well," Aram said. "That is what will happen, then."

He checked his watch and finished off the last dregs of his coke.

"I'm late for a meeting. Thank you for seeing me." His father stood.

"Will you allow me to visit Frieda?"

"It is not *my* decision that keeps you away. Only the Council can make such a ruling. I will bring it up with them, however. You will be able to speak to her within the week. I promise."

"All right," Haatim said, standing too.

He felt like a huge weight had lifted from his shoulders. Even though they hadn't decided a lot, at least it provided an opening of a dialogue between him and his father, and it felt good getting filled in about what had gone on. They could move forward now and overcome the separation between them.

"I will keep your secret," Haatim said.

"Thank you," Aram said. "Once all of this is over, I am hoping that we will be able to spend more time together. Things have been rather hectic these last few months with everything going on with Abigail and now Frieda, but I would like for the chance to reacquaint myself with my son."

"Me too," Haatim said. "Everything has just been so ... crazy."

"It is nearly over. Things will go back to normal soon."

Haatim chuckled. "What *is* normal?"

Aram smiled, and it was the first time Haatim had seen his father smile in a long time. It looked good on him, transforming him into a completely different person.

"I suppose we can make a new normal. Together."

"I'd like that."

"I'm so glad that you're here now. With you here, we can make the Council great again."

"And no more lies?"

"Never again," Aram said.

Haatim held out his hand so that they could shake, but Aram stepped in and gave him a hug instead. "I missed you, my son," he said. "I love you."

Then he left, leaving Haatim standing in the center of the room, more conflicted but also happier than he had been in weeks.

Chapter 16

Haatim noticed that the external security grid seemed to ramp up around the hotel each time another Council member showed up. Eleven such members resided here now, counting Frieda, which meant that only two more were on their way before deliberations could begin in Frieda Gotlieb's trial.

Haatim grew used to seeing the armed guards parked at every entrance. It felt like a prison state, and they and the electric fence had become a part of the scenery.

It had to be insanely expensive paying for all this security, which explained why they rarely gathered in one location. It seemed like even more of a waste because of the conversation he'd had with his father the night before. Now that the trial would only be a formality, it seemed like a complete waste of money.

Dominick stayed busy more often than not now, often driving or flying in Council members, depending on the weather. Haatim hadn't spoken to him since their last meeting and knew Dominick remained annoyed with him. They had trained this morning, but neither of them had spoken more than a handful of words.

Haatim didn't know what to say. He couldn't tell Dominick the secret that his father had told him, and he couldn't think of a good lie to explain why he'd blown Dominick off.

Instead of talking, Dominick put his emotions into the fight and beat the crap out of Haatim, leaving him bruised.

Still, in the grand scheme of things, he felt healthy and happy with how things went. Haatim worried almost constantly about Abigail and how she'd gotten on. Also, he worried about whether or not his father had told him the truth. The more he thought about it, the less sure he felt. No way could the kind-hearted girl he'd met do something like that.

He didn't know where she'd gone, if she remained safe, or what she might do, but at least his father had called off the hunt for her for now. After the trial finished, Haatim would try to find her and prove her innocence.

But, for now, he grew bored. Barely after noon, he had nothing else to do with his day. The trial hadn't started, Dominick wasn't around, and he had a lot of pent up energy and nothing to spend it on.

Luckily, the Council traveled with an extensive library of books, and Haatim pored over them with a voracious appetite. Many of them covered the history of the Council of Chaldea or the Order of Hunters. Some of them spoke about the cults and creatures they'd battled throughout the years, and all of them proved interesting.

The records seemed rudimentary and incomplete. By his best guess, the Council had formed around the twelfth century with a group of four men and a woman, all peasants, in response to the times. They had expanded in the ensuing years and branched out, becoming a multi-faith and multicultural organization dealing with otherworldly threats.

Now, Haatim relaxed in his room, engrossed in an account from the sixteenth century about the life of a renowned Hunter. His phone buzzed. He slipped it out of his pocket and glanced at it.

His mother.

He'd gone to visit her a handful of times while at the Council building, but it felt exhausting. She knew nothing about this life that he shared with his father, and so it became difficult for him to speak with her at all.

Haatim didn't like to lie to his mother, yet the situation demanded that of him. He sympathized with his father's decisions because, as much as he wanted to tell his mom the truth, it remained in her best interest to keep it from her.

As a result, they couldn't exchange any conversation beyond pleasantries. Still, he liked visiting her because the first remark she always made was about how much healthier and stronger he looked and how proud she felt of him.

He clicked the answer button. "Hey, Mom," he said.

"Haatim?" she said. "Can you come see me? We need to talk about something."

"What?" he asked.

"I just need to see you. It's important. Can you come to my apartment?"

"What is it?" he asked. "Is something wrong?"

"No," she said. He could hear the lie in her voice. "Nothing is wrong. I just need to talk to you about something."

He hesitated, not sure if something was off or if, maybe, she might have overreacted to something. His mom considered most things to be meltdown events, but Haatim detected a hint of fear in her voice.

Had she discovered something about the Council? Had he (accidentally) given her clues about what he and his father did?

Or something less sinister? Like, perhaps, he should have called her and had forgotten. Most probably, the list of things she'd asked him to do in the last few months that he never accomplished would be a long one. They all seemed like silly things now.

"All right," he said. "I can come tomorrow."

"I need you to come over now," she said.

"I'm busy, and the weather is supposed to storm tonight," he said.

"This is important, Haatim," she said. "I need to see you right away."

He sighed. "Okay, I'm on my way."

He hung up and headed out of his room. Along the way, he grabbed his coat; they'd forecasted one hell of a storm tonight.

When he made it to the lobby, he spotted Dominick sitting in the foyer and talking to an old man, who wore orange robes. He looked to be from a Southeast Asian monastery. Probably Theravada Buddhist—something Haatim had grown familiar with in his studies.

The man rose, bowed, and smiled when Haatim approached, and he returned the gesture. Then the man headed toward the elevator. With a hint of jealousy, Haatim watched him step inside. He couldn't remember the last time he'd ridden in one of those.

"There you are," Dominick said, as Haatim came up to him. "I haven't seen you all morning. Was about to come looking for you."

"I was just up in my room reading."

"You should have exercised," Dominick said.

"It is exercise," Haatim said. "For the mind."

Dominick chuckled. "Working out your mind won't make your abs any tougher. Where you headed?"

"Back to the city," Haatim said. "I need to talk to my mom."

"Oh? What's she need?"

"No clue," Haatim said. "She seemed particularly vague tonight."

"Mothers," Dominick said, laughing and shaking his head. "Need a lift?"

"No, I'm good."

"I've seen you drive on snow. You shouldn't be behind the wheel."

"You don't have anything else to do?"

"Nah, I'm in the clear. Savin was the last to arrive. The trial starts tomorrow.”

“Wow,” Haatim said.

It had taken such a long time to start Abigail’s trial that he found it hard to believe it had only taken a few weeks to commence this one against Frieda.

“I’ll drive you in,” Dominick said. “I need to refuel the helicopter and get it ready before I start flying people out. It’s supposed to storm all night, so I’d rather get this stuff done sooner instead of later.”

“All right,” Haatim said.

He followed Dominick out of the building. Though windy, no snow fell yet. The days grew shorter, but they’d almost reached the solstice and would start lengthening soon. Haatim looked forward to having more than a couple of good hours of sunlight each day.

It took ten minutes of waiting for the gate crew to clear them this time. A lot of faces, Haatim didn’t recognize, but once the pair got on their way, they made good time. Dominick drove up the roads with practiced ease, and Haatim had to hand it to him for how well he could control vehicles. A natural.

“I’m worried for Frieda,” Dominick said, as they drove. “I didn’t think it would come to this. I thought they would drop the charges against her before calling in a full trial.”

“Neither did I,” Haatim said.

“Your father has never been Frieda’s biggest fan. After she let Abigail escape, he must have decided he would push this to the final conclusion.”

“Maybe,” Haatim said. “But I don’t think things will go too poorly for Frieda in this trial.”

“What do you mean? Did you speak to him about it?”

“I did. When I left you the other day, they wouldn’t let me in to talk with Frieda, but I went to my father and confronted him. I’m sorry I brushed you off. I just didn’t want you to get involved in family stuff.”

“No, I get it. I’m not mad or anything. I felt a bit hurt at first, but I’m over it. How’d that meeting with your father go?”

“Still finding out, for the most part,” Haatim said. “I’ll let you know how things went after the dust settles. I did talk to him about Frieda.”

“Oh?”

“I told him I disagreed with his opinion, and that Frieda doesn’t deserve treatment like this.”

“How’d he take that?”

"He said he'll stop pushing so hard and that he'll try probation and re-evaluation after a few years without her having control of the Hunters."

"So she won't be in charge of us anymore, but she'll still be on the Council?"

"Essentially," Haatim said.

"That seems reasonable, I suppose. In my opinion, they should just free her and admit this was all a stupid error of judgment, but I guess that's why I'm not in charge. After all, failing to stop Abigail from escaping isn't the same thing as freeing her."

"She *did* let Abi go," Haatim said.

"They don't know that," Dominick said, giving him a look. "Besides, the alternative meant allowing them to finish murdering Abigail, and we don't want that."

"No. Definitely not."

"Then, that means Aram won't even push for her execution anymore. He doesn't even want her removed from the Council? But just wants them to strip her of the Hunters and give them to someone else to command?"

"Himself," Haatim said. "I'm sure he's next in line."

"Bingo," Dominick said. "I talked to a bunch of Hunters out in the field, and they won't be too happy with any regime changes. Aside from a few bad apples, Frieda has complete control. Even if Aram gets control for a couple of years, he won't manage to do much before the Council reinstates Frieda."

The words reassured Haatim. He'd met a few of the Council members, and they all seemed intelligent and forthright people, and not quick to react or make snap decisions. The one obvious thing was that they all had a healthy respect for, or fear of, Frieda Gotlieb and her family name.

The name had come up many times while Haatim read the history books. Two of her ancestors stood among the original founding members. He'd seen mention of divinity and angels in the earliest stories, which meant that the original four remained highly revered.

Frieda made for the last living relative of that blood line, and from everything that Haatim had garnered, she didn't have any children or a husband, which meant the line would probably die out with her. He'd hoped to ask her about that before the Council put the ban in place to keep him away from her.

They reached the apartments his mother occupied, and

Dominick drove up to the lobby entrance.

"Need me to stick around and wait?" he asked.

"No," Haatim said. "I have no idea what she needs, so this could take hours."

"Just call me when you're ready to head back," Dominick said. "I'll be at the airport."

Haatim climbed out and went into the complex. Dominick disappeared down the road, heading east.

While Dominick's words had reassured Haatim, they also worried him. Right now, the Council sat divided and looking inward, but as soon as the trial finished, they would turn their attention outward again.

Their first target would be hunting down Abigail.

Worse, his father would be in charge of the Hunters. He had no doubt that Abigail could take care of herself, but he'd also seen how ruthlessly efficient some of the other Hunters were. Surviving against all of them …

That seemed like something else entirely.

He would need to act fast if he were to find Abigail first. He had no doubt that his father would hold up his word and let Haatim go after her first, but too many unsuccessful attempts and his father would revert to his original plan.

Would Abigail even trust him? Things hadn't ended well, so if he did reach out and try to find her, would she steer clear? How could he convince her of his intentions to try and keep her safe?

Moreover, if he did bring her in, would it be to face another trial and execution? To leave her out would mean they would hunt her down and kill her, but bringing her in might end up getting her killed regardless.

He didn't know what to do but would need to figure it out soon. The trial would be over shortly, and his father would take charge.

Haatim reached his mother's hotel room on the third floor and tapped on the door.

"It's open," she called from within.

He turned the knob and stepped into the room. She stood in the center of the seating area. His father stood next to her.

Haatim tensed up. Had she discovered their secret? Did she plan to confront them? Or, was this just an innocent get together that she'd organized to try and have a family dinner—something they hadn't had in a while?

"Dad? What's up?" he asked.

Aram frowned and glanced at the floor, clearly uncomfortable. "Haatim ..."

"Is everything all right?" He turned to his mother. "What's going on?"

His voice trailed off when he saw a third person step out of the bedroom, gun in hand. Nausea overwhelmed him when he recognized her. The room spun in his vision.

A tall woman in her early twenties, wearing traditional garb from his hometown, stood there. She looked as beautiful and sweet as he remembered. They'd grown up together.

"Nida," he breathed.

His sister smiled. "Hello, Haatim," she said. "Did you miss me?"

Chapter 17

The trip back to Lausanne passed uneventfully for Abigail. She kept expecting to see Colton, Anong, and Jack coming after her, but during her two days on the road and flying in, she never came across them.

Maybe they had given up. Or, more likely, they had gotten called back to help protect the Council with Frieda's upcoming trial. It seemed insane to imagine so many Council members gathered together in one place; a risk she felt was completely out of hand.

She'd heard nothing more about the upcoming trial since leaving Mitchell behind, and the closer she got to turning herself in, the more nervous she became. It meant her death because no way would Aram forgive her for everything that had happened.

Abigail could make no other decision, though. Dangerous and out of control, everything he had said about her, as well as all of the other people who had hated her throughout her lifetime, had proven true. She *was* a monster and couldn't be trusted.

She didn't even trust herself.

Abigail drove to the small airport inside the city where Dominick kept his helicopter. Spinner, an apt yet preposterous name. Though an old monstrosity that barely stayed up in the air, he loved it like a father loves his child.

Hopefully, he wouldn't be here. Abigail stood a fairly good chance of finding him somewhere out in the air yard, probably gabbing with a mechanic or working on his baby. It would be easier to leave the sword with him if she found him, and she didn't want just to leave it and hope no one else stumbled across the old weapon.

On the other hand, she didn't necessarily want to talk to Dominick. Though the sword would be safe with him, if he talked to her, she felt afraid that he would try to talk her out of her decision. Right now, she just didn't want to deal with that.

However, she couldn't take the sword with her. The Council would confiscate the weapon and lock it up somewhere. Arthur's legacy didn't deserve to be forgotten like that. Better to leave the sword with Dominick so that at least one good thing would survive this mess.

She found his ugly little helicopter resting on a pad on the eastern side of the yard. The cockpit door hung open, and music spilled out.

Jazz. Of course. He usually played Coltrane or listened to Marvin Gaye. The music meant he must be here, and no way could Abigail slip the sword in without him noticing. She would have to face him.

Just outside the launch pad, she hesitated, attempting to muster up the courage to approach. With a deep and steadying breath, she edged toward the cockpit.

✳✳✳

Dominick leaned back in his seat, one leg stuck out and holding the door of his cockpit open. A best of Coltrane record played, and he hummed to himself, glancing down at his watch every couple of minutes and frowning.

He had expected Haatim to call him by now to come pick him up from his mother's hotel room. Dominick had spent the last two hours checking over the engine on his little bird, and then occupied himself by cleaning out old wrappers and trash.

He could do only so much cleaning, however, and he grew more worried about Haatim. He doubted anything serious had happened with his mother, or the man would have called.

Maybe dealing with whatever his mother had called about had him too occupied. Worrisome, all the same. Dominick hadn't called yet to enquire, but he would if no word came in the next couple of minutes.

"Hey, Dominick."

The voice came from behind him, inside the back of the chopper. He let out a little yelp and nearly fell out of the cockpit, completely caught off-guard.

He steadied himself on the doorframe and glanced over his shoulder to see Abigail sitting there. She wore a bemused expression.

"Dammit, Abi," he said, composing himself. "Don't do that."

"Your door was open."

"To let in air. Not ninjas. How are you always so quiet?"

She shrugged.

158

He glanced down. A long blade rested across her knees. He recognized it instantly.

"Arthur's sword. You found it?"

Abigail nodded and held it up to him. Gingerly, he took the hilt and held up the weapon, sliding out the blade partway. It looked beautiful and pristine.

"Frieda told me where to find it."

"I haven't seen this thing in years. Not since ..."

He glanced back at Abigail, who frowned but didn't say anything. He handed the blade back to her.

"What are you doing here?" Dominick asked, wanting to change the subject. "I thought you were hiding like Frieda told you to do."

"I came back to turn myself in," she said. "And I'm leaving the sword with you."

"What?" he asked, shocked. He spun in the seat to face her more completely. "What are you talking about?"

"They're going to execute Frieda instead of me," she said. "I won't allow it."

"They won't execute Frieda," Dominick said, shaking his head. "There's no way. She's too important, and Haatim said his father already took that possibility off the table."

"It isn't worth the risk," Abigail said. "I won't let her get punished because of me."

"Frieda made her choice. Do you think it will help anything if you don't honor the decision she made?"

"I don't care," Abigail said, looking down at the sword in her lap. "She *can't* be at risk because of me. Not after ..." The words died in her throat.

Dominick hesitated, and then said, "After what?"

She looked up at him. "I'm a monster," she said. "They were right about me. All of them. They should have killed me when Arthur pulled me out of that cult."

"Don't say that."

"It's true," she said, and a tear slipped down her cheek. "They should have murdered me instead of letting Arthur protect me. If it wasn't for me, he might ... he *would* be alive. He would never have been put in that prison or killed those people."

"Don't say that, Abi," Dominick said softly. "You helped put him in the prison, but it was all the years of battling evil that corrupted him. He just couldn't handle it anymore and snapped."

"No," Abigail said, wiping away a tear. "Fighting evil didn't corrupt Arthur. I did."

✳✳✳

A cool breeze whipped through the cockpit and ruffled Dominick's hair. A long moment passed while he tried to digest what Abigail had said. "What do you mean? You did what?"

"I can't get into it right now," she said. "All you need to know is that Arthur gave up *everything* for me. More than I ever imagined. Frieda too. She's all I have left, and I can't let her die because of me. Not for me."

"I can't let you turn yourself in," Dominick said. "We can figure this out."

"There's nothing to figure out," she said. "My mind is made up, and if you try to stop me, then I *will* consider you an enemy."

The finality in her voice came out undercut with something that made the hairs on Dominick's neck stand on end. Just a touch of a boiling rage laced her tone, most of which she held back.

Dominick hesitated, trying to decide his best course of action. If he did try to stop her physically, he had no doubt that she would make good on her threat. Could he handle Abigail in a fight? However, if she intended on killing him, then he would have no choice but to try and kill her as well. No way could he beat her with kid gloves on.

If he let her go, then she would get locked up in a cell until after Frieda's trial and the Council could decide what to do with her. At the very least, if Abigail did turn herself in, then they might find some way out of her execution once they freed Frieda and she became better able to help.

Better to live and fight another day.

The decision *definitely* not because she scared the crap out of him.

"Do you want me to fly you in?" he asked. "The weather is supposed to turn bad in a couple of hours, but I think I can get you there before it hits us."

She shook her head. "No," she said. "I just wanted to bring Arthur's sword to you and thank you for helping me all these years. You've been a true friend, even though I never deserved one."

"Come on," he said. "Don't get so melodramatic on me. This isn't the last time I'll see you. I'll head back to the Council in a while after I run some errands, so I'll see you when I get there."

"I'll probably be dead already," she said.

"Don't say that," he said. "Frieda will never let that happen."

Abigail bowed her head and let out a long sigh. "I should go."

"Chin up, Abi," he said. "This isn't goodbye. It's just 'see you later.'"

She looked up at him, a frown on her face. Then, carefully, she handed him the sword once more, and then climbed from the helicopter and onto the tarmac.

A few steps away, she glanced back at him. "Goodbye," she said.

And then Abigail had gone.

Dominick watched her disappear around one of the old storage buildings.

"Dammit, Abi," he mumbled, slipping his phone out. He needed to get back to the Council before anything happened to make sure that Abigail would be okay. He wouldn't put it past Aram to try and execute her as soon as she arrived. "Always have to get the last word in, don't you?"

He dialed Haatim's number. They needed to get back to the Council building post haste to make sure that Abigail didn't do anything stupid. The line rang straight through to his voicemail, though.

Dominick growled in frustration and climbed out of the cockpit, heading toward his car. He didn't care how important Haatim's conversation with his mother might be; this meant life or death. He would drag Haatim out of there if he had to.

Chapter 18

"But you're ... you're ..."

"Dead?" Nida grinned. "I was, but I am no longer."

"How?" Haatim asked. "How is this possible?"

"Maybe you should ask *him.*" Nida gestured toward Aram.

Haatim looked at his father. Aram appeared as a man broken, looking down at the floor with a resigned expression and slumped posture. He refused to make eye contact with Haatim.

"Dad? What's she talking about?"

"I couldn't just let her go," Aram said, his voice low. "Haatim, you have to understand. I couldn't just let your sister die. Not if I had *any chance* to bring her back."

"What do you mean? What do you mean, you couldn't let her die?"

"When the doctors told me she only had a few weeks left, I ... made arrangements. I couldn't let her go, not without at least trying."

Haatim let out a sharp breath. "The deal you made. You went to Arizona to bring Nida back."

"They promised they would be able to do it, and I believed them. I needed to see her again. No parent should ever have to watch their child die. I wanted to see her again so badly."

"I'm standing right here," Nida said. "You don't have to talk about me like I'm not."

Aram glowered at her. "You are *not* my daughter."

"Oh, Daddy, Daddy. Why must you be so persistent in your dismissal of me? You wanted to have me back, and here I am!"

Aram turned back to Haatim. "They betrayed me. They promised they could bring Nida back, and I felt desperate enough to believe anything. And, for a while, I thought it *was* Nida. But it isn't her, Haatim. She never came back. This ... this *thing* came in her place."

"Who?" A lump rose in Haatim's throat. "Who betrayed you?"

"The Ninth Circle," Aram said.

A wave of dizziness washed over Haatim. "You mean *this* is where it all started?" He shook his head. "You didn't just make a deal for peace, you did *this?*"

"I believed this would be the opening of negotiations, and that we could sue for peace after we took care of this. I never thought ... they told me that if I didn't pay them ..."

"All of this—*all of this*—is your fault?" Haatim asked, incredulous. "You try to kill Abigail and ruin Frieda *after* you made a deal with the Ninth Circle?"

"You don't understand." Aram held his palms up in the air and, finally, met his son's gaze. "I did all of this for you. For us. I knew how hard it was for you after she died and—"

"Don't you *dare* bring me into this," Haatim shouted. "I miss my sister and have wished, every single day, to see her. Not once, though, did I ask for something like this."

A heavy silence hung in the atmosphere.

"Touching, isn't it?" Nida said. However, rather than her words breaking the tension, they only enhanced it. "Oh, how I've missed you, brother."

Part of Haatim—a large part—heard those words and wanted nothing more than to break down and weep. All of the grief and pain he'd put behind him for his lost sister had come back, and it felt as stingingly painful as it had only moments after her death.

He wanted Nida back more than anything else in the world. But he also knew that wasn't possible. Never mind all of the truths he'd found out about the demonic creatures that possessed people or a Council battling an underground war to protect normal people. He knew in his heart that such a proposition could never be right.

This wasn't *right*.

"You aren't my sister," he said.

"I am, Haatim. You know that I am."

"I know that you are not. Nida is dead."

"I look like her, though," the demon said. "Isn't that enough?"

"Why are you here?"

"I have some business to attend to. I must say, you've changed quite a bit since I saw you in Raven's Peak."

The hairs rose on the back of his neck and forearms. "You were there?"

Not-Nida pulled an ornamental dagger from behind her back. Long and curved, it glimmered in the light.

164

"I went there for this," she said. "You'd be *amazed* at what it can do." Then she pursed her lips. "I suppose I should say that you *will* be amazed at what it does. It's nearly time for things to begin."

"Why are you doing this?"

"Do you expect me to give you an honest answer? Am I to regret the error of my ways and repent? I could give you a myriad of reasons. Maybe I'm just angry that Father, here, has tried so hard to *kill* me over the last few months. He sent Hunters to try to murder his child."

"You are *not* my child."

The demon ignored him. "Or, maybe, I could just say that it's fun. I've had a *lot* of fun killing people, and ever since your father gave me this body, I've enjoyed so much more than I ever thought to find on the surface."

Haatim's mind scrambled. "You killed the Hunters?"

"Of course," Nida said.

Haatim turned to Aram. "The ones you told me that Abigail had killed?"

"I didn't know—"

"Spare me." Haatim turned away from Aram. "Spare me the lies. I'm done. You brought me here, demon, so what do you want. Why are we here?"

"A family reunion, of sorts," Nida said. "I need our father's assistance, and I wanted to ensure his cooperation."

"Why would he help you? All he does is manipulate and lie."

"True, but I think that underneath the ignorance and stupidity, he has a good heart and loves his family." It turned to Aram. "Tie them up."

Aram looked at Haatim. "I'm sorry."

Haatim ignored him. He'd never felt so hurt or betrayed in his life, nor so helpless.

"Come here," Aram said, grabbing a length of rope from a nearby counter. "Don't make this harder than it has to be."

"Don't do this," Haatim said. "Whatever she's planning, it's worse than *anything* she can do to us."

"Oh, I wouldn't say that," Nida said in a silky tone. "I have a *very* vivid imagination."

"Don't," Haatim said, as his father approached. "Please, don't do this."

"Poor, sweet, innocent Haatim," Nida said. "Our father couldn't bear to lose me even when my time came to go. Do you think he will allow you and your mother to die if he can stop it?"

Aram grabbed Haatim's arm, refusing to make eye contact, and dragged him over toward his mother. She stood there, terrified and crying, barely conscious. It looked as if she'd received a beating sometime earlier.

Aram pulled two chairs back-to-back and sat mother and son down, and then he tied the rope around them. He pulled it tight, making sure they couldn't move.

Nida gestured with the gun for him toward the table where a duffel bag lay. "Open it," she said.

Aram did. Haatim couldn't tell what lay inside, but Aram's face fell when he looked in it.

"Enough C4 to take out the adjoining rooms as well," the demon said. "I set it for two hours, and if you get me inside fast enough, you'll get back with plenty of time to turn it off."

"It'll take forty minutes just to drive to the Council," Aram said.

"Then, we'd better hurry. Put it at their feet, and then get moving. If you try anything ... *anything* at all, then by the time you get back here, you'll only find chunks of your family left."

"Don't go through with this," Haatim said. "She won't let us live either way."

Haatim understood, now, the demon's plan. It wanted to break into the Council and bypass the external security. With the numerous armed guards, it would prove nearly impossible to breach their defenses. Yet, no one would think to challenge one of the Council members, especially the one in charge of security.

Aram refused to look at Haatim, and the expression on his face was one of utter despair.

"It was ..." He let out a shuddering breath. "This was never supposed to happen. I'm sorry, Haatim, but this is the only way to keep you safe."

He dropped the bag next to them and headed from the room. The demon walked past the chairs, leaning down to Haatim as it passed. It carried a bathroom rag and roll of tape. It shoved the rag into his mouth, and then put a line of tape over it.

"Don't worry, big brother," it said. "You'll see the real Nida soon enough."

And then it went out through the doorway, closing the door behind it. Haatim sat there, shocked and confused and with no idea of what to do.

166

✳✳✳

Nida—or, rather, the creature that had called Nida's body home these past several months—sat in the passenger seat of Aram's car while they drove toward the gate of the Council building. With assault rifles, half-a-dozen guards watched the entrance. They wore heavy, cold gear, and the snow fell on them.

It should begin storming imminently, perfect for what the demon had planned. Aram had quite a few mercenaries on site, as well as a few rapid response teams in the surrounding area to call in case of emergencies, but the weather would slow their timing down by quite a bit.

"I have your word?" Aram asked, as they pulled slowly up to the gate.

"Of course," Nida said. "I only want Frieda. Let me take her, and I'll go peacefully."

"What do you want with her?"

"That is between her and myself," Nida said. "Once I have dealt with her, I will leave, and you will never see me again. But, if you mess things up now, your entire family will die."

The car pulled to a stop in front of the gate, and one of the guards came up. Aram didn't respond, except to roll down his window. He handed his identification through to the man. His hand shook ever so slightly, but it could have been from the cold, and the demon doubted the guard would notice.

The man looked at the card and then at Aram. He glanced at Nida in the passenger seat. "She's with you?"

"Yes," Aram said. "She is with me, and I have given her full clearance."

"We'll need to check your car," the man said. "No exceptions."

"This is a special exception," Aram said. "And I'm in a hurry."

"Sir, I was told not to allow *anyone*—"

"Do you want me to speak with your supervisor?" Aram asked. "I have full authority over who is allowed or denied from your team."

The man hesitated, and then handed the card back to Aram.

"Of course, sir," he said. "My apologies. Have a nice day."

Then he stepped back and signaled for the other guards to open the gate. It slid apart, and Aram eased the car through the opening. He let out a sigh, hands clutching the steering wheel.

"Well done, Father."

"I'm not your father," Aram said, bitterness in his voice.

"Perhaps not, but perhaps indirectly," the demon said. "After all, *you* gave me this body and life."

"A decision I regret with every breath I take."

Nida chuckled softly while the car drove to a stop next to a side door of the hotel and out of sight of the main gate.

"You can regret it all you want, but right now, you need to just live with it."

Guards patrolled this area, Nida knew from her earlier surveying of their defenses, but none would patrol here for another ten minutes. They climbed out, and Aram used a keycard to get them into a loading area behind the hotel for services and storage. Packed with boxes and supplies, it had a ramp leading down with a concrete floor.

"You are inside our defenses now," Aram said. "You wanted Frieda. Now, you can go get her."

"Where is she?"

"Fourth floor, third door on the left. Only one person stands guard over her. I'll wait for your return to drive you out."

"Yes," Nida said. "You will wait here."

She turned and kicked him in the side of the knee. It cracked when the cartilage snapped, and Aram staggered. He let out a sharp cry of pain and grabbed something under his shirt. He drew it out, hands shaking, but she caught his arm and swatted it away.

The gun skidded across the floor and came to a stop against the wall of the ramp. The demon forced Aram down to the ground, and then dragged him in through the doorway and out of the cold. He cried out in pain when his knee buckled under him.

"Don't be such a wuss," Nida said, closing the door behind them. "You planned to betray me?"

"I never planned for you to leave," Aram said through gritted teeth. "You are an abomination. I created you, and I fully intend to destroy you."

"I am your daughter."

"You are *not* my daughter." Aram's words came out low and snarly. "My daughter died."

"A pity you didn't learn that lesson months ago," Nida said. She moved to nearby pipes and eyed them over, looking for a gas line. Then she reached up and grabbed hold of one, yanking on it. The seal proved a lot tougher than she'd expected, and it would take a few tries to break it loose.

"And to think, *this* was your plan? You thought you could bring me here and deal with me alone?"

"You are my responsibility," Aram said.

"You are weak." Nida shook her head. "If you wanted to betray me, you should have done it at the gate when you had your cronies with you."

"I did," Aram said, and then chuckled.

Nida hesitated, and then glanced over her shoulder at him. "What?"

"There are *no* exceptions for searching cars, even for me. They know that, and they also know certain codes for danger. Right now, they have surrounded this room to eliminate you. You won't escape *this* time."

Nida growled and yanked on the pipe, snapping the connection and tearing it from the wall. A hissing sound erupted while gas poured out.

She ran over to the door that led outside. A dozen men stood out there in the snow, approaching slowly with rifles ready.

"Damn it," the demon said.

From his spot on the floor, Aram chuckled. "It's over," he said. "I made a terrible mistake bringing you back to life, and I'm sure I'll pay for what I did, but at least this nightmare is finally over."

"Oh?" Nida strode over to him and raised the pipe. "*Nothing* is over."

Then she swung it down, cracking him in the shoulder with the lead tube. The bone shattered, and Aram let out a scream of agony.

The demon rushed over and retrieved the gun from the floor just as the outside door breached. A canister of gas bounced across the floor, spewing as it went. It rolled to screaming Aram, releasing its contents into the air.

Nida ran to the far door, which led out of the storage room and further into the building. This one opened as well, and another canister rolled inside. She fired through the doorway, hitting one guard in the shoulder as he tried to duck out of the way.

They started to close the door, planning to let the gas knock her unconscious. The canister spewed its fumes, but they had no effect on her. Nida charged straight into the door just before it latched, slamming it open with her entire body weight. The edge hit one man squarely in the chest, knocking him back and into the others.

Four guards in total. She caught her balance and raised the pistol, firing it into the face of the nearest man.

The others tried to respond, raising their rifles to react in kind, but they stood too close for such long-range weapons to be of much use. The demon stepped in and kicked one man in the chest, knocking him to the ground, and then fired two more bullets into the chest of another.

The first man, whom she'd shot in the shoulder, swung his gun around one-handed and pulled the trigger, firing off a spray of wild shots at her. One clipped her shoulder, but the rest went over her head. She turned and fired, shooting him in the throat and silencing him, for good this time.

The last guard had just begun to get his bearings and recover from the initial attack, but Nida reacted considerably faster. She fired off the last few shots from her clip into him. He staggered back into the wall and slid to the floor, head hanging on his chest, and a trail of blood above and behind him.

Behind her, the other team had fully breached the loading area and now charged into the room, wearing masks. The gas from their canister still hung in the air, obscuring their sight of her, but the domestic gas also filled the area from the pipe she'd ripped from the wall.

One of them saw her and raised his rifle, pulling the trigger. The spark ignited the gas, and a cloud of fire appeared in the center of the room, washing over them. A wall of hot air buffeted the demon. The ignited gas disappeared in a flash, but not without consequences. A few men dove aside in terror, and one man's coat caught on fire.

Many of them, however, kept shooting and ignored the distraction. Nida grabbed an assault rifle from a guard and returned fire, forcing them to duck and find cover. Then she slipped a knife loose and cut the shoulder strap to separate the gun from the guard.

The demon threw the door shut behind her and sprinted down the hall, and bullets tore through the wood behind her and ripped into the walls.

Another shot clipped her leg, but not squarely enough to disable her. Nida rounded the corner and headed into the boiler room, where the furnace was located. Also where the backup generator lived, which should kick on and maintain the electric fence if the external power got cut.

There would be more guards alerted to her presence now, but that was to be expected. Things had actually gone rather well, considering. She ran to the huge gas storage tank and pulled a two-kilogram brick of C4 out of her pocket, as well as a detonator.

Nida put them on the valve, attached the detonator, and set the timer for fifteen seconds.

Then she sprinted further into the building, heading for the stairwell leading up. Shouting came from behind as the guards gave chase. She made it to the second-floor landing, turned back, and waited. A guard rounded the corner, and the demon opened fire into his chest.

A few more guards hesitated, popping around the corner and shooting up at her. Nida ducked back, satisfied that she'd held them up long enough, and given them a reason to be more cautious. She sprinted up the stairs, and a few seconds later, the C4 detonated.

The building shook, and a rush of hot air blasted up the stairwell. The tank wouldn't completely explode, but the detonation would have ripped a hole in the side. At the very least, it had taken out the generator and sparked countless fires that would keep going for hours. The gas would continue to spill out and burn, causing significant damage difficult to contain.

Nida heard no more guards behind her while she ran up the flights of stairs. She hadn't caught them all in the explosion but doubted they would be ready to continue the fight, at least for a few more minutes.

The demon hadn't expected Aram to betray her but had prepared for it. To be honest, she even felt a little impressed that he hadn't just lain down and taken everything she threw at him.

She'd hoped to have Frieda and be on her way out before calling in her soldiers, but it looked like she would need to improvise.

Nida pulled a small device from her pocket and pressed a button. It sent a signal to the two teams of mercenaries hidden in the woods outside the hotel. Their first action would be to cut the power, and with the backup generator already out of commission, they would have no trouble breaching the fence.

With the distraction and chaos happening inside, they would have no trouble launching their small war against the Council.

Their orders were to kill everyone.

With ease, Nida found the room that Aram had mentioned. No guard stood out front, but a chair did show where a guard should have been sitting. It looked like he had abandoned his post.

This was, indeed, where they held Frieda. Aram hadn't even managed to lie to her about it and cost her more time. Alarms blared now, filling the halls with noise and contributing to the chaos.

A few seconds later, the power went out. The hallway went completely dark, and it took a second for her eyes to adjust. They would scramble now to get the generator back online, and if there had been only minimal damage, it might only cost them a couple of minutes, but it would be enough.

Nida opened the door to Frieda's room and stepped inside. Movement registered a second later, and the demon ducked just as Frieda swung a cabinet door at her head. It hit against the wall, snapping in half, and then Frieda came charging out at her with a flurry of attacks.

Nida danced back, creating some distance, and then she burst out laughing. "Wasn't expecting that!"

Frieda didn't respond. Instead, she charged forward, dropping the broken pieces of the cabinet onto the floor and launching another strike at Nida, aiming for her face and chest with her attacks. Frieda wasn't terrible, and with the recent wounds on Nida's body, the demon noticed it becoming more difficult to move but realized that Frieda wouldn't be a match for her.

Frieda had modest training but wasn't a soldier. Nida deflected her first several attacks, and then countered with a series of blows, knocking Frieda back into the wall, kneeing her hard in the stomach, and then elbowing her in the back of the head.

Frieda collapsed to the ground with a groan, trying to pick herself up. She fell again, disoriented.

"Surrender," Nida said, stepping away.

Frieda rolled over and kicked out at Nida's legs. The demon backpedaled, easily avoiding the attack, and Frieda found her feet. She charged back in, swinging with abandon and trying to take the demon down.

Nida stepped back, and her left leg almost gave out because of the bullet wound. She staggered, caught her balance, and then waited for Frieda to approach. This time, when Frieda came in, she hit her hard in the chest with an open palm, and then followed through with a low kick to the back of Frieda's legs, throwing her to the ground once more.

"I don't want to kill you, but I don't need you alive either. All I need is your blood."

Frieda tried to get up again, but Nida stepped on her chest, pinning her down.

"Why?"

The demon smiled, sliding the ornate dagger free and holding it up to the light. "Your blood is special."

Frieda reached up and grabbed Nida's leg and rolled, throwing her off-balance and toward the floor. The demon hit the ground and rolled, finding her balance a few feet away just as Frieda stood.

She rushed back in at Frieda, deflecting a few clumsy attacks and hitting the woman hard in the face, breaking her nose. Frieda staggered back, dazed, and Nida caught her arm. She sliced the wrist, and Frieda jerked back as blood dripped out.

Nida chanted a few quick words, holding the blade up with the blood on it. After a few seconds, the hallway grew hot, as though someone had turned up the temperature by twenty degrees. The blood that had fallen to the floor sizzled and boiled, and then ate through the carpet like acid.

Frieda watched it in horror. "What the hell is that?"

"Your blood has power," Nida said. "I don't need much of it, but a renewable source is always preferable."

Frieda stared at her for a second, and then turned and sprinted down the hallway, heading toward the stairwell. The demon caught her after only a few steps, knocking her to the ground and slamming her head into the floor. Frieda groaned and thrashed, but Nida had no trouble keeping a hold on her.

She tore off a part of Frieda's shirt and tied it around her wrist, staunching the flow of blood.

"There we are, that's better."

"You won't get away," Frieda said, dazed.

"On the contrary," Nida said. "I already have."

She forced Frieda to her feet and pushed her toward the stairwell. Blue security lights flickered to life, and the alarms sounded again, but all too late. The demon's soldiers would have had plenty of time.

As soon as they headed down, gunshots echoed up. The sound brought a smile to Nida's lips. Her small army had breached the fence and had set about cleaning up the defenses outside while the disorganized and scattered guards tried to mount countermeasures.

By the time they made it to the lobby, Nida's forces had complete control of the exterior of the facility. The team totaled twenty soldiers, most of them human, but with a few demons mixed in. One of them came over to her as she pushed Frieda to the exit.

"Is our train ready?"

"Yes, sir," the soldier said. He might have been attractive, once, but his rotted face betrayed that he'd been dug up a few weeks ago. "It will arrive in fifteen minutes and wait for us. We've locked down the station."

"Good. Send the soldiers door-to-door. Kill everyone," Nida said. "No one can be left alive."

"Yes, sir."

"And do it fast. We leave shortly. We have what we came for."

The man nodded, and the soldiers moved into the building. Nida pushed Frieda out into the snow and toward one of the parked cars. Outside lay the bodies of several soldiers, who had gotten gunned down when the attack started. A few of the casualties came from her team but most belonged to the Council.

The demon pushed Frieda into the backseat and turned to survey the havoc she'd wreaked. The hotel had set on fire and smoldered on the far side of the building where she'd blown up the generator. Part of it had collapsed. It would burn slowly for many more hours, and with the storm, it would take a long time before any help could arrive.

By that time, the Council would be gone.

Gunshots sounded from inside the building while her team mopped up the Council members. All of them in one location: she couldn't have asked for a better present from her arrogant father.

A glorious day, indeed.

Chapter 19

Dominick sensed that something had gone wrong even before he made it to the hotel room where Haatim's mother stayed. The lobby stood nearly empty with few guests staying at this time of year. Not down to anything in particular that he saw, but just a feeling he had that something seemed wrong—too quiet—and he'd learned to trust his instincts.

He knocked, but received no response. The door proved locked, and it sounded silent inside the room. Dominick drew his pistol, chambered a round, and then knocked once again. More to justify what he was about to do than anything else.

He stepped back and kicked the door open. It blasted back when the lock splintered, and he walked inside, pistol ready.

The room stood in shambles. Luggage lay scattered everywhere in the suite, and the kitchen had been torn apart. In the center of the room sat Haatim and his mother, tied back-to-back on chairs and gagged.

A large bag of plastic explosives and a timer sat on the floor next to them. Though counting down, it still had ten minutes to go.

Haatim saw him and screamed into the gag, trying to get his attention. Dominick stepped around the bag and removed the gag from Haatim's mouth, and then he set about untying he and his mother.

"She has my father," Haatim said.

"Who?" Dominick asked, trying to undo a persistent knot. It had pulled too tight, so he slipped a knife out instead and sawed at it. "What the hell happened?"

"She's taking him to the Council and planning to use him to break in. We need to get there and stop her."

"Who?" Dominick asked. A sick feeling settled in his stomach. "Abigail?"

Haatim looked at him like he'd gone crazy. He shook his head. "No, not Abigail. It doesn't matter. We need to go now before something terrible happens."

Haatim's mother seemed groggy and barely conscious. After untying her, Dominick carried her over to one of the beds and laid her down. He checked her pulse. Though she would be all right, it looked like she'd been drugged with some heavy stuff.

"We need to get out of here," Haatim said. "The bomb will go off. We need to evacuate the building."

Dominick shrugged. "We have nine minutes left," he said.

"Do you know how to disarm a bomb? What happens if you cut the wrong wire?"

"Why would I cut any wires?" Dominick raised his brows. "This is a bag of plastic explosive with a timed detonator."

"What do you mean?"

"I mean, when the clock reaches zero, it triggers the explosive, but there aren't any failsafe's or backups. No cell phone trigger. Just a normal timer counting down."

"So, how do you stop it?"

Dominick reached into the bag, grabbed the clock, and unplugged the wires connecting it to the bricks of C4.

He glanced at Haatim and smiled wryly. "Voila," he said.

"Fine, but we still need to go."

"What's going on?" Dominick gripped Haatim's knee and held his gaze to secure his attention. "What happened?"

Just then, his phone buzzed. He glanced down at the coded alert. Nausea rolled up his through his chest and into his throat, which both tightened up.

"What?" Haatim asked. "What is it?"

"The Council has been compromised," Dominick said. "It's under attack."

"I told you. We need to go," Haatim said. "We need to get back there and help."

"No kidding. Come on. We'll take the helicopter. Way faster."

"What about my mother?" Haatim asked.

"Leave her," Dominick said. "The drugs will wear off in a couple of hours, and she'll be fine. Probably won't remember a thing."

Haatim nodded and headed for the door. Dominick followed, but then hesitated and glanced back. With a shrug, he went back into the room and grabbed the bag of C4 from the floor.

One thing he'd learned was never to turn down high-powered explosives.

✳✳✳

Abigail, on the road driving back to the Council building to turn herself in, saw a line of cars speeding in the opposite direction toward town. They came on fast, taking up the entire road and forcing her off to the side.

Her tires skidded across the loosely packed snow before finally coming to a rest, and she watched the line of cars go past.

Seven cars in total, heading toward Lausanne. It didn't make any sense to Abigail. Why would such a large group of people be leaving the Council building in anticipation of the storm?

The snow came down already, but only a light dusting at this point. Whoever occupied those vehicles would have a hard time getting back down these roads in a couple of hours, so she doubted it was a member of the Council. Who else would warrant such a convoy of vehicles, though?

Something didn't feel right.

And then she noticed small holes in the last few vehicles in line when they passed by. Bullets. Something had happened. The Council had been attacked.

But by who ...?

... and who'd won?

Abigail turned her car around and headed up the road behind the convoy. They snaked through the mountains. Something had gone tremendously wrong.

Her phone rang, and she slipped it out of her pocket. Dominick calling; she answered.

"What's going on?"

"The Council got attacked," Dominick said. "Someone breached the defenses and did some serious damage."

"What?"

"I don't know any specifics and haven't been able to reach anyone. I've got Haatim, and we're heading to the airport to get Spinner."

"Who did it?"

"I don't know, but they used Aram to get inside. We need to get to the hotel and stop them."

"It's too late for that. Whatever they were after," she said. "I think they got it."

"What do you mean?"

"A convoy of cars just drove past me, headed back into Lausanne."

"How many?"

"A lot. Been in a firefight."

"Can you tail them?"

"Already am," she said.

"All right. We'll get airborne, and I'll call you back on the satellite connection. Don't lose sight of them."

"I won't." Abigail hung up. Then she turned off her lights and followed the line of cars up the mountain.

While she drove, a myriad of questions ran through her mind. Who would have attacked the Council, and why? What were they after? Did it have something to do with her? She doubted it, but at this point, she had no way of knowing.

The biggest question, though, was how they had managed it at all. The council had turned the hotel into a fortress, which meant that it must have been an inside job. Dominick had said that they used Aram to get inside, but she couldn't believe he would betray them. As much as she hated him, she couldn't imagine him as a traitor.

Was Aram still alive?

Once they reached the outskirts of the city, Abigail turned her lights on again. Enough other vehicles used the road to keep her from looking suspicious, and she worried about someone else hitting her.

They drove for another ten minutes, into Lausanne, before she realized their destination: the train station. It sat just outside the city center, and the tracks had been designed to withstand even the most extreme of winter weather.

It made sense; many of the main roads outside the city had closed already in anticipation of the oncoming storm. The train provided one of the few reliable ways into and out of the city at this point.

Another call came in to her phone. Dominick's number from inside his chopper. This time, Haatim spoke when she answered, and she could hear the distinct sound of the helicopter starting up in the background.

"Abi?"

"I'm here," she said. "They're heading for the train station."

"Why?"

"They want to get out of the city," she said. "There's a train waiting. We can't let them get away."

"We won't," Haatim said. He relayed to Dominick that they were going to the trains, and then he came back to her. "Dominick said to wait somewhere outside the station, and we'll pick you up."

Abigail pulled into the parking lot behind the convoy, which parked near the loading ramp. People piled out of the cars and headed up to the platform. She counted fifteen armed soldiers in total.

In the center of the group, soldiers half-dragged and half-carried a figure to the train.

Even beaten and battered, Abigail could recognize her anywhere.

"Frieda," she breathed.

"What?" Haatim asked.

"They have Frieda," Abigail said. "She was their target."

"Ten minutes out," Haatim said. "Dominick said we'll be there in ten minutes. Wait for us."

"No," she said. "There isn't time."

Abigail ended the call and stepped out of her car. The parking lot stood nearly empty and had the lights off. Highly doubtful that this train was scheduled.

As cautiously as possible, she moved forward, making sure to stay out of sight of the group while she made her way up to the loading platform.

Twelve railcars lay in a line, and they all looked like passenger cars. The engine released billowing clouds of smoke into the air at the front, and it looked almost ready to leave. Several additional armed guards stood on the platform, looking around and patrolling the area.

The group she had tailed went to the third railcar from the back and climbed inside, pushing Frieda on in front of them. Abigail got a clear sight of one of them, and then saw that she carried an ornate dagger in her hand.

The dagger. It had to be the one from Raven's Peak that Belphegor had gone after. Whoever she was, she must have been the one who'd found it in the tunnels and nearly killed her and Haatim.

Abigail needed to get on that train. The guards seemed heaviest at the rear, and so she slipped around the building and to the front of the train. The doors all sat open right now. She waited until one of the guards looked in another direction, and then quick-stepped across the platform and slipped inside. The falling snow dampened the sound as she entered the passenger car.

In the first-class railcar, she looked around for somewhere to hide. It held a fully stocked bar, and she climbed behind it and rested down in the small alcove where a bartender would stand. The lights were on, but it stood empty and silent.

A few minutes slipped past, and then she heard movement. One of the guards came onto her first-class car, and the doors slid closed. A few seconds later, the train moved underneath her. It started out slow, and then gradually picked up speed as it headed away from the station and Lausanne.

The guard paced back and forth in the railcar, carrying his rifle and not paying attention to anything. Clearly, he didn't think anything would happen on this trip, much less that an enemy combatant occupied the same railcar as he.

Abigail waited until he walked past her, heading toward the front, and then climbed atop the bar quietly. Her foot scuffed on the faux-wood, and he started to turn toward her, but she leaped out at him before he could react. She kicked him in the face and knocked him to the ground.

He hit hard but tried to find his feet immediately. Abigail rushed forward, kneeing him hard in the jaw and grabbing the gun so that he couldn't get a good hold on it.

He managed to land a solid punch to her stomach, knocking her wind out, but she retaliated by kicking him hard in the testicles. He winced and let out a groan, and then she punched him in the throat.

Abigail followed that by slamming his head into one of the seat backs of an aisle chair, and he fell to the ground, unconscious. Then she picked up his rifle, hoping she wouldn't need it, and headed toward the rear of the railcar.

The door leading out, while latched, wasn't locked. She slid it open. The wind whistled in around her. The sound of the train intensified.

A small metal platform connected the two railcars. Hitched at the center, it had a pathway no more than half a meter wide. Each car extended a pair of railings, about waist high, that met in the center, making it a little easier to cross from one car to another.

The train hadn't reached full speed yet, so she had no trouble in stepping across to the next passenger car. The air felt bracingly cold as she went, whipping over her skin and raising gooseflesh on her arms. A latch held the outside of this car as well, and it also proved unlocked.

Seats packed the otherwise empty railcar, two on each side of a central aisle. Abigail headed down the row. The lights flickered overhead occasionally as the third rail disconnected. It felt eerie moving through the quiet railcar with snow falling outside. It had a detached feeling to it.

Without incident, she made it to the far side and looked through the window at the next car in line. This one seemed empty too, and so she made the trek across the snowy divide. Bitterly cold, she wished she'd brought a heavier coat. To be honest, she hadn't expected to spend any time outdoors.

When she moved into this next car, the opposite door opened a crack. Someone was coming in the opposite way; probably guards doing a sweep to make sure no one like her had come aboard.

Quickly, Abigail slid the door closed behind her and ducked down into the seats. She glanced through an opening in the chair backs and watched two bundled up men enter the railcar and move forward through the aisles. They carried assault rifles and walked toward the front at a brisk pace.

Abigail ducked low, knowing she wouldn't have anywhere good to hide when they made it up to her seat. She still had the assault rifle but didn't want to use it. The gunshots would alert everyone in the nearby vicinity to her presence, and that would change things from dangerous to hopeless in but an instant.

Crouched as low as she could, Abigail slid partway under the seat and scrunched into a ball. The footsteps approached, and she grabbed the hilt of her revolver. The rifle wouldn't do any good in such close quarters and would serve more as a liability than an aid.

She weighed her options: either she had to jump up now and use her momentary surprise to take out the two guards, or she would have to hope for the best—that they might walk by without noticing her.

If she stayed tucked into her little cubby, and they spotted her, it would take several seconds to extricate herself. Too long, and most likely, they would execute her before she could mount a defense.

Still, taking them out now meant alerting the entire train to her presence and giving up her surprise. Having all fifteen guards descend on her at once would be a worst-case scenario.

Better to stay low and pray for the best.

Luck stayed with her. The lights flickered just as the two men reached her section of the train. They went off for a few seconds, and by the time they came back on, the men had passed. The door she'd entered from slid open to allow the men to pass to the railcar she'd just vacated, and then it closed, leaving her alone once more.

It would only take a few minutes for them to find their downed compatriot. Abigail regretted not dragging him behind the bar, but she couldn't worry about that now. She climbed out of her hiding place and rushed down the aisle and toward the door leading further along the train.

The snow had picked up outside, and she could barely see through the windows anymore. When she opened the door, she saw that the train headed into the mountains, weaving up and down switchback trails and across rocky terrain. No sign of the city remained behind them, or any other sign of life.

Hopefully, Dominick would manage to navigate through the storm, but it seemed doubtful. Though not snowing too heavily yet, the storm had picked up and would make flight dangerous.

Still, if any pilot could handle weather like this and make it through to the other side, Dominick could.

As a little girl, she'd always loved riding trains. Abigail had even—though she would never admit it—wanted a toy train set of her own to snake around her room.

Arthur had taken her across the US from east coast to west, and once, they'd even managed to ride the trains in Siberia, though only for a short leg of the journey while he went on a mission.

Abigail kept moving further back down the train until she stood in the car ahead of the one where they held Frieda. She crouched low and moved slowly, carrying the rifle and trying to decide her best course of action for freeing Frieda.

Though she had a healthy respect for assault rifles, she'd never gotten accustomed to using them. Arthur considered them a crutch because they were too difficult to obtain in most countries.

He had forced her, instead, to train endlessly with holdout pistols and small arms and only shown her rudimentarily how to shoot anything heavier. She'd fired them enough, though, to know she could hit her target.

At sixteen, she got her first gun. Arthur had asked what kind she would prefer, and she'd told him she wanted a revolver just like his. At the time, it proved almost too big for her to carry, and the kick enough to put her on her butt. Now, though, the weight felt comfortable, and she loved the reliability.

Abigail moved to the window and glanced into the next car. Another first-class railcar with a bar and only a handful of seats. In the center of the car, in a ring, stood a group of six. She couldn't see Frieda, but she did see the young woman standing at the center of the group with the curved dagger in hand.

One guard stood ready with a rifle, and the rest held hands, chanting. The girl stood near them, watching carefully and supervising the group.

The sight brought a flash of images to Abigail's mind. She remembered being younger and strapped to a table. A group of cloaked people stood in a circle around her, chanting and performing some terrible ritual.

She didn't remember what they were saying or even how old she had been when this happened. These memories, she'd buried and tried to forget about, and so they remained hazy and unfocused. She pushed them away, shaking her head and focusing on the situation at hand.

Abigail didn't have a lot of time. Whatever they were trying to do, it involved Frieda, and she needed to get her out of there.

Carefully, she slid the door open just enough to slip through, and then closed it behind her. Stood on the walkway between cars, she checked the clip on the assault rifle and prepared herself.

No going back now.

With a steadying breath, Abigail threw open the door to the first-class car, picked a few targets, and opened fire.

Her first shot hit the guard carrying the rifle in the shoulder, staggering him. He dropped his gun and fell back against the seats, crying out in pain. She held down the trigger and swept across, emptying the clip into the crowd of cultists.

The nose of her gun pulled up, and she ended up losing half of the shots over their heads, but it served its purpose. They ducked into seats and scrambled in confusion and terror, and she knew she'd hit about half of them with at least grazing shots.

The clip emptied a lot sooner than she'd expected, however, and she drew her revolver.

Abigail took aim at the woman with the dagger and pulled the trigger. The woman reacted too fast and managed to duck behind the seats and out of sight.

Abigail continued firing anyway, not sure if she hit her or not. Her bullets would rip right through the soft red cloth of the seats, so she sent bullets in a spread pattern to cover as much area as possible. Abigail aimed for every spot where she thought the woman would hide.

Once she'd emptied her gun, she spun open the cylinder, spilling shells onto the tracks beneath her. Then she reached into her pocket to scoop out another load of shells. Just then, three cultists leaned out of their hiding places to fire back at her. The rest had dropped under her barrage of fire, and two of these three men looked wounded but still able to fire at her.

They forced Abigail to dodge back out of the way of the door. She slid under the side rail and put the metal wall of the railcar between her and the attackers.

Bullets thudded into the metal walls, and occasionally, one ripped through and hit the next car in line behind her. Glass shattered when they blew out the windows around and above her.

A metal ladder, built into the railcar next to her, gave her something to hold to keep her balance while she hung over the tracks. She used her free hand to finish reloading her revolver, snapping the cylinder back in place.

Abigail grabbed hold of the railing and pulled back onto the walkway, waiting for the barrage of suppressing fire to end. As soon as a break came, she leaned in and took aim at one of the targets.

Her first shot hit a cultist in the stomach, who had rushed toward her position. He fell back in surprise, collapsing into one of the seats with a scream of agony. The other two men still stood busy reloading and managed to duck out of sight, but she fired at their hiding places anyway. She felt certain she'd hit at least one of them.

As soon as Abigail had fired her last round, the woman reappeared from her hiding place behind the seats. She bounded overtop and dove into a roll. She landed nimbly in the center aisle and rushed forward.

Abigail tried to reload her spent shells, but wouldn't have time before the woman fell upon her. Instead, she slid her gun away and pulled out the blade strapped to her lower back. She stepped up into the railcar and stabbed out just as the woman came in.

Up close, the woman looked younger than Abigail had anticipated, maybe early twenties. Dark skinned, she may be of Middle-Eastern descent. Difficult to tell with the flickering lights in the middle of a gunfight.

The woman dodged Abigail's first attack, and then kicked out at her, forcing her to duck back out of the train. She backpedaled nimbly onto the narrow walkway and slashed back and forth with her knife, forcing the woman to maintain separation between them.

One of her cuts drew blood on the girl's stomach, but she didn't seem to notice. She stepped right through the attack and punched Abigail in the side with a fist. Then she followed that with a kick to Abigail's knee, and then another to her chest, knocking her roughly into the door of the railcar behind.

Then the woman spun and slid the door closed, trapping them both out on the narrow walkway. Abigail caught her balance and darted forward, avoiding another kick and stabbing with the blade again.

The woman countered, slipping under her attack and catching Abigail's wrist in an iron grip. She yanked Abigail forward and knocked the blade out of her hand. It bounced against the side of the train and disappeared into the snow.

Abigail kicked out, hitting her opponent in the knee, and then punched her twice in the face. The woman seemed to barely notice, maintaining her lock on Abigail's wrist and keeping her close.

Abigail tried to counter, ducking back and pulling the girl toward her, but her plan backfired. The woman yanked Abigail toward her instead, off-balance, and then threw her over the railing and toward the side of the train.

She went flying into the air and scrabbled at the side for something to grab onto. Just in time, she caught the ladder built into the side of the train and clung to it, clutching the cold and slippery metal.

Slowly, Abigail pulled herself back onto the ladder and climbed the freezing bars, refusing to give up the high ground.

The girl leaped out at her, catching onto the ladder beneath and grabbing hold of her foot. Abigail kicked down, hitting the woman in the jaw, and kept climbing.

When she reached the roof of the railcar, she slid onto it, finding her footing a few meters farther away on the roof of the train. It jostled underneath her, and it felt like standing on a sheet of ice in an earthquake.

The girl followed her, stepping lightly onto the roof and rushing forward at Abigail. She launched a flurry of attacks, sliding across the icy surface, yet somehow maintaining her balance.

Abigail dodged and punched, receiving a kick to her right leg but landing a few solid hits herself. They moved back along the train, and Abigail found it difficult to maintain her balance.

She'd reached the back end of her railcar, and the one behind lay about two meters away. The closer she got, the harder it would be to make the jump. Abigail waited until they stood only a few steps away, and then turned and sprinted.

She leaped into the air, clearing the distance and landing roughly on the next roof, where she fell to one knee and slid about another four meters before finding her feet.

The woman pursued her, leaping the distance and landing in a rush. She tried to barrel into Abigail, who dodged her and let her slip past.

The girl came to a stop several meters farther, turned, and then came sprinting back in, launching another series of attacks. Abigail countered, hitting her several times in the kidney with what should have been debilitating blows, but her opponent didn't even seem to notice.

Abigail connected twice as often as her opponent, but none of her attacks had any effect. They both slipped across the roof, and this was a battle of attrition, Abigail held the disadvantage. Quickly, she needed to find an opening and take out her opponent.

A long and tall bridge drew nearer. It disappeared into the snow in front of the train, and when they passed onto it, Abigail couldn't see the bottom of the canyon beneath them. It had to be several hundred meters high at least.

With the snow whipping around them and freezing her skin, it gave her an intense feeling of vertigo.

Abigail kept attacking, trying to find some weakness in her opponent. The snow had let up once more, but the roof had grown slippery and difficult to maneuver on as they fought.

In the distance behind the train, a speck of light approached, but she couldn't identify it from this distance. Hopefully, Dominick and his helicopter, but impossible to tell.

Desperate and wanting to end things, Abigail drew her second blade, the one she kept tucked in her boot, and stabbed forward. She pierced the girl in the shoulder and drew a deep cut, but received a nasty blow in return.

Abigail fell back, landing on the roof and sliding toward the edge. She scrambled, catching her balance, but her opponent refused to let up.

The demon—the woman had to be a demon—kicked her in the side of the head, dazing her and knocking her farther down the train. Abigail stumbled back, reeling, and fended off a quick series of punches and kicks while she backed up and tried to put distance between them.

186

Abigail tried to regain her composure but realized too late that the attacks were feints, as the woman repositioned to her side. She'd set Abigail's back to the edge of the train, and they remained overtop the bridge.

Only emptiness lay behind her.

The demon came forward in a rush. Abigail tried to move and reposition herself back to the center of the roof, understanding what her opponent intended to do, but moved too late. She dodged a punch, but the following kick caught her full in the chest.

Her feet left the train.

Her body flew backward into open air. Abigail watched in slow motion while the train ran away from her. The demon girl, still on the train, watched as Abigail flew backward.

✳✳✳

"What was that?" Haatim asked, squinting forward through the snow. They flew just behind the train and had caught up quickly. Something, however, had just gone flying off the top of one of the railcars, maybe twenty meters in front of them.

"Hold on," Dominick shouted.

Haatim glanced over at him, trying to figure out what he meant, and then the seat dropped under his butt. Luckily, he'd strapped in, so it dragged him down with it, but he had an intense moment of vertigo during those first few seconds.

Dominick aimed the helicopter down at a sheer angle, pitching them toward the ground of the canyon. Then he rolled the helicopter sideways so that the blades wouldn't have any air underneath them, and the helicopter plummeted.

Alarms blared, warning them of the ill-advised maneuver. Haatim couldn't help but agree. He hadn't been in many helicopters during his life but felt fairly certain that they weren't designed to do this.

"Throw out the ladder!" Dominick shouted.

"What?"

"The ladder! Get it to her!"

Haatim, all at once, understood, and his heart skipped a beat. "That was Abigail?"

Dominick didn't reply but turned his attention back to the dashboard in front of him. Rapidly, he threw switches, tilting the helicopter further and powering off the engine.

Haatim froze in fear when the helicopter fell. He stared out of the window, unable to move, and with only the realization that he was about to die flying through his mind.

"Move!" Dominick screamed at him.

Haatim came back to reality, blinking, and unbuckled himself. He climbed into the back while the helicopter jostled in the wind, and then grabbed the rope ladder and pulled it free from its restraints.

The rotors stalled out above them just as he opened the side door of the helicopter. His body moved mechanically while terror gripped him. The helicopter went into free-fall, nothing more than a huge brick heading for the ground. Haatim clutched the sidebar, and the frigid wind whipped into the area around him.

Dominick punched controls while alarms whistled and whooped.

"Throw it now," Dominick yelled, flipping a switch repeatedly. "Throw the ladder."

Haatim pushed the ladder out of the helicopter, but no way could Abigail reach it. He could see her falling just below them, maybe ten meters and off to the side. No way that the rope ladder would be long enough to get to her.

The engine restarted, and the blades spun to life once more. In only a few seconds, it would—hopefully—pull them back up, but Abigail would continue to fall, out of their reach.

With a steadying breath that sounded a lot like a gasp, Haatim pushed the ladder back into the helicopter behind him and grabbed the safety line sticking out of the side of the craft. Body shaking, he wrapped the cord around his wrist a few times, clutched the rope as tightly as he could, and dove out of the helicopter.

The spinning rotor blades stopped the descent of the behemoth machine. The line pulled out. Haatim had about twenty meters of slack before it caught him up.

He angled his body and aimed for Abigail. She tried to slow her descent as well, moving toward him to close the gap. He tried not to think about what he was doing, or how they might both fall and die, or how he might not have enough slack, and she would fall and die anyway.

Instead, Haatim focused on reaching her. He extended his free arm, reaching out to grab Abigail, and their fingers touched. He only needed a little more slack ...

They came together just as the line ran out and tightened. Abigail caught his wrist and pulled the two of them together. Haatim hugged her to his chest, and she wrapped her arms around his body, clutching him, and her warm breath gasped against his neck.

They swung on the taut line. Haatim clutched the rope and Abigail as firmly as he could. After a few seconds, the line retracted while Dominick manipulated the controls from the front, drawing them back up to the chopper.

Abigail climbed inside first, then helped pull Haatim in, and closed the door behind them. The alarms had stopped. The cab seemed silent now, with the helicopter simply hovering.

Haatim untangled himself from the rope and tried to get his teeth to stop chattering. He had severe burns on his wrist from the rope and couldn't stop his body from shaking.

"Thank you," Abigail said, staring at him and still holding his hand. Her eyes had turned red, the same as in the holding cell before she'd escaped.

He must have reacted in surprise because he saw a hurt expression settle on her face.

"Your eyes ..." he said.

She didn't respond, except to look away.

"Come back up here," Dominick hollered, flipping more switches and getting them in motion once again.

Haatim looked one last time at Abigail, and then climbed up next to Dominick, who said, "Nice catch."

"What now?" Haatim asked.

Abigail leaned into the cockpit. "Get me back on that train."

"I radioed in for backup," Dominick said. "Response teams are less than ten minutes out and—"

"Get me back up there," Abigail said. "Before they kill Frieda."

Dominick didn't reply, but instead, flew after the train. Haatim buckled himself into the copilot's seat, still shaking head-to-toe but starting to relax. Each second that passed made his wrist throb more, but he barely felt it.

He heard noise in the back of the helicopter and shifted in his seat. Abigail rifled through bags and scattered tools. First, she grabbed a long and slightly curved sword, which she slung over her shoulder, and then she picked up the bag of C4 that Dominick had taken from his mother's apartment.

"What do you need that for?" Haatim asked.

When she looked at him, her eyes glowed faintly. Her expression looked like a mask of calm, but it was her red eyes that sent a shiver down his spine.

"To end this," she said.

Haatim gulped and nodded.

"We have a problem," Dominick said.

They both looked forward. A mountain loomed in front of them. Huge, it grew larger by the second while they approached. The helicopter, though going as fast as it could and gaining on the train, still left them a ways behind.

The train headed for a tunnel in the side of the mountain, not that far away. In only a few seconds, it would disappear completely.

"How long is the tunnel?" Haatim asked.

"A few kilometers, at least," Dominick said. "Maybe eight minutes for the train."

"Too long," Abigail said. "Get me on there."

"I can't fit in that tunnel," Dominick said. "And even if I could—"

"Fly faster," she said.

Dominick exchanged a worried glance with Haatim, and he could sympathize: right now didn't seem like a good time to argue with her.

Dominick groaned but did pick up speed.

"Never thought I would be playing chicken with a mountain," he muttered.

Abigail moved to the side door and slid it open once more. She climbed out onto the railing on the side of the helicopter, and then crawled to the back, getting into position as if about to pounce.

"Can we make it?" Haatim asked.

"I don't know."

"What happens if we don't?"

Dominick sat in silence for a few seconds. "Let's not find out."

The train remained ahead of them as they zoomed toward it, and Haatim reckoned it would be close. They flew so fast that he couldn't even feel sure that they would be able to stop now if they wanted to.

The mountain grew, and a jagged cliff wall filled the entire windshield. Dominick made gasping noises, and Haatim tried to look away, terrified and helpless. He couldn't get his eyes to follow his mental commands, however, and just watched the cliff face approach.

"We're not going to make it!" Haatim screamed.

He couldn't even see the train anymore, or anything except the mountain in front of them. If the caboose hadn't entered the mountain tunnel, it was about to.

190

"Hold on …"

"Stop!" Haatim shouted. "Stop now! We can't make it."

The mountain loomed only a handful of meters away, and still they flew full speed at it.

"Now!" Dominick roared at Abigail.

He spun the helicopter back in the other direction just as Abigail leaped from the side railing and for the train below. The momentum propelled her forward, and she disappeared from their sight into the dark tunnel.

The helicopter continued gliding toward the mountain, fighting against momentum. The blades chipped against the side of the cliff face, and pieces of metal flew loose and crashed into the sides and windshield. A huge crack appeared in front of him, but whatever had hit the glass didn't make it through.

Somehow, amazingly, they came to a stop. When he looked through his window, it felt like he could reach out and touch the cliff face if he wanted.

Haatim let out a breath he hadn't realized he'd held and tried to calm his frantic heart.

"Did she make it?" he asked.

"I don't know," Dominick said.

"What now?"

"Now," he said. "We fly around."

✳✳✳

Abigail caught the back rail of the caboose with only one hand, swinging down hard against the metal and hanging off the back of the train. Pain made her grunt, but she managed to keep a hold on it and pull herself up and onto the walkway.

Her entire body hurt, and she felt exhausted, but also angrier than she ever had. Frustrated with everything that had happened, starting with the trial and culminating with this, left her boiling. Arthur had always taught her never to give in to her anger, but she'd gone past that point now. Enraged, she embraced it wholeheartedly.

Abigail had done with fighting back against her nature. Done trying to be what Arthur had wanted her to be.

Now, she would be what she wanted: what she was always meant to be. She returned to the little girl Arthur had stolen from The Ninth Circle. The girl who had wanted to hurt things.

Abigail strapped Arthur's sword around her waist and dropped the bag of C4 onto the walkway. Quietly, she moved forward to the doorway leading into the caboose.

In the pitch-black tunnel, the only light came from the train. Inside the caboose, a pair of guards milled around. Both of them carried rifles and looked rather bored.

They wouldn't stay bored for long.

Abigail drew and reloaded her revolver, and then opened the door to the car. The guards looked up in surprise, but too late. She raised her pistol and fired off two rounds. Both guards collapsed, one with a bullet in his head and the other in the neck.

Abigail didn't hesitate but sprinted forward through the railcar. The doors stood open between this car and the next, and she leaped clear through the opening and into the adjacent railcar.

Two guards occupied this passenger car as well. They'd heard the gunshots and had come to investigate, but pulled up short when she approached.

Abigail raised her pistol and fired two more shots, dropping the closest man, who had prepared to fire. Then she slipped Arthur's sword free and charged the other man.

He got his gun up, but she swatted the barrel aside with her sword and impaled him in the stomach. Further down, another man stood on the walkway between this railcar and the next.

Abigail fired her last two shots at him, hitting him in the arm and chest. He fell to the side, over the railing, and disappeared into the dark tunnel behind the train.

Then she jerked her sword free, letting the dying man fall to the ground, limp. With no more shells for her revolver, she tucked it away and picked up a rifle from a downed guard. Then she ran toward the far door, which led into the next railcar, the one where they had Frieda.

Through the window, she saw that the remainder of the guards had gathered. Maybe eight of them, but they had taken up positions behind furniture and out of sight, so she found it impossible to tell. They didn't come toward her, and had, apparently, decided to hole up and make her come to them.

Fine with her.

The girl hid with the guards, on the far side of the first-class car. She had picked up Frieda and used her as a body shield. Frieda looked only barely conscious, being mostly supported by the girl.

"You're too late," the demon shouted. "The ritual is complete. I have what I came for."

Then she threw Frieda forward onto the ground and turned to the guards.

"Kill them both," she said, heading out toward the front of the train.

Abigail dropped to a knee and took aim, but not at any of the guards. She aimed, instead, at the lights over their heads.

She fired. Glass exploded, casting their railcar into darkness. Startled, they fired at her, forcing her to duck out of the way. She dodged behind the seats, out of their line of sight, and then shot out the lights in her car as well, casting it into darkness too.

Abigail ducked down and shifted her position to further back in the train. She waited until the shots had died down, watching for muzzle flashes. Once they stopped firing, she lined up a shot and pulled the trigger.

As soon as she fired, she dove to the other side of the train. They set off another barrage of shots at her. Bullets thudded into the area she'd just vacated. Windows exploded. A cacophony accompanied the railcar getting torn apart all around her.

Even when the firing died down again, she waited.

"Do you see her?" one of the guards shouted.

"I think she's down."

"Check it out."

"*You* check it out."

Movement came from up ahead when one of the men climbed across the walkway to come check on her. Abigail waited until he reached the walkway, and then rushed forward. She stayed low, using his body to block line of sight between her and his friends.

When he noticed her, he raised his gun and let out a shout, but too late. She kicked the gun away, grabbed him, and then threw him sideways into the wall of the tunnel. He disappeared with a thud and scream, fading into the darkness behind them.

Abigail didn't hesitate, just dove into the darkened train car and drew the sword once more. Though pitch black inside, somehow she knew the exact location of the guards.

On instinct alone, she stepped in and stabbed to the side with her blade. It sliced into flesh, and a man let out a scream of surprise and pain.

Several gunshots fired into the area, but Abigail had already moved on. Each muzzle flare came like a flash of lightning. The train car became a series of random images, highlighting everything for a split second and then gone once more.

Abigail ignored it all, focusing inward instead. She kept moving, diving and weaving over and around the seats to close the distance between each guard. She ran across the tops of the seats, stabbing one man, and then bounding off to land on another, driving her blade into his chest and riding him to the ground.

Abigail hit the floor in a roll, coming up slashing to cut the arm off another opponent, and then the head off yet another. She never stopped, taking erratic turns so that they couldn't anticipate a pattern in her movements.

With the sword an extension of herself, Abigail cut and stabbed and dropped each of them while she moved through the railcar.

All of a sudden, the train filled with light when they exited the tunnel. Though cloudy outside, and the sun setting, she'd spent so much time in the darkness that it felt blindingly bright.

One man remained standing, but looked the other direction, evidently thinking her still behind him and toward the rear of the train.

He turned, searching for her, and raised his rifle when he spotted her. He stood a good eight meters away; too much distance to close. Abigail rotated and threw the blade end over end, embedding it deep into his chest. It sunk in almost to the hilt.

He collapsed onto his side with a grunt. The train fell completely silent, the only sound the chug of its wheels rolling over the tracks.

Abigail looked around. Realized what she'd just done. Body parts lay strewn all around her. Now, she stood near Frieda.

She'd killed all those men over the span of a few seconds. Blood covered her hands and clothes, and she grew lightheaded. She'd always thought she hated killing people because Arthur had raised her to think such.

Never should taking life be done lightly, and yet, she'd just murdered fifteen people. And the only thing that concerned her was how little she cared.

Evil lived in her. Pure and complete. She'd become the very thing that Arthur had taught her to hunt for so many years.

And the scariest thing was that a part of her felt thrilled that she'd accepted her place in life at last.

The demon-girl she'd chased had gone. Must have gotten away during the firefight. Frieda lay on the floor, eyes open but unfocused. She breathed shallow breaths and looked to be severely hurt.

Abigail rushed over to her. A cut stood out on her right wrist, and a lot of blood had drained out. She seemed barely conscious.

Quickly, Abigail wrapped up her wrist, staunching the flow of blood, and then tapped her on the cheek to wake her. It took a few tries before Frieda's eyes opened. She let out a groan, tried to roll over, and her eyes had difficulty focusing.

"Stay with me," Abigail said. "Hey! Focus, Frieda."

She groaned and shook her head, blinking. "What the hell happened?"

"A lot," Abigail said. "What do you remember?"

"She took my blood."

"Who?"

Frieda hesitated. "Haatim's sister."

Abigail looked at her in confusion. "She's dead, right? She died months ago."

The look on Frieda's face said that she didn't have an answer to that question.

"She was ... trying to summon something, I think. I only heard bits and pieces of what they chanted."

"Summon?"

Frieda nodded. "She wanted to bring something into this world."

"And she needed your blood?"

Frieda looked at her helplessly. "I have no idea. Apparently. They drained a lot, and then started chanting, and at some point, I passed out."

"I need to get you out of here," Abigail said. Then she retrieved her phone with the intention of calling Dominick, who'd called multiple times from the looks of the missed calls list. She punched in the number to call him back.

He answered on the first ring, "Abigail, you okay? We're three minutes out."

"I'm fine," she said. "I've got Frieda."

"Where is she?"

"Third car from the back. This isn't over. I'll detach the back cars, and you can grab Frieda."

"What? What about you?"

"Don't worry about me. Get Frieda to safety."

Abigail hung up the call before Dominick could respond. She found her bag of C4 back in the caboose and carried it to the next walkway. The bag held several pounds of plastic explosive, along with a number of timed detonators.

It wouldn't take much to detach the three cars. Abigail placed a small chunk of it around the hitch, which connected the two railcars together, and then attached a timer. She set it for thirty seconds.

When she looked back into the car, she saw Frieda sitting in one of the chairs and holding her wrist. She looked exhausted and beaten up, but Abigail felt sure she would be all right.

"Once you're loose, Dominick will come get you and take you to safety," Abigail said. "Stay here and keep pressure on the wound."

"What are you going to do?"

Abigail grimaced and slung the bag with the rest of the C4—at least ten more pounds—over her shoulder.

"Stop this train."

"Be careful," Frieda said.

"We're a long way past careful," Abigail said.

Then she turned and headed into the next railcar, intending to go after Nida.

Chapter 20

Abigail ran through the train, leaping across the walkways and heading toward the engine. Nida must be somewhere up ahead, but she couldn't see her yet. The demon proved easy to follow, however, because she'd left all of the doors open along the way.

The snow came down in a heavy blanket now, dropping visibility to almost nothing. No lights shone outside the train, as it passed through the mountains alone, making it all feel detached.

Abigail ran through two cars before she heard the detonation behind her. When she looked back, open space grew between the detached cars while they receded into the distance. Frieda would stay safe now, and Dominick would have no trouble picking her up and getting her warm.

No going back now. Determined, Abigail hurried forward through the empty train, down the center aisle, hearing only the motion of the train around her. After another few minutes, she caught her first glimpse of Nida.

The girl moved up ahead, limping and leaning heavily against the seats as she went. Badly injured, by the looks, and having trouble keeping her body in motion.

Abigail caught up with her on the third railcar back from the engine. She jumped through the open doors and into the car, just five meters behind Nida.

The demon turned to face her, a furious expression on her face. "Why won't you just die?"

"It's over," Abigail said, edging toward the demon. "Surrender."

Nida laughed, leaning heavily against one of the seats, knife in hand and looking like she had trouble staying on her feet.

"You think you've won, but this is only the beginning."

"This is the end," Abigail said. "At least, for you."

She drew her revolver and fired.

Nida sprang to the side, diving out of the way of the shot. The train lights flickered, and Abigail fired again, trying to trace her movement, but Nida disappeared behind the seats.

Abigail kept shooting after the demon, and then drew her sword. She rushed forward just as Nida leaped out over the seats, stabbing with the dagger.

Abigail blocked the first attack, and then sliced back, narrowly missing Nida's shoulder. She followed through with a kick, knocking the girl back several steps and sending her off-balance. The demon staggered on her wounded leg, and Abigail rushed in after her, slicing back and forth.

Nida rolled, avoiding the series of attacks and keeping her distance. The seats made it hard to get a good angle with her big blade, but Abigail pursued and refused to let her opponent catch her feet and retaliate.

Finally, she managed to connect, slicing Nida's thigh with the blade and hobbling her. She followed that by cutting deeply into her arm, severing tender muscles there. Nida managed to twist her body and avoid the brunt of the attacks, but Abigail could tell that the demon had a hard time keeping the body moving. It had begun to give out and wouldn't last much longer.

"Last chance," Abigail said.

Nida leaped out at Abigail, stabbing with the blade, and Abigail knocked the dagger out of her hand. It bounced under one of the seats, out of sight. The demon dove past her, back toward the doorway leading further back down the train.

She pulled something out of her pocket and flashed Abigail a grin. Her mouth had filled with blood, and one of her eyes had swollen shut.

"I'd hoped I wouldn't have to waste this," she said. "I don't have a lot to spare."

A vial of red something. Then Abigail realized that it contained Frieda's blood. Nida dumped it onto the ground between them.

As soon as it hit the floor, it steamed and hissed. Abigail hesitated, not sure what was happening, and watching it warily. She'd never heard about anything like this before.

Nida chanted, performing some sort of ritual. The words sounded guttural, no language Abigail had ever heard spoken. She didn't know enough to recognize the intention of the ritual.

However, she did realize, quickly, that it was something terrible.

The material around the blood burst into flames, spreading rapidly through the car as though oil coated everything. Abigail stepped back, watching the flames rise to encompass the entire area, blocking her off from Nida.

"A little present," Nida called, stumbling away and toward the exit leading to the rear of the train. "Have fun!"

And then she disappeared out of the passenger car and into the snow. Abigail cursed in frustration, trying to find some way around the fire to get to the demon.

Something crawled in the fire.

At first, Abigail couldn't identify it, but then she made out its humanoid shape. It crawled toward her, growing in size and climbing to its feet. It looked like the burning seats and flooring of the train had formed into a humanoid creature, maybe three meters tall.

"Uh oh ..." Abigail took a cautious step back.

It turned toward her and charged, still aflame.

Abigail turned and ran.

✳✳✳

"Get her in here," Dominick called from the pilot's seat. "Hurry."

Haatim ignored him and pushed the ladder out of the helicopter. It fell down and stopped a few feet above the walkway connecting the two railcars.

The snow fell thick now, making everything slick, so he wasn't about to rush and slip off and break his neck.

Of course, he realized that was a funny sentiment considering what had just happened not even ten minutes earlier. He could still hardly believe he'd jumped out of a helicopter, and if he'd had even a few seconds to think about it, he never would have gone through with it.

Haatim descended the ladder to the walkway between two of the stopped railcars. Three of them rested on the tracks, blanketed in snow. His hands and body chilled at speed, but to be honest, it didn't feel that bad. After his time spent with Dominick, a bit of cold weather didn't bother him like it used to.

Dominick had the helicopter hovering, keeping it steady even as the wind picked up. The storm rumbled nearby, and they'd nearly run out of time.

As soon as his boots touched the slick metal, Haatim slipped and almost fell over the side railing. Below, the rough ground waited for him. The raised tracks sat about a meter above the ground. A lot of snow had packed, but a tumble would still hurt. He held onto the rope ladder, pulling himself up, and then worked his way into the railcar.

It had no lights, and it took a minute for Haatim's eyes to adjust. The entire place looked demolished. Seats torn up, bullet holes everywhere, and half the glass missing. The wind blew snow in through the openings, and it swirled in the air in small tornados before settling to the ground.

"Holy hell," he muttered, eyeing the devastation.

Hopefully, Abigail hadn't gotten wounded during this firefight, but Haatim couldn't think of a single way in which she might have gotten out of this unscathed. Bodies of at least six dead men lay strewn about, maybe more.

Then something moved near the front of the carriage. Haatim stumbled back with a cry, trying to jerk his pistol loose.

"Who's there?" he shouted, raising the weapon. He attempted to sight down the barrel, but his hands shook too much.

"It's me, Haatim." Frieda walked toward him, clutching her arm to her chest, wrapped in a cloth bandage. She looked weak and barely able to stay on her feet.

He slid the gun away and grabbed her, helping her stand.

"Are you all right?"

"I'll be fine," she said.

"Where's Abigail?"

"She went on ahead. We need to hurry and get to her."

"Is she safe?"

"No. She went after Nida, but it isn't Nida."

"I know," he said. "She tried to kill my mother and me."

"We need to go."

"Stay here. I'll drop you a harness."

"Okay," she said.

Haatim climbed the rope ladder, and then dropped down the line with a harness attached. Frieda slipped into it, and he hauled her up. Once he'd gotten her safely into the helicopter, he closed the door.

"We're in," he said to Dominick, who nodded.

"Let's go get Abi." Dominick pulled out of the hover.

They flew after the train, once more chasing it down. It moved slowly, but the wind forced them to keep their speed low too. It buffeted the helicopter around and made piloting difficult for Dominick.

"Do you know what happened to my father?" Haatim grabbed a blanket and wrapped it around Frieda.

"No. I never saw him. Nida took me and got out of there."

"Why did Nida come after you?"

"I don't know. Something to do with my blood, but I'm not sure what. All I know is that she plans to summon something here."

"What?" Haatim's eyes grew wide. "What do you mean?"

"I mean we need to hurry and catch up because Abigail won't stand a chance against it alone."

The creature moved fast but clumsily and had a hard time getting around the seats. Abigail dodged and weaved, trying to get away from it, but it had too large a reach.

It swung a huge arm down at her, clipping her shoulder and launching her through the air. She flew over the countertop of the bar and smashed into the line of bottles. A few broke, glass and liquor flew, and many jarred loose and went rolling across the floor.

Some of the liquor ignited, spreading the fire further. As the fire grew and filled the area, so did the creature. Already, it towered near the top of the railcar, looking down at her and smoldering.

The only part that didn't look like a conglomeration of seats, metal, and floor were its eyes. They stared at her, filled with hate and rage. It moved through the aisle toward her, jerking seats out of the way as it went.

Abigail scrambled, diving over the bar and running toward the front of the train. She managed to get up and out of the way before it could maneuver toward her.

The fire spread after the demon, raging through the carriage. The smoke made it difficult to see or breathe, and she crouched low to try and stay under it.

Abigail felt, more than heard, something come flying at her and ducked just as a section of a seat flew over her head. It burned and bounced down the aisle in front of her. A guttural roaring sound came from behind her as the demon kept coming.

She made it to a door, but it stood closed. She flipped the latch and opened it a little.

As the creature came at her, swinging its burning arms, Abigail turned and raised her sword to deflect the first attack, but it pushed right through, slicing its arm off.

The broken chunk kept flying, spreading hot ash and clipping her on the shoulder. Some of it hit her, burning her skin. She stumbled back and finished pulling open the door. The demon roared at her again, but she managed to stumble outside onto the narrow walkway.

Hurt, she tried to pull the door shut behind her, but the demon stuck an arm through the opening, stopping it from closing. Quickly, Abigail opened the door to the next railcar and climbed inside just as the demon exited the first. It couldn't quite fit, but grabbed hold of the metal sides of the train and pushed them apart.

It crumpled as easily as a tin can. The demon looked enormous now, and nearly filled the entire section between carriages.

Abigail scrambled, sliding her door closed. This time, the monster couldn't stop her. Only a split second later, though, something slammed into the wall.

The metal caved in, almost giving way. Abigail spun, sprinting through the railcar just as the demon broke through the wall and came in after her.

Abigail had no idea of how to deal with something like this. She'd never even heard of things like this, let alone been trained in dealing with them. Stuff like this never made it to the surface, and every second it stayed here, it seemed to grow larger.

She couldn't let it get to any city centers or places with innocent people. Something like this would continue to spread and grow, and it would wreak immense devastation before they managed to stop it.

If they managed to stop it.

The demon charged into the railcar after her, trailing fire and roaring as it came. The roar sounded guttural and unlike any creature or animal she'd ever heard. More of a grinding sound than anything else.

It picked up part of another seat and threw it at her. Again, Abigail sensed more than saw it happening and ducked just in time, so it didn't hit her in the back of the head.

An idea came to mind. She slung the bag of C4 off her shoulder while she ran, pulling out the last few bricks and clumping them together. Then she attached a detonator just before she reached the next door in line.

The demon chased her, but this car—doubled up with seats—didn't have open space. As the monster grew, it could barely fit down the aisle.

Not that it stopped coming.

Abigail threw open the door and ran out into the cold, but instead of jumping into the last car, she climbed the ladder. The last carriage didn't have an opening to reach the engine.

The metal felt slick and damp, hard to hold onto, as the snow billowed around her. She made it onto the roof, sliding on the slick surface. Smoke and ash billowed from the engine up ahead, making it even more difficult to see as she moved forward.

Abigail set the timer on the detonator for thirty seconds, and then moved again. She crawled across the roof, stuffing the C4 back into her bag. Beneath her, the creature roared, but instead of following her, it burst into the railcar below.

The roof wobbled under the creature's impact, and she slipped across the rounded metal surface and toward the edge. Panicked, Abigail turned the sword sideways and stabbed it into the roof just before she fell over the side.

She swung out into the air, holding onto the grip of the sword. They traveled overtop solid ground for now, but just up ahead lay another long bridge over another canyon.

Abigail looked into the railcar. The demon charged down the center aisle. It pushed through the seats, ripping them out and tossing them to smolder behind it.

Just as it reached the window in front of her, Abigail swung her legs, kicked against the slick metal, and rolled her body. The demon punched through the glass, reaching for her, and missed her leg by a few centimeters. She could feel the heat and fire pouring off it as she rolled back onto the roof.

She slid the blade free, got her bearings, and crawled toward the engine. She didn't know if anyone drove this thing or if it ran on automation, and didn't much care right now. A gap lay between her and the engine, about a meter across.

The demon pounded against the front of the train. Though more solid than the other connection doorways, the monster would burst through the metal after only a few more hits.

Abigail backed up a few steps and climbed to shaky feet. With a deep and steadying breath, she sprinted toward the edge and jumped, landing on the engine just behind the smokestack and grabbing on. It gave her nothing easy to grip, but she managed to catch onto a pipe jutting out of the side and catch her balance.

Then she descended to the bottom of the engine and stuffed the bag into a crevice. The timer said she had another eight seconds, and they'd moved over the enormous canyon, the bottom of which she couldn't see because of the snow.

The demon slammed against the metal wall again, which gave way as one of its arms smashed through. It pulled its arm back in and looked through the opening at her, roaring in rage.

Abigail smiled at it, waved, and then jumped from the train.

✳✳✳

Haatim dropped into the co-pilot's seat as they approached the train. The wind picked up and jostled them constantly. The snow had brought visibility down to almost nothing. The sun had gone, yet he still had no problem seeing the train: it looked like the front several cars had set on fire.

It glided across a bridge high in the air, maybe a hundred meters ahead of them. He couldn't make out any details, just the fire, as they flew in toward it.

"Why is it on fire?"

"No clue," Dominick said. "Radio Abigail again."

"I did," he said. "Not answering."

"Try again. When we get close, I'll lower you and try to—"

Just then, a huge explosion lifted the front of the train by the engine. It rocked the tracks and broke the rails, knocking the train off the runners. It skidded forward across the bridge for another twenty or so meters, and then the tracks curved.

The train didn't. With so much forward momentum, it ran right off the edge, pulling the rest of the attached railcars with it. The engine nosedived into the wall of a cliff, crunching under the weight of the attached cars, and then it all fell toward the ground.

It dropped another sixty or so meters, and then hit the bottom with a sharp crack. Part of it landed in the running river and sank.

"What the hell was that?" Haatim asked.

Neither Dominick nor Frieda answered, but just stared at the smoldering wreckage. Dominick flew the helicopter down toward the train. The weight of the metal pulled the front cars into the river as well, and slowly, the water put the fire out. In silence, the train slipped beneath the surface.

"Do you see her?" Dominick asked.

"No," Haatim said. "Get us closer."

The wind felt worse in the crevice, forming a wind tunnel. Dominick flipped on a spotlight on the front of the helicopter and scanned the area.

"Keep your eyes open," he said. "The water is cold. If she's down there, she won't survive long."

Haatim didn't reply. He watched the spotlight as it ran over the surface of the river, scouring the area, but couldn't see anything other than random pieces of wreckage floating on the surface. The water moved at speed, pulling everything along with the current.

"How long can she survive?" Haatim asked.

"Ten minutes," Dominick said. "Maybe. Probably less."

They searched for another twenty minutes, scouring the entire length of the train and the surrounding area. The wind speed increased yet more, and by the end, Dominick had to scramble just to keep them from slamming into the wall of the canyon.

"We need to go," Dominick said. "I can't keep this up. The storm has come."

Haatim didn't answer but kept searching for any sign that Abigail might still be alive.

"Haatim?"

"I heard you," he said.

"I'm sorry."

Haatim let out a sigh, sick to his stomach, with all hope ripped out of him.

"We're low on fuel. And I won't be able to fight this wind."

"We have to find her."

"I know," Dominick said. "But we can't stay out here right now. We can come back first thing in the morning and search for her."

"Search for her body, you mean," Haatim said.

Though Dominick said not a word, his expression said exactly what he meant. He turned the helicopter around, and they flew toward the city. The wind and snow gave them a bumpy ride, but Haatim barely noticed it. He'd never imagined he could feel so devastated.

"How could she be gone?"

"The Council," Frieda said. "We need to get back there."

"What happened?" Dominick asked. "Is the Council all right?"

Frieda didn't respond but just stared out through the window.

Epilogue

Dominick flew the helicopter back to the hotel. Wrecked, it looked like the center of a war zone. Not too far from the truth. Various sections of the building blazed or smoldered, and an entire wing of it had cracked open like a clam shell.

The fence remained intact except for a few sections that someone had cut through. It looked like the building had power, but only minimal and, probably, that came from a backup generator. The bodies of the mercenaries they had hired over the last several months to keep them safe lay littered around the guard posts.

Somewhere inside the building, an alarm blared in useless warning of an attack.

Haatim, in the copilot's chair next to him, looked exhausted and beaten down. Frieda still just sat and stared through the window in the back, her expression unreadable while she surveyed the devastation.

Dominick had radioed ahead multiple times to try and raise a response. He had prayed that someone might have survived the attack, but so far, no answer had manifested. He landed the helicopter, and they stared at the demolished hotel for a few minutes.

"We need to check," Frieda said.

"You know what we'll find," Dominick said. "Maybe, we should just go."

"We need to know for sure."

He let out a deep breath. The storm didn't seem as bad here, but it still snowed heavily. With the engines off, they climbed out of the helicopter and headed toward the wrecked building to search for survivors.

An endless sea of bodies waited outside, murdered and left out in the snow. He hated leaving them like this and knew they would need to gather them in the morning, once the storm had moved through.

Frieda followed him into the main lobby, and Haatim wandered around the side of the building. Dominick thought to stop him but decided to let him go on his own. Probably, the guy just needed a few minutes to wrap his head around it all.

They all did.

Dominick went upstairs. Many of the Council had died in the firefight, but many more had only been wounded and then summarily executed. He moved through the building into the sections not on fire and looked through all the rooms in which the Council members had stayed.

Some had been executed in their sleep. Others had tried to fight back and escape, but they all lay dead.

He found Frieda down in the lobby. She looked devastated and hardly able to stand. Was it from the blood loss, the exhaustion, or the emotions of seeing her entire life's work and her friends and family all dead around her?

Probably all three.

"Six Hunters left in the world," she said. "Counting you. I'm the last Council member."

"I'm not done searching," Dominick said. "I've only accounted for ten."

Frieda looked at him, her expression one of sheer devastation. "Do you think you'll find any more?"

He didn't answer. Instead, he said, "How was this possible?"

She could only shake her head in response.

Dominick couldn't believe the sheer destruction of what had taken place. Whoever had planned this, had been incredibly thorough. He'd known many of these people his entire life and had thought the Council could never be brought down, let alone so quickly and efficiently.

"This is insane," he said.

"I know," Frieda said. "We lost everything."

"We have a lot of funerals coming up."

"Those will need to wait," Frieda said. "This isn't over."

"You think Nida will come back?"

"I know she will. Whatever she's planned, this is just the beginning."

"What do we do now?" Dominick asked.

"Rebuild. Call in every favor owed. Find every friend we can. Prepare for what's coming."

"And what is that?"

Frieda looked at him and sighed. "War," she said.

Dominick looked at the ruins around them, smoldering in the snow.

"It isn't coming," he said. "It's here already."

Haatim found his father's car on the south side of the building, near where the explosion had taken out a huge section of the hotel. The door leading inside hung open, and a ramp led down into a storage room, where he found the bodies of several soldiers scattered.

Some killed by the impact of the explosion and others filled with bullet holes. A few small fires still burned in the area, filling it with smoke that poured out of cracks in the ceiling.

He stood there, listening to the crackling of the flames and trying to come to terms with everything. So many people dead. Unfathomable. Only just introduced into this world, and already, it had turned on its head.

Abigail gone. Too difficult to process. Even with how much he'd worried about her possible execution these last months, he'd never imagined what it might feel like to lose her.

The worst part about it was that he'd never, in fact, had her. Different from anyone he'd ever met, he cared more for her than he'd believed he could care for any human being. Too late to tell her, he realized just how much she meant to him.

Now she'd gone, and he stood alone in the world.

A noise came from further in the room. A dragging sound. Haatim looked around. A pistol rested against the wall. He picked it up and edged his way through the dim space, searching for whatever had made the sound.

He came upon it around the corner, tucked behind machinery. His father struggled to drag himself across the floor with one arm, and his other shoulder hung twisted and broken. Though bloody and weary, his eyes flashed when he saw Haatim standing in front of him.

"My son," he said, his breath coming in ragged gasps. He smiled. "Thank God, you're here."

Haatim stared at him, feeling a mounting rage in the pit of his stomach. "You did this," he said.

Aram's smile faded. "I tried to stop this—"

"It's your fault. You got them killed. You got them all killed."

The words spilled out, and he took a menacing step toward his father. His hand squeezed the grip of the gun, and his father seemed to notice it for the first time.

"Haatim, please ... think this through."

"I am." He raised the gun. Never in his life had he felt such fury. Could he pull the trigger and take his father's life? He wanted to.

And, his father deserved it. After everything that had happened, *he* shouldn't be the only one allowed to survive. Moreover, if he shot him now, it would look like just one more dead body. No one would ever know what he had done, and it would serve to balance the scales.

Justice.

"*You* got her killed."

"Haatim, *please.*"

Haatim hesitated, struggling to decide whether or not to pull the trigger.

End of Book II
Lincoln Cole

About the Author

Lincoln Cole is a Columbus-based author who enjoys traveling and has visited many different parts of the world, including Australia and Cambodia, but always returns home to his pugamonster, Luther, and wife. His love for writing was kindled at an early age through the works of Isaac Asimov and Stephen King, and he enjoys telling stories to anyone who will listen.

Intentionally Left Blank

Intentionally Left Blank

Intentionally Left Blank

Intentionally Left Blank

Intentionally Left Blank

Intentionally Left Blank

Intentionally Left Blank

www.ingramcontent.com/pod-product-compliance
Lightning Source LLC
Chambersburg PA
CBHW060551190726
48283CB00003B/962